ASH

BRATVA BLOOD BROTHERS #1

JAX KNIGHT

Ash
Bratva Blood Brothers #1
Copyright © 2024 Jax Knight
Published by Hudson Indie Ink
www.hudsonindieink.com

Jax Knight has asserted her right under the Copyright, Designs and Patents Act 1988, to be identified as Author of this work.

All rights reserved.
No part of this publication may be reproduced or transmitted in any form or by any means, electronic or mechanical, including photocopying, record, or any information storage or retrieval system, without prior permission in writing from the publisher.
Thank you for respecting the hard work of this author.
This is a work of fiction. Names, characters, places, brands, media, and incidents are either the product of the authors imagination or are used fictitiously. The author acknowledges the trademark status and trademark owners of various products referred to in this work of fiction, which have been used without permission. The publication/use of these trademarks is not authorised, associated with, or sponsored by the trademark owners.

Ash/Jax Knight – 1st ed.
ISBN-13: 978-1-916562-71-4

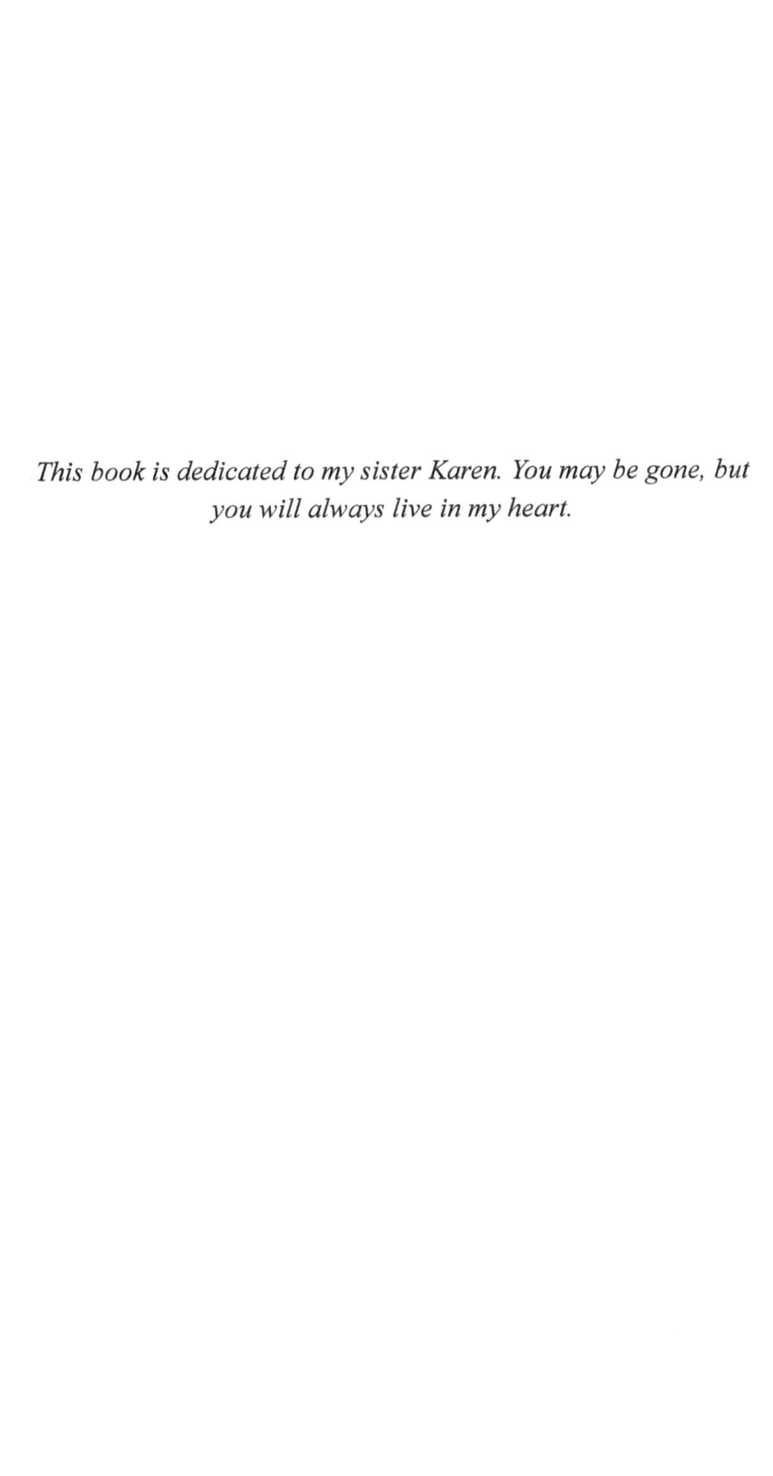

This book is dedicated to my sister Karen. You may be gone, but you will always live in my heart.

PROLOGUE
ASH ROMINOV

JUNE - EARLY HOURS OF FRIDAY MORNING

pushed a shaky hand through my hair, took another deep breath, and tried not to notice the almost overpowering metallic smell of the blood saturating the floor. It had been a long night, and I was tired. I needed to get some sleep.

"I'm heading home, Marko," I told my younger brother as I headed for the door.

"No worries, I'll take out the trash," he said, referring to the now-dead thief who lay at his feet wrapped in a body bag.

"I'm on clean up tonight," Romi said as he prepared to hose the place down.

"Brill!" I raised my hand in a slight wave and left the room.

I showered, changed, and headed out to my car. Once inside, I pumped up the air con and the music. Heavy metal blared out at me along with the cool air as I drove down the long driveway towards the main road. This would keep me awake for the short drive to the city apartment, where I planned on crashing tonight.

My family owned a country estate on the outskirts of the

small town of Harpenden in St. Albans, Hertfordshire. We lived there most of the time, but we kept a couple of apartments in the City for when we couldn't manage the forty-minute commute or needed to entertain and wanted some privacy.

I needed to be up early for a meeting with the event coordinator in the morning to go over the final preparations for the opening of our new club on Saturday. After that, I had to check in with my friend Anton, who was providing extra security at the event, so I was staying in the City tonight.

Anton and I go way back. We went to school together. I was only nine when we moved to London from Russia, and I was nervous on my first day of primary school.

My dad had ensured we were given English lessons for almost a year before he decided to move to the UK, and while I was a quick learner, I hadn't been quite fluent yet. My Russian accent was still pretty thick. I liked school when I was a kid, so I was worried about not understanding things and falling behind. I never expected to be bullied. That was a shock.

Back home, everyone knew who I was or, more importantly, who my family were, and nobody would have dared to bully me. In the UK, they didn't know anything about me, so as the new guy in my year, the bullies figured they had found a new target.

Unlike now, I was small and slim for my age then. Shy and a bit nerdish, too, to be honest. So, getting pushed to the ground and having four larger boys looming over me demanding I give them money was unexpected.

I didn't know what to do at first. I'd lain on the ground where I had fallen, looking up at my tormentor, my bottom lip trembling, fighting back the tears that threatened.

"Give it back," I'd shouted as Peter fucking Johnson had torn my bag from my shoulder, and his red-haired friend tipped the contents all over the playground. The four boys just laughed and taunted me about my foreign accent. Peter kicked me when I tried to get up, and the red-head threw my empty bag at my head.

Then, an anger I hadn't felt before grew from the pit of my stomach, and the shock of what was happening to me started to lift as another boy showed up. He was tall and blond, and he grabbed Peter by the back of his jacket and swung him around before slamming his fist into Peter's stomach.

While the other three boys were momentarily distracted by the blond boy's attack, I was spurred into action. I ran at the nearest one, the red-head, and shouldered him, took him down to the ground, and then hit him in the face as he fell.

When I looked up, I saw Peter on the ground also.

With their friends down, the other two bullies turned and ran off like the cowards they were. Peter and the red-head weren't far behind as they struggled to their feet and ran off after them.

The boy who came to my rescue remained. He was a few inches taller and broader than me at that time. His dark blond hair was long on top with an unruly strand that fell into his blue eyes. I turned to look at him, and he smiled before we both burst into laughter.

"That was so much fun. We make a great team. I'm Anton, by the way," he introduced himself, clapping me on the back and grinning; "Nice to meet you, newbie!"

"I'm Sashenka, but you can call me Ash," I said. "Thanks for helping me out."

"Anytime." He smirked. "You are in my class, and I am supposed to be your class buddy, so I guess it is my job to help you and keep you out of trouble. Though I have a feeling you might end up getting me into plenty," he chuckled.

From that day on, we were inseparable, and he's been my best mate since. He was right. I did get him into plenty of trouble over the years, but he was not averse to getting me into plenty, too, that was for sure.

Even though he went away to fight in the military for a few years, we remained close. Now that he had come home and opened his own security firm, I knew I could rely on him to help keep my family safe. Anton wasn't just a friend; he was one of my blood brothers, part of our Blood Brother pact, and one of the few people I could trust.

In a rare flash of emotion, I realised I was smiling at the memories. It felt strange. These days, I didn't feel much of anything except rage and guilt. It must be the aftereffects of the adrenaline, I guessed. Still, feeling something else for a change was nice, even if I knew it wouldn't last.

I sighed as I felt the darkness returning to encroach upon my brief moment of happiness. I tried to push it away by focusing on the road ahead and turned the music up even louder to drown out my inner demon as it reminded me of my failings.

I'd noticed my inner darkness taking over and leaving me spiralling out of control more often lately. It was getting more difficult to ignore and even harder to pull myself together when I was spiralling. But I kept trying. When I finally got my revenge, things would be better. I hoped.

Not allowing myself to sink into the blackness that threatened to engulf my soul took a lot out of me, though, and by the time I reached home, I was drained and ready to collapse.

Once I got into the apartment, I set my alarm and crashed on the bed, exhausted. I closed my eyes and allowed the world around me to fizzle out of existence…for just a little while.

CHAPTER 1
GRACIE JAMIESON
FRIDAY MORNING - LATE AGAIN

BLEEP, BLEEP, BLEEP!

"Ugh!" I grunted, buried my head under the pillow, and blindly grappled for the alarm clock to hit the button on top and stop the god-awful sound. I'd get up in a minute…or maybe five…

Mr tall, dark, and dreamy was just about to lean in for a kiss, his lips a mere breath away from mine, when there was a loud pounding sound, and his face disappeared. My eyes flew open.

"What the hell?" I shouted, annoyed and a little disorientated before I realised; I was in bed, and Mr Tall, dark and dreamy, was a dream; damn it! But the pounding was real… Damn it again!

"Gracie, it's Friday morning. You need to haul your ass out of bed and get to work, or you will be late again, and you know your boss said he'd sack you if you were late one more time!" my cousin Claire shouted, pounding on my bedroom door.

"Oh god!" I groaned.

I checked the clock. It was eight a.m., an hour after I'd

turned off my alarm. Shit, I was going to be late for work again. I needed to stop reading so late.

"I'll run you to the station if you can be ready in ten minutes," Claire shouted from the kitchen.

Christ, I needed to get ready super quick. I jumped out of bed and grabbed some underwear on my way into the bathroom.

I didn't have time for a shower and needed to multi-task if I had any hope of being ready in ten minutes. I peed and brushed my teeth with one hand and sprayed body mist under my arms with the other. Ugh! After that, I sprayed my feet and private area, hoping things weren't too whiffy down there. I'd had a bath before bed, so fingers crossed! My mother would be appalled, but thankfully, she would never know.

Unfortunately, she passed away from cancer when I was twelve, and as she had been a single parent, I was sent to live with my aunt Carole and my big cousin Claire, who was fifteen at the time. Claire became like a big sister to me, and my aunt Carole was a kind and caring woman, so I was lucky to have them.

Sadly, my aunt Carole died almost six months ago, in January. She was a police officer on her way home during a snowstorm when her car skidded off the road and went down an embankment. Her vehicle overturned, and she died at the scene.

I remembered the look on the faces of the officers who came to the door to inform us. I would never forget it; they weren't just delivering a death message, one of the hardest jobs a police officer must do, but they were delivering a death message for one of their own.

Aunt Carole had been a Sergeant with the Metropolitan police force here in London and was well-known and liked by her colleagues. The cremation occurred three weeks later, and officers lined the roadway, coming out in droves to pay their respects. It was a horrible yet beautiful day, and I still couldn't believe she was gone.

"Hurry up!" Claire shouted again, and I blinked as I realised I had been standing in front of the mirror, lost in my dark thoughts.

Shit, I hated when I started spiralling; I could zone out for ages when that happened.

"I'm coming!" I shouted.

I threw on jeans and a T-shirt, quickly pulled on some socks, and stuffed my feet into my trusty Sketchers, which were great for running. I grabbed my bag, phone, and keys from my bedside table and rushed out the door.

"Here you go," Claire said, handing me a to-go coffee mug and a slice of buttered toast to eat in the car.

"Thanks," I said gratefully.

I glanced at the time on my phone. I made it with two seconds to spare. Fantastic!

Usually, I had to take the bus, so getting a lift from Claire today was a godsend. I sat back, munched on my toast, and sipped my homemade latte in the reassuring knowledge that it only took five minutes to get to the station by car. The next train was due two minutes after that, and then it took twenty minutes to get into the city centre, which gave me just enough time to get to work by nine a.m. if I ran.

When the train arrived, I took a seat and smiled smugly. I'd made it!

"Ha, you won't be sacking me today, Mr MacGrumpy!" I said out loud before sticking out my tongue in a childish gesture of defiance against the man who was my nemesis. Not that he was here to see it.

The old gentleman in the seat in front did, though, and frowned at me over his glasses. Oops!

"Sorry," I said.

He frowned again and pursed his lips, muttering something about young people and no manners, before returning to reading his newspaper. Embarrassed about being caught acting like a child, I squirmed.

I hated conflict and tried to avoid it whenever I could, so I often apologised for things I didn't need to. True to form, I felt the word "Sorry" on the tip of my tongue again but bit it back and turned to stare out the window instead. It wasn't as if I had been talking to the old guy. He didn't need to listen or take offence at my ramblings. I definitely wouldn't apologise again.

I smirked. It felt empowering not to give in to the urge to apologise again. Claire would be proud. She always told me I needed to be more confident and stand up for myself. Of course, that was easy for her to say. Claire had always been confident and outgoing and had what she liked to call a sassy nature, although some might call it aggressive, and indeed do! It was what made her good at her job. Claire was a lawyer in her fourth year since qualifying, so she was now a mid-level associate at a renowned law firm in the City and doing well.

I, on the other hand, lacked confidence and hated confrontation. I could also be painfully shy, mostly with members of the opposite sex, especially if they were young and hot.

I put it down to having been a child carer for my mother during her long battle with a brain tumour. I had no siblings or other family to help. Unlike my few friends at the all-girls school I attended in Glasgow before moving to London, I hardly ever got to socialise or mix with boys. I never got to have sleepovers or friends around to visit. It was just too tricky, especially when Mum was feeling poorly and had headaches and couldn't bear a lot of noise.

I did get a few hours of respite each week when I went to a charity-run programme for young carers like me, but it was not enough to *"bring me out of my shell,"* as Claire would say. The rest of the time, when I wasn't at school, I was needed at home to help Mum.

She rarely well enough to leave the house. Mainly, when we did, if the weather was dry, we went for walks in the park, or I pushed her along in her wheelchair if she found keeping her balance hard. We would chat about anything and everything, and Mum would tell me funny stories about growing up in the countryside with her wild sister, my aunt Carole, and the mischief they got up to.

They were always getting themselves into trouble, usually at my aunt Carole's suggestion, like when they snuck into the local farmer's greenhouse and stole the tomato plant he was cultivating for the annual *Best Local Grower* competition. Aunt Carole loved tomatoes, and these were apparently huge, so she decided she just had to have them!

So, with my mum acting as a lookout, she sneaked into the greenhouse and stole them. Who would have guessed she would turn out to be a police officer?

The farmer realised who the culprits were when he found one of my aunt Carole's ladybird hair clips near his precious plant, and he turned up at my grandparents' house, furious. My mum and aunt Carole were grounded for a whole week after that and then had to muck out the farm stables for another week to make up for it.

Aunt Carole wasn't sorry; she loved eating those tomatoes.

Tomatoes were her absolute favourite snack growing up. My mum and most of their friends loved to snack on sweets or even rhubarb dipped in sugar. Aunt Carole loved tomatoes. She cut them in half, sprinkled them with some salt, and munched on them like apples.

She still often ate them that way as an adult. Every time I

saw her eating one, it reminded me of my mum telling me that story and it made me smile.

Mum and I also spent a lot of time people-watching. We often made up stories about who they were and what kind of life they lived. One man sitting in the park reading a newspaper might be a Russian spy, while another was an undercover agent for Interpol. A woman in a beautiful dress would be on her way to meet her secret lover. Another woman would be a real witch disguised as an ordinary woman, like in Roald Dahl's book *The Witches,* looking for a child to spirit away. We would laugh at all the lives we created for the people we saw. It was a great game. I loved it, which was probably why I developed such a creative imagination.

We read book after book together, too. My mother knew she couldn't give me much of a life in a physical way, so whenever she was up to it, she did her best to make up for that by stretching the bounds of my imagination. That's where my love of reading came from and why I did a degree in English and Literature.

Reading also helped entertain me when my mum was too ill. Escaping into a world of make-believe helped me cope with those times and her eventual loss. I lived vicariously through the characters in the books I read and while I don't regret that, it didn't make for being a confident person in real life. I often wish I was as confident as the female characters I read about. If I were, I could write those types of characters myself! I'd always wanted to be a writer. I'd wanted to write romance novels since I was a teenager, but so far, I hadn't even managed to start one.

I sighed loudly, disappointed in myself. I had lots of ideas in my head, but I kept procrastinating. I felt like my characters and story ideas were not good enough to be published, so I had yet to begin anything. One day, I promised myself I would do it. One day! In the meantime, I was stuck selling advertising space for a small local newspaper. A far cry from my dream job.

The tinny voice over the tannoy brought me out of my reverie as the train slowed to a stop. There was a slight delay due to a broken-down train at the station which needed to be moved.

Oh, bloody heck, that was all I needed!

Served me right for counting my chickens too soon. My mum always said, *"You should never count your chickens before they hatch,"* and I did. Bugger!

Twelve minutes later, I jumped off the train when the door opened.

I sprinted to the building that housed my newspaper's office and raced up the stairs to the third floor, praying I got there before Mr MacGrumpy arrived.

I hoped he would be delayed getting into the office, too. Or someone from HR would want to see him and he'd head there first, if I were lucky.

"Please let him be late. Please let him be late," I chanted, hoping by doing so I could somehow circumvent the inevitable as I took the stairs two at a time, moving faster than I had in years.

As I threw myself through the door to the landing where the offices were located, panting hard from the exertion, my heart plummeted when I saw him standing outside his office door with a scowl.

He wasn't late, and I was so screwed!

"My office, now, Miss Jamieson!" he bellowed.

Sacked? I had been sacked! I stared at my nemesis, unable to comprehend what he was saying.

Shit, what was I going to do now?

I hated selling advertising space. I did. It was a shitty job with a shitty boss, but it was my only job and my only source of income. I felt panic rising; I needed this job!

"Please, Mr Jones, I promise not to be late again. Can I have just one more chance?" I begged the grumpy bastard.

My boss wasn't actually called Mr MacGrumpy. He was called Jones, Mr John Jones. Yep, a very nondescript name for a very nondescript person. He was a small, thin, pale man in his mid-forties with a receding hairline, no chin to speak of, and a constant dour expression with a perpetually grumpy personality to match. Hence, my name for him. If I were English, it would simply be Mr Grumpy, but I was not; I was Scottish, so he was Mr MacGrumpy to me!

He wasn't just grumpy, though; he liked to shout, usually at me. While none of the other staff in the office were immune to his rants, he seemed to reserve his loudest and most prolonged bouts of shouting for me, and today was no exception. He was a bully who delighted in chastising me for the slightest thing because he knew how easily upset I was.

Of course, being late most mornings had not helped my case. That was why Mr MacGrumpy told me on Tuesday that I was on my final warning, and if I were late again, I would be out of a job. He had been off work tending to personal business the last few days, so being late wasn't a problem, but not today, and my goose was cooked!

"I am sorry I was late. There was a broken-down train on the track and…." I started to say.

"I don't want to hear any more excuses from a pathetic little mouse," he interrupted, and I felt myself tearing up.

I stood there, ashamed, and tried desperately to tune him out while he ranted at me, and so, I only caught bits and pieces of what he was saying, "useless," "always late," "can't even get out of bed in the mornings," before I burst into tears.

The whole office was watching, and I'd never felt so humiliated!

"Get out and don't come back!" he shouted, and I turned and ran for the door as tears streamed down my face. I didn't stop running until I got back to the station.

I sat in the back of the train and sobbed.

I didn't go home right away. I couldn't. Going home this early in the day, instead of my usual time, meant facing up to the fact that I no longer had a job.

Instead, I walked to a nearby park, sat on a bench, and spent most of the morning people-watching.

When my stomach grumbled loudly, I finally moved. There was a café nearby, so I grabbed a coffee and muffin, then returned to the bench. The coffee tasted good, and I sipped it slowly. I couldn't stomach the muffin, though. After a few bites, I felt nauseous, so I threw the rest into the pond with the ducks.

I read my Kindle for a bit. It was comforting and distracted me for a while. Then I took a slow walk through the park and pretended to admire the flowers, anything to avoid the problem I faced.

Eventually, I couldn't put it off any longer and headed home. By the time I got there, I was replaying the morning events in my mind, and the tears were flowing again.

I realised, however, that they were for a different reason this time. This morning, they had come from shock, embarrassment, and humiliation due to my confrontation with my boss and losing my job. This time, they were due to an overwhelming sense of anger. Of course, I was angry at that appalling little man, but I was more furious with myself. I was angry that I had allowed him to bully me all of those times and annoyed that I had taken his shit in the first place. I might not have been in this situation if I had stood up for myself more or been on time for work more often.

I was also annoyed that I'd run off like a coward. I should have been confident enough to tell him he could stick his job or at least have walked away with my head held high and my dignity intact. Instead, I'd skulked away sobbing like the pathetic little mouse he'd called me.

"Aargh, I need a drink." I practically screamed; I was so frustrated with myself.

As soon as I got into the house, I ran straight to my room and grabbed the bottle of gin I'd bought for a colleague's birthday.

Well, I won't see them anymore, so why not? I thought as I opened it and took a slug straight from the bottle.

It burned my throat, and I instantly felt better. I took another couple of large gulps, put in my earbuds, and started my favourite playlist to cheer myself up. Pink's sultry voice filled my ears, and I started humming along before I reached for the takeout menu.

Some gin, some sounds, and some comfort food sounded like a plan to me!

CHAPTER 2
ASH

At nine a.m. sharp, I met up with my event planner, and everything looked great as we dotted the I's and crossed the Ts.

Marcie Matthews was as thorough as me, and I liked that about her. She was a strong, confident, and attractive woman of mixed race who was fast becoming one of the best event planners in London. I'd used her a couple of times before, albeit for smaller events. Nevertheless, she was my first choice for the club opening because I knew she would get my vision for the place. I knew she would be happy to work with my little sister, Sonia, and let her have some significant input even though Sonia had been away at University.

Marcie was also one of the few women who didn't hit on me. I was rich and reasonably attractive, with a powerful family, so I wasn't short of female attention, but I didn't mix business with pleasure. Business was important, and business came first. Apart from family, of course. If I needed a woman, I could get one, but I didn't want a relationship. Not right now. So, I steered clear of involving myself with any women I worked with. That would only ever lead to complications I didn't need.

I used to dream of having a wife and children, but not for a long time. My lack of emotion and my obsession with revenge didn't make for a good basis for a relationship.

Besides, finding a woman who was capable of being a partner to a man like me wouldn't be easy, even without the darkness consuming me. The type of life I led wasn't for everyone.

There were some women, like my sister, who were brought up in families like mine and were used to my lifestyle, but I hadn't met one yet that I wanted for my own, and I definitely didn't want an arranged marriage. If I married, I wanted it to be for love. I doubted very much that love was in my future, though. With the darkness inside me, I thought that was probably for the best.

After I chatted with Marcie, I grabbed a coffee with Anton to discuss the extra security arrangements for tomorrow night. Some of his men would be outside, and others scattered throughout the club along with our own guys. Romi would be solely responsible for Sonia's safety. My brothers Miki, Marko, and I, along with our friend Luca, were tasked with schmoozing the guests. A task I hated but would do out of necessity. This meant that we'd be somewhat distracted, so I arranged for Anton himself to work the room both before and during the event, keeping an eye on everything. With the recent threats we'd been facing, I didn't want to take any chances.

"So, what happened with the Polish lot to cause the current issues then?" Anton asked as we stood to leave.

"Two of Janusz Glowacki's men were caught stealing from our street team again and trying to muscle in on our territory," I said.

Anton had been around my family long enough to see and

hear things that let him know the rumours about us were true, but his knowledge was still somewhat limited, for his own good more than anything. The less he knew, the more legit he could stay, but I always told him the basics.

My family were Russian Mafia, Bratva. We ran most of the South of England and the south and west of London. My father, Alexi Rominov, was the Bratva Pakhan until his death. My older brother, Mikhail, who we call Miki, now held that position. I was his second and oversaw security and most of the legitimate side of our businesses. Our younger brother Marko was our Intelligence officer, and our cousin Romi was our Enforcer and head of our team of personal bodyguards.

"Thought you guys had an alliance of sorts? Is that shot out of the water then?" he asked.

"Seems someone wants us to think that. Somebody is setting Glowacki up, and the guys involved were double-crossing him while carrying out the attacks on us," I told him.

"Turns out they believed they were working for the Albanians, although something doesn't quite ring true about that; I doubt they are strong enough."

The Albanians certainly hated us after we almost wiped them out before, and they might be slowly rebuilding, but they were not in a position to go up against both us and Glowacki.

"The alternative is that they have formed an alliance of their own with someone, but you know, the Albanians, ruthless and brutal bastards who don't play well with others. So, I can't see that happening."

"Nevertheless, the guys stuck to their story until the end, so whether the Albanians are involved or not, that seems to be what they believed. It is more likely someone wants us to believe the Poles and the Albanians are working together. Someone not too bright!"

"Well, if not Glowacki or the Albanians, who do you think is involved then?" he questioned.

"My money is on the Somali lot."

He shook his head and sighed. "Seriously, those Malia Boys never seem to learn, do they?"

"No, they don't. We have gone easy on them in the past so as not to upset the balance of power between them, the Albanians, and the Broxley Estate Boys, but it seems like it's time we finally taught them a lesson," I replied.

"Well, you know I am legit, but you are like a brother to me, Ash, and if you need me, bro, I'm there for you!" he said. "I haven't forgotten our pact."

Years ago, when we were all kids, Miki, his best friend Luca, Marko, Anton, Romi, and I all hung around together, and we entered a Blood Brother pact. It was a bit like the thing that the Native Americans did years ago. We cut our fingers and merged blood with each other, vowing to be blood brothers and have one another's backs forever. So, I knew I could count on him.

"I appreciate that, but I promised when you started your firm that if I hired you, I would try to keep you out of things that are less than lawful, and I will try my best to keep that promise. See you tomorrow night," I told him, clapping him on the back as we headed out to the street.

I dwelled on the subject of who was behind the attacks all the way back to the apartment to collect my car.

One thing I was sure of: it wasn't the Polish.

The Polish Mafia and Bratva had been rivals even before we came to the UK. When Janusz Glowacki took over, he was young and ambitious and had tried, on several occasions, to muscle in on our territory, but my father subdued him quickly each time.

Despite that, both men held a grudging respect for each

other as neither Brotherhood ran girls nor did any form of human trafficking. We kept to the same moral code that despite what was going on, you didn't touch women and children, even those of rival families. Only the Italians, some sections of the Irish Mafia, and one or two other gangs I knew of had similar views.

So, over the years, they learned to tolerate each other and generally attempted to steer clear of the other's business. However, when Glowacki's eldest son and my folks were murdered by the Albanians five years ago, we went from rivals who barely tolerated each other to needing one another. In our joint grief, an alliance was formed.

At the time, it was necessary, to prevent the Albanians from muscling in on both our territories and to be able to win a war we could not have handled on our own. So, we formed the alliance to bolster numbers and resources. Joining forces had its desired effect and the deaths of our family members were avenged.

Unfortunately, we were not quite strong enough to wipe them out entirely, but the Albanians took a massive hit to both their numbers and business. They were left leaderless and in chaos for some time as members fought from within to take over. They remained weakened even now.

However, with the initial threat to our families over, the alliance could have fallen apart, but instead, the ties formed in desperation held strong. Despite facing a devastating blow a couple of years ago that could have torn the alliance apart, it had, in fact, gone from strength to strength since then.

I hoped that continued. I respected Glowacki and his sons and liked them, actually. Still, if my latest information was accurate, the alliance not only needed to remain strong, but it looked like we might need to think of a way to build an even closer bond with the Polish. A war was coming, I knew it, and we'd need the Polish on our side to win. We were definitely stronger together. We trusted Glowacki, and he trusted us. That was a rare thing in our line of business.

While we were Bratva, we nevertheless made the majority of our money from legitimate business and white-collar crime these days, especially money laundering and cyber crime.

My uncle Maxim was the Pakhan in Russia, and his son Viktor ran things in New York. However, they were more heavily involved in criminal activities than us and less involved in legitimate stuff.

We kept more of a low profile here in the UK, so the majority of our businesses were legit. We appeared to be nothing more than Russian Oligarchs, which simply meant Russian businessmen, at least on the outside anyway, and that was how we liked it. While the authorities might have their suspicions at times, so far, we'd managed to stay off the radar of the local Metropolitan Police and, most significantly, the National Crime Agency and FBI.

The Poles were mainly involved in counterfeit goods like cigarettes, alcohol, perfume and, more recently, vapes and drug trafficking, supplying everything from prescription painkillers to heroin. However, like us, they also owned numerous legitimate businesses and had several other businesses they used to launder their money through.

Unfortunately, we still dabbled in the supply of drugs, but only cocaine and ecstasy.

We hated our drug side of things. I never used drugs; none of my family would, but we sold them, and we knew what they could do to people. None of us were immune to feeling a certain level of guilt at being a part of the hard drugs problem in the world. But being born into the Bratva, our lives had always been mixed up in drugs, and it was not so easy to walk away.

We wanted to, but it wasn't that simple. Miki had managed

to cut back on the type of drugs we dealt, and we now only sold the two, having handed the provision of all other hard drugs along with the prescription drugs to Glowacki over the last few years.

We also ran a large and very crucial part of the routes used for trafficking drugs and guns through the UK. We did this on behalf of our family in Russia, the USA, and several other associates with whom we did business from Ireland and Scotland.

We were keen to offload this side of the business, too, so we could concentrate on the legit stuff and the white-collar crime only, but we would need to find the right people first.

These were the areas others tried to muscle in on occasionally, and it seemed like it was happening again with the recent infractions into our territory and attacks against us.

These areas of our business, in the wrong hands, would be a disaster for my family here and our Russian and American counterparts. It would also upset the balance of power and cause chaos in the UK. Any war that ensued would not just have severe consequences for the crime organisations involved but would no doubt have an impact on innocent lives, too. So, before we could offload anything, we needed to ensure it was to people we could trust.

Glowacki would have been a good bet to take over the rest of the drug supply and the management of the supply route part of our business, but he wasn't in the position to take on much more right now. He had problems inside his brotherhood and would need to recruit more members from Poland, assimilate them into the UK, and strengthen his own business again before he would be strong enough to take on anything else.

I called Marko and checked in with him. He informed me that our spies, or rather *intelligence officers* as he liked to call them, had been working overtime, and the rumours were that the Polish thieves actually worked for the Malia Boys, just as I had thought.

It seemed like they were hoping to set up Glowacki and thus split up our alliance, pin it on the Albanians, and then watch the inevitable war ensue. They could then muscle in on our territory while we were all otherwise occupied trying to kill each other. It was not the first time they'd caused trouble for us, of course, but they had definitely never tried to go up against us directly in such a manner. This was certainly an issue we would need to address with Glowacki, sooner rather than later.

I called Miki to let him know, and he agreed to arrange a meeting to discuss this with Glowacki when we saw him at our club opening tomorrow night.

I jumped into my car and headed to the gym to work out with some of the guys before I returned to the Estate.

CHAPTER 3
GRACIE

SATURDAY MORNING - HUNGOVER

My head was pounding from the bottle of gin I drank last night.

"Hi," Marcie said, bursting into the kitchen like a mini tornado with Claire close on her heels. "I hear you got yourself fired from that shitty job at last!"

I covered my ears and winced at her loudness.

"Sorry," she said, "You a bit worse for wear?"

"Eh, yeah," I mumbled with my head in my hands.

"Can you please turn down your volume?"

Marcie was Claire's best friend and acted like another big sister to me. Marcie was great but loud, and her voice was always set a few decibels above everyone else's. Marcie was also hyper and did everything at top speed, and while I loved her to bits, even on a good day, she could be exhausting. And today was definitely not a good day.

"About time. Maybe now you can start that book of yours, huh?" Marcie said, just a tiny bit quieter.

I groaned, feeling a bit distraught.

"Aw, hon, I can see you are still upset, but you should look at this as a good thing because now you have more time and can put it into your writing."

She had always said that I was not cut out to work for a small newspaper like the London Local.

"You need to be doing what you dream of and writing that book instead of wasting yourself on selling advertising space," she told me for about the millionth time this month alone.

"I know," I sighed. "But I just don't seem to have a good enough idea yet."

"Well, at the very least, you need to get a job where you can actually write articles, and maybe that will help inspire your creativity," Claire interjected.

"Easier said than done!" I huffed.

"I sent my CV to so many places before the London Local. I only got an interview with them and Nostar Publishing, and you know what happened there," I reminded them.

Feeling dejected, I hid my head in my hands again.

"Yes, honey, but you cannot let a minor setback and an idiot boss stop you from fulfilling your dreams," she replied.

"You call being told, and I quote, '*you need a personality to write and, dear, you just don't have one!*' minor?" I practically screamed in frustration.

"That woman was an idiot. You need to forget what she said and move on," Marcie said, sounding exasperated, having told me this so many times before.

Oh, oh, here we go, I sighed; time for a *let's lecture Gracie episode*! We had these every few weeks or so because the girls didn't believe I was meeting my *"fullest potential."*

I knew they meant well, but I was really not up to this today.

It was easy for them; they both had their life put together. Claire was the up-and-coming big thing in defence law, and Marcie was a highly sought-after event planner with a very successful events company of her own. They were both confident, strong, and successful women who knew what they wanted in life, had gone out and grabbed it with both hand.

While I, on the other hand, was so not.

"Marcie's right, Gracie," Claire agreed. "You need to get over that. You are a great writer, and anyone would see that if you could just be a bit more confident in yourself."

"Why don't you apply again and send your CV out with that short story you wrote in college that won you the award? It was great," she encouraged.

"Yeah," agreed Marcie. "Once they actually read something you have written, I am sure they will jump at the chance to offer you a job."

"I'll do it on Monday," I said, thinking, *nope, not happening, I am not risking the abject humiliation of last time ever again.*

"She's procrastinating again," Claire said.

"Yep." Marcie nodded; her lips pursed.

That was it; I had officially had enough. I couldn't handle this today.

"I said I'll do it!" I shouted before storming out of the kitchen.

I stomped off to my room and banged the door. I winced as the loud noise caused by my immature temper tantrum made me feel even worse.

"Urgh!" I cried and flopped heavily onto my bed.

I wished I could be more like them.

I sat there huffing while I replayed yesterday's humiliation over and over in a loop, along with the added comment, *"You need a personality to write, and dear, you just don't have one!"*

I hated that man! I hated that woman!

Never again, I thought as my anger bubbled up inside me. Never again would I let anyone walk all over me like that!

I was going to be much more assertive and only apologise for things when I was in the wrong.

From now on, I vowed, I would be as confident and sassy as Claire. After all, we were cousins; we came from the same gene pool, so I had to have some sass buried inside me somewhere. Didn't I? I would just have to dig deep to find it! I might not be confident, but I remembered that saying, '*Fake it until you make it!*' Yes, I told myself, that was precisely what I needed to do! With this decision made, I took a deep breath and felt the tension leave my body as I exhaled.

There was a soft knock on my door, and Marcie stuck her head in.

"Sorry, sweetie, I didn't mean to upset you. I just want you to be doing something that will make you happy," she said, looking contrite before sitting on the bed and hugging me.

"I know," I said. "I am going to try to be a bit more confident, I promise!"

"Great," she smiled, "I know just the thing to help you with that, and it will give you some cash while you look for another job."

"Eh, what would that be?" I asked suspiciously.

"Nothing bad," she laughed, "I just got a call from Derrick. One of the staff booked for tonight quit unexpectedly, and there is nobody to replace her. Since we have two big events this evening, we are really short-staffed as it is. How about helping me out?"

"What do I need to do?" I asked tentatively.

"Just carry around some trays of drinks or canapes and offer them to the rich guests schmoozing at the opening of that new club, easy peasy!"

"Sure, okay," I nodded. It did sound easy enough and exciting, too.

I had read about the new club that was opening up. It was

for members only, and the membership to a place like that would probably set me back at least a year's wages, so there was no chance of me ever going there as a guest. Now, at least, I would get to see inside it, ogle all the wealthy clientele and their outfits, and get paid! It's not like I had anything else planned anyway.

Besides, what could possibly go wrong?

CHAPTER 4
ASH
SATURDAY - GLITZ OPENING

sighed in pleasure as the hot water cascaded over my body. I lathered myself all over, cleaning off the sweat and grime from this afternoon's intense workout. The spray was focused on the back of my neck and shoulders as I leaned back, my muscles relaxing under the massaging pressure.

I enjoyed showers. They always made me feel clean inside as much as they did outside. It was as if the warmth of the water flowing over my body cleansed not only my skin but also my soul. Heaven knows I needed it.

I was oddly excited tonight but wasn't sure why. I had a feeling that something important was about to happen, and I was strangely happy at the thought.

I hadn't felt truly happy in years, so the feeling was a strange one and not something I was comfortable with. My guilt ensured that.

Usually, these days, I only felt happy or excited when I was about to take revenge on one of my enemies, and only for a very brief period. Like when I was pounding on the thief last night. So, it was odd that I felt this way when all I was doing tonight was going to the opening of my family's new club.

It was an invite-only event for some minor celebrities and local businessmen and women, and there was plenty of security. We had our own guys working the door and inside, plus the extra security staff from Anton's firm. Technically, it was probably overkill on the amount of security staff we had working the event, but with the recent attacks against our family businesses, we were taking extra precautions. Especially since Sonia had just returned home from university.

Regardless of these attacks, I doubted there would be any issue at tonight's event. It would be foolish for anyone to attack us so openly, especially with all the security in place. So, it was unlikely I'd be dealing with any enemies tonight. This made me wonder why the hell I was feeling this way, but I couldn't shake it as I finished showering and dried off.

The odd sense of excitement lingered while I dressed.

I checked my watch, and it was almost time to leave. I needed to collect Sonia in a few minutes. She was the youngest of my siblings and the only girl now, and with three older brothers, she was spoilt, or as she would say, "suffocated," by us.

We were very protective of her, always had been, but over the last two years, we'd become even more so. I supposed we could be rather intense. However, it was a necessity. As a mafia princess, she always needed to be protected, but with the current situation, even more so.

Sonia had returned home a few days ago, and I was glad. She was studying for a business and project management degree at the University of Edinburgh, where she had also taken some courses in interior design. Sonia was off for the summer break but wouldn't be returning for her final year. Instead, she would be completing it on placement, initially with Marcie Matthews at her events company and later with us in the family business. The last two years with her away with only two bodyguards had been difficult for us all to cope with, especially me, so I was pleased to have her home where we could protect her more easily.

I was proud of the woman she was becoming. She was strong and beautiful with a fiery personality and a wicked sense of humour. She could even occasionally make me laugh, and that was a difficult task these days.

I seemed to have lost my humour when I lost my ability to feel two years ago after *the incident*. That's how I thought of it, *the incident*. I didn't like to think of what happened or any of the details, especially not about the person involved or the overwhelming loss my family suffered. Whenever I did, I was overcome by guilt. It was why I couldn't seem to feel anything but anger and a burning need for revenge against those who had caused my family so much pain.

It was the second time my family had suffered a terrible loss in just a few years, and that made it even harder to cope with. In fact, the only way I did cope with *the incident* was to focus entirely on revenge, so much so that I'd become absolutely consumed by it. Frighteningly so.

Sometimes, I spiralled out of control with it. It concerned me, even though I pretended overwise. However, it worried my family more.

Miki had been the most concerned for me and forced me to see a psychologist last year. Not that it did me much good. The idiot didn't tell me anything I hadn't already known.

He said I had shut my emotions down to focus on revenge so that I didn't have to deal with my grief and guilt. That I was using my obsession as a means of disassociating myself.

He tried to get me to talk about things. He said that if I faced things, I would see that I was not to blame, and I would eventually find a way to get over it. Stupid shit! You didn't get over something like that; you just found a way to keep going.

But the guy was right; I was disassociating myself as much as possible. Hell yeah! Damn right, I was. It was the only way I could keep functioning.

I accepted *the incident* happened, and a person I loved was gone. I accepted that I was primarily to blame. I accepted that before I could move on with my life, I needed to get justice, and the only way to do that was to take revenge. Bratva style.

I felt guilty because I was guilty. I felt anger because the situation should never have happened and because if I hadn't been late, it wouldn't have.

I needed to atone, and until I did, I would lead a half-life. I would feel the guilt and anger that was my due, my punishment.

I accepted all of that, and as far as I was concerned, that was as much facing up to things as I needed.

The only way forward for me was to put an end to everyone who had played a part in *the incident*. Once I had done that, I believed I could eventually move forward, shake off some of the overwhelming guilt and then come to terms with my grief.

Unfortunately, the last person involved was currently out of my reach, which meant the final piece of my revenge was out of my reach. One day, that would change, but not for a long time. Although, if I had my way, it would be sooner rather than later.

The thing that concerned me was that the longer I waited, the more my control slipped, and the harder I found it to cope. The recent attacks were making things worse. My family was in danger again, and so were our allies.

After *the incident*, I swore that I would never allow anything to happen to any of my family members again. That extended to Glowacki and his family. I was determined to ensure that this situation would be dealt with swiftly and without any of my loved ones being hurt. So, until I could get my final revenge for *the incident*, I would focus all my rage on our newest enemy, and if it consumed me, so be it! I only hoped it wouldn't and that, one day soon, I would be free of it.

This isn't the time to be thinking of these things, I chastised myself.

I poured a shot of vodka and gulped it down. The liquor burned as it slid down my throat, and I felt myself relax. I took another shot and relaxed some more. That felt better.

Tonight's event was important. I had to schmooze with the guests. A difficult task for me at the best of times but made even more difficult when I was in a sour mood. I needed to stay in control.

I took a few steadying breaths while studying my reflection in the full-length mirror.

I looked sharp in my made-to-measure charcoal grey suit with my white shirt and matching charcoal tie. I nodded in approval. The tailor was right; the colour suited me well and made my dark grey eyes look lighter. I had my dad's dark, brooding looks and dark grey eyes but my Italian Mafia princess mother's olive skin and full lips. I felt a tug in my heart, thinking about my parents. I missed them.

My mother was a beauty with eyes as blue as the sky and long, dark brown hair. Sonia was becoming the image of her and had the same blue eyes. That's why we referred to Sonia as *malen'koye nebo*, which means little sky. All of us took our looks from our father except Sonia, and… I cut off the thought.

My body tensed, and I clenched my fists and ground my jaw. My eyes narrowed, and my vision blurred. I shook with rage as my thoughts returned to their all-too-familiar dark place. I was starting to spiral again. I'd let myself indulge in my dark thoughts too much tonight. I needed to regain control. Fast.

I closed my eyes, focusing on my breathing while reciting my mantra.

"I will get revenge." Breathe. "I will get revenge." Breathe. "I will get revenge." Breathe.

Thankfully, after a few moments, my thoughts were back under control, and my breathing had calmed once more.

This was something I did when I felt myself spiralling, and although it didn't always work, it seemed to be doing the trick tonight.

I downed another shot of vodka and rechecked my watch. It was eight p.m.

I headed across the hall and knocked on Sonia's door.

"Time to go."

She was ready, as I knew she would be. Sonia was always on time and never liked to be late.

I had taken a few girls out on dates in the past who wanted to keep people waiting, either because they couldn't decide what to wear or because they wanted to make an entrance for attention. I couldn't stand that. I never waited for anyone more than once. If a girl kept me waiting without a good reason, she never got the chance again.

Not that I dated much; I preferred to pick up a girl, fuck, and then leave. There was less need to deal with their emotions when I didn't have any of my own. Less hassle that way. Yeah, I could be a jerk. I was aware of that, but I didn't really care.

Sonia snapped her fingers in my face. "Hey, bro, you in there? Looking a bit spaced out," she said, pulling me out of my thoughts.

I sniggered at her attempt to sound American.

We were all born in Russia but had come to live in the UK as children. We were now British citizens, and although Russian was our first language, English was our second and the one we tended to use on a daily basis. Father had wanted it that way so that we would quickly become fluent. We usually only spoke Russian now, though, when we were in Russia, or when we were discussing the family business with each other in a place where we didn't want to be overheard. Our mother was Italian, so we spoke that too, but generally, English had become the norm.

Nevertheless, we all still had traces of Russian in our accents, to varying degrees, most noticeably when our emotions were heightened, but Sonia had the least as she was only three when we came here. She was the most British of us all, with absolutely no trace of a Russian accent unless she was actually speaking Russian. In fact, Sonia often sounded the epitome of a well-bred English Lady. Though tonight, she was obviously channelling our American cousins by the sound of things. She did that when she was in a playful mood. I found it cute.

"Yeah, sorry, I was just thinking about security for tonight."

"Are there likely to be any issues?" she asked, concern in her voice and accent back to normal.

"I don't anticipate any, but we still need to be cautious. Especially with the recent threats. You just make sure I know where you are at all times tonight, Sonia."

She sighed dramatically and rolled her eyes.

"Yes, Ash, I will. I always do."

"Your safety is important," I told her. "Nothing can happen to you."

She looked at me, and I saw a flash of sympathy in her eyes before she quickly covered it.

She knew I didn't like or want sympathy.

"I know." She smiled sadly up at me.

"I promise I will be careful and will stay by your side, or Romi's, all night."

"Unless I see a gorgeous male specimen who sweeps me off my feet, of course." She winked, then laughed at my scowl.

"Come on," she said, taking my arm.

"I promise to be good. Bet you can't say the same." She smiled at me knowingly.

I smirked. "Probably not."

Romivik was waiting for us outside; he was driving us tonight. Our late uncle Petior was his step-dad, so Romi became our cousin through marriage. Romi and his family moved to London with us after Uncle Petior passed away and so we grew up together. Aunt Letitia and Romi's brother, Dimitri, returned to Russia not long before my parents were murdered, but Romi remained with us and took over as the head of our personal bodyguards.

Natural blood cousin or not, he was family, and we trusted him with our lives, literally. He was also a member of our blood brothers pact. Tonight, since Sonia was home, he would be taking care of her throughout the evening when I wasn't with her. He loved her like a baby sister, so she was in safe hands with him.

"Hey, Romi," she greeted him with a bright smile.

"You look beautiful, by the way," I stated, realising I hadn't told her yet.

"You certainly do!" Romi agreed, and the way he was looking at her, if I didn't know better, I would say it was with more than familial appreciation.

Nah, I dismissed the thought immediately. Ridiculous.

"Well, hopefully, that tall, dark, and droolificent male specimen I am hoping will sweep me off my feet and carry me off over his shoulder might actually notice me then!" She laughed and winked at me again, then at Romi.

"There will be none of that nonsense, young lady, or we turn this car around right now, and you will be getting locked in your room for the rest of the holidays. Maybe longer," I said, growling.

She laughed again, and I huffed out a breath.

This was my baby sister. I didn't like to think of her with any man. She was far too young. They had all better stay away. I pursed my lips, feeling annoyed. If any man came near her, I would definitely let out my inner demon on him. I knew I was being unreasonable in that respect, but I was her big brother, so tough.

"Relax, bro. I'm teasing," Sonia chuckled, placing her hand on my arm as the car slowed to a stop.

"I'm not planning on meeting anyone new tonight, but at some point, I am going to want to set my sights on someone in particular, and you are going to have to deal with that," she said with a serious yet sympathetic look.

"We'll see," I replied huffily, but I was thinking, '*I know what men are like, and there's no way in hell they are getting anywhere near you!*'

If Sonia could tell my thoughts didn't align with my words, she didn't say anything. Instead, she smirked at me and turned to look out of the window.

I decided to push all thoughts of any man with Sonia right out of my head before it soured my mood even further. We spent the rest of the drive in silence while I thought through the checks I needed to make when I arrived to ensure everything was running smoothly.

Before long, the car slowed, then Romi opened the door and helped Sonia out. We'd parked off to the side near the end of the long driveway which led up to the entrance. Sonia was thrilled to see our new club, Glitz. She was practically humming with excitement as we walked towards the entrance.

Sonia was the one who'd named the club and worked with our architect on the design. She had also helped Marcie with planning tonight's event but hadn't actually been inside the building. I knew she was longing to see the finished product.

"Oh my God, look at those lights!" she squealed in delight. "I knew they would look great."

Despite myself, I felt a tug on my lips as I fought to hide my smile at her enthusiasm. That was Sonia, though; she was a bubbly person with an infectious laugh that would get even the darkest, most soulless being to smile. She giggled and pointed at the water feature with coloured dancing lights that ran along the outside of the wall in front of the entrance.

"Just like the Bellagio," she clapped her hands. "I love their show with the dancing water lit up in beautiful colours. I've always wanted a water feature like that, and now we have one of our own. It's great!" She jumped up and down excitedly like a small child.

I smiled indulgently. I had to agree; it was. I even felt a brief moment of pride as I looked at it.

Romi chuckled at her and nodded. "It sure is."

She turned her head to look at the beautifully designed entrance.

"Stunning!" she said breathlessly, looking awed.

"Yes," he agreed, but there was something in his eyes when he looked down at her that gave me pause. I narrowed my eyes, but it was gone in a flash, and he turned to stare at the doorway. I shook my head. I was obviously imagining things. These recent attacks and Sonia's comments in the car were making me paranoid.

I turned to look at the entrance myself and listened to Sonia gush with pride.

It was a great-looking building. The outside was black marble with *Glitz* written in foot-high letters of gold leaf, done to look like glitter. It sparkled against the flickering light from the lamps that burned on either side and looked like real flames. It was elegant and sophisticated, the sort of entrance you would expect from an exclusive members-only club. The tall, heavy, dark wooden double doors were wide open, waiting for the guests to arrive.

"Come on, let's go see the inside," I said, hurrying her along.

I needed to get in so I could check with the security team that everything was as it should be.

Sonia linked arms with both of us, and we entered the building. As I stepped through the door, the feeling of excited expectation I had felt earlier returned full force. I pursed my lips, wondering what it meant.

I nodded at my brother, Miki, who was chatting to Luca. Luca Orlov was Miki's best friend and Bratva. He oversaw the management of all our other clubs and was now going to run this one for us as well. His dad, Stefano, had been a close friend of our Dedushka's (grandfather) in Russia. When we came to London, he came with us to act as a second and mentor to my dad.

Stefano helped us all out a lot before he retired. He was older than my dad and acted like a father figure to him and a surrogate grandfather to us. Luca was his son from his marriage to a much younger woman and was the same age as Miki. We'd all grown up together, but he had an even closer bond to Miki than the rest of us.

Although I was Miki's second, it was often Luca that Miki took with him whenever he needed backup, both in legitimate and non-legitimate situations.

The guests hadn't arrived, and Marko wasn't here yet, either. He was still busy finishing something off on his computer when we left. Sometimes, that man was tied to it. He would follow along later, with two of our bodyguards, Vlad and Trigger, no doubt late as always.

Maria, our Italian housekeeper, and surrogate grandmother, who we lovingly referred to as Nonna, wasn't coming. She'd suffered from a headache earlier in the day and so had decided to go to bed early. She planned on visiting the club another time when she felt better.

I was glad no guests had arrived yet. I didn't really like people much anymore, and I didn't like events such as this. I used to be a fun, sociable guy. I found it hard to have fun now. Still, opening a club required an event such as this, so I told myself to suck it up.

Besides, I knew there was a change coming, and I still couldn't shake off that unusual feeling of excited expectation that was bubbling up inside me again. For the first time in a very long time, I was actually feeling things, and I didn't quite know what to make of it.

I left Sonia in Romi's capable hands and headed off to find Anton to brief the security team.

CHAPTER 5
GRACIE

Thankfully, after a large glass of water, a couple of paracetamol, and some sleep, I felt much more human again. Showering and washing my hair helped immensely, too, so by the time I checked myself out in my full-length mirror, there was no trace of my hangover from earlier.

I was wearing a pair of black trousers with a white cotton shirt and flat black shoes. I'd tied my long blond hair up in a high ponytail, and I'd even put on a bit of make-up, not too much, but enough that I thought I looked natural but pretty.

A tiny bit more, I decided, as I added a touch more mascara to make my blue eyes pop and slicked on some light pink lip gloss.

Okay, I nodded in approval. I looked the part of a competent waitress, so now all I needed to do was act it. I had been known to be incredibly clumsy in the past, especially when I was young, but I hadn't had any real issues in years. I was sure that I'd be fine tonight. So much so that I was excited when Marcie picked me up in time for me to be at the event an hour before things kicked off to help Derrick.

Derrick was Marcie's assistant and our good friend who

would be overseeing the opening of the club while Marcie organised the other event. A leading politician was holding a conference at a hotel nearby. It was supposed to be next week but had to be unexpectedly brought forward. Hence why she was so short-staffed tonight.

Derrick was competent, so there shouldn't be any problems. I loved Derrick to bits and was really thrilled to be working this event with him. I felt a bubble of excitement as we approached the venue. It was going to be so much fun!

―――――

"Hey, sweetie pie, thank goodness you're here," Derrick greeted, giving me a tight hug.

"Now, chop, chop, tons to do!" he cried as he bundled me into the kitchen.

We helped the caterers unload the catering boxes from their van and then started unboxing the food onto the large oval platters made of real silver with ornate edging, not the cheap disposable tin foil versions I was used to. They were gorgeous.

The food looked utterly amazing, too. There were seared scallops with a honey and Dijon sauce, miniature shrimp cocktails, smoked salmon and cream cheese blinis with figs, blue cheese tarts with Waldorf salad, mini ricotta bruschetta with sweet and sour tomatoes, little sandwiches filled with smoked salmon, cheese and caramelised onion pickle, ham and avocado, chicken with Caesar salad dressing and, of course, those garden party favourites, cucumber! I smiled to myself at that; posh people always liked their cucumber sandwiches.

There were also several varieties of dessert shot glasses, all laced with alcohol. My favourites were the pina colada cream with filthy cherry compote and one called Glitz Mess, which was a variation of the famous Eton Mess, I assumed. It had golden syrup and cream laced with champagne and was decorated with gold spray, with Glitz spelt out at the top of its little spoon. I loved that! There were also some tasty-looking mini cupcakes decorated with gold-coloured cream icing and a letter G made from dark chocolate.

They all looked delicious and beautiful, and it would have been sacrilegious if I'd ruined any. Thankfully, I did not. Not one thing fell on the floor or got overturned on the platters while I set them out, and I couldn't help smiling as I put the last dessert on its tray. *Score one for me.*

I have so got this! I thought, pleased with myself, as I looked at all the beautifully arranged trays.

My mouth watered at the sight of all that gorgeous food, and I couldn't resist stealing a couple of the desserts for later. There was a ton of everything, and with only three hundred people on the guest list for tonight, there would be plenty of leftovers anyway. So, I didn't feel guilty.

"Caught you, Missy!" Derrick said, winking and giving me a knowing smile as I hid the last of my treasures away.

"Bet you did the same!" I said, smiling back.

I'd known Derrick for a few years now, and I knew how much he liked his food. There was no way he had his hands on all of those goodies and didn't snaffle some away for himself.

He just winked and laughed.

"Okay, folks," he said, gathering all of us waiters around.

"Time to get this show on the road. Start mingling. Get out there and offer the guests drinks, then come back, and pick up a tray of food once your drinks have been handed out. You can then alternate between food and drink trays for the rest of the night."

There were several drinks on offer. Expensive champagne, straight Russian vodka, and freshly squeezed orange juice for non-alcohol drinkers. These were to be handed out by us waiters. For anything else, the guests ordered directly from the free bar. Lucky them!

I grabbed a tray of champagne and headed off into the main room, excited to get a look at the main club.

The guests had begun to arrive, and the hall was already filling up. Music played softly in the background as people milled around looking at the décor or stopped to chat with folk they knew. I felt a bit nervous at first as I weaved in and out of the guests, but after a while, when I hadn't spilt anything, I started to relax and felt much more confident.

I looked around at everyone and all the lovely clothes. Most people were in couples, I noticed; the men were all in expensive tailored suits, and the women were all beautifully dressed in outfits and jewellery, which probably cost more than I made in a year.

I wandered around checking everything out as I worked. The décor was beautiful, very tastefully done, with either black marble or mirrored walls and gold and black light fittings and accessories. Everything was sleek and minimalistic and very expensive looking.

I managed to alternate between handing out drinks and food for a couple of hours without any issues before I got to take a short break. In a quiet corner of the kitchen, I grabbed some water and my hidden dessert stash and ate them with relish. They tasted even better than they looked, and while I ate them, I daydreamed about being one of the guests instead of a waiter.

In my dreams, I was wearing a lovely, long, tight-fitting, expensive silver dress and was on the arm of a handsome, dark-haired man. We sipped champagne, chatted, and laughed, just like some of the couples I had seen. He was looking deeply into my eyes with his arm around my waist. He pulled me closer, leaning towards me, and I felt my breath hitch in anticipation of his kiss.

A glass smashed, startling me out of my dream just at the good part. Typical! My spoon had dropped onto my lap when I'd jumped at the noise, splattering the last bits of cream from my dessert onto my trousers. Aargh! I got a wet cloth and mopped at the mess. Thankfully, I managed to get it off, leaving only small damp patches on my trousers. It could have been worse. I sighed and checked my watch. It was time to get back to work.

Back in the main hall again, I stopped beside a young couple with my drinks tray. The young woman was beautiful with her long dark brown hair. She was wearing a gorgeous bronze-coloured sparkly dress, which hit her mid-thigh, showing off her slim, tanned legs. The man she was talking to was tall and muscular, with dark brown hair cut very short and neatly trimmed facial hair. His tie matched her outfit. They made a gorgeous couple.

The man murmured something and then moved away, but she turned towards me. Just as she took a glass of champagne off the tray, I was jostled from behind, and the champagne spilt all over her hand.

"I'm so sorry. Let me get you something to dry off with," I apologised.

I put my tray of drinks down on a nearby table, picked up a serviette, and gave it to her.

"Don't worry, it's fine." The woman smiled reassuringly at me. "It wasn't your fault. In fact, it was my brother's," she said, looking pointedly at someone behind us as she dried off.

"Sorry, malen'koye nebo," a male voice said, and I felt the hair on the back of my neck stand up at the trace of a Russian accent.

I turned to see the most handsome man I had ever seen. Oh my god! I blinked in surprise. He could not be real. Surely, nobody looked like that in real life? Even the book boyfriends conjured up between mine and the author's imagination combined could not have created such perfection. He was tall, around six feet two inches, muscular, clean-shaven with dark hair, and the most gorgeous dark grey eyes that matched his beautifully tailored suit. Wow!

He was looking at his phone, and I assumed that was what had distracted him enough to bump into us. I was openly staring. Gawking at him was more accurate, and his sister was smirking knowingly at me. I felt like a clumsy fool, and even though it wasn't really my fault, in fact, it was his, I couldn't stop myself from apologising yet again.

"Sorry… I'm sorry," I stuttered.

So much for being more assertive and less apologetic, I inwardly chastised myself.

His eyes turned slowly in my direction. Oh my! I gulped hard and felt my face flush with embarrassment. My body heated, and my heart raced as I looked into the most beautiful yet cold eyes I'd ever seen.

I saw his sister grin before I took to my heels and ran off towards the kitchen. Gosh, I needed air and a safe place to hide for a few minutes before I said or did anything that would make me look like even more of a fool. Which would not be unusual for me when faced with someone hot and male. Not that I had ever seen anyone hotter than him.

Aargh! Had I really thought this was going to be fun? Had I honestly thought it would be easy and my clumsiness was over? I was such an idiot!

CHAPTER 6
ASH

STILL SATURDAY NIGHT - ANOTHER ATTACK

My phone buzzed in my pocket as I headed towards Sonia and Romi. I checked it. There was a text from one of our guys, Sergei. He texted me earlier to say that one of his street dealers was missing. So, I knew I needed to read it.

Although we had cut down on the types of drugs we sold, we still made our own Molly, otherwise known as ecstasy, and cut the cocaine we brought into the UK in our lab. We then sold the pills and powder to our dealers. We had several top-level dealers who sold our stuff to the more affluent clients, as well as numerous street dealers. Sergei was our go-between.

He managed the whole dealing side of things, keeping the dealers in line and ensuring everything operated as it should. He also enabled our family's connection to the drugs we distributed to be kept to a minimum, thus keeping us away from all police scrutiny.

This was him confirming that the guy had been found dead, his stash and cash gone. Shit, I couldn't believe this.

I was so distracted I bumped into someone.

"I'm so sorry; let me get you something to dry off with," a female voice said.

"Don't worry, it's fine. It wasn't your fault. In fact, it was my brother's," my sister replied.

I glanced at her to see her looking pointedly at me as she dried her hands off. Oops!

"Sorry, malen'koye nebo," I said and leaned down to kiss her on the cheek.

I sent a quick text back to Sergei, saying I'd call him back soon.

"Sorry… I'm sorry," a female stuttered.

I looked up just in time to see a waitress stalking off towards the kitchen, her long blond ponytail swinging. *Cute ass*, I thought before turning around to my brother Miki who had just joined us.

"Miki, we've had another situation."

Miki's eyes turn hard along with his expression.

"We need to talk with Glowacki as soon as possible."

He nodded.

"I'll arrange it. You wait here until Romi gets back. Then get Marko and come meet me in the office," he said before leaving.

"Where is Romi?" I asked, looking around.

"I'm here," Romi answered, coming up behind us.

"There's been another incident. I'll catch you up later. Stay with Sonia," I told him.

As I walked away, I smirked when I saw him being unceremoniously dragged towards the dance floor by my dance-loving sister, knowing he would be kept there for quite some time if she had her way.

I noticed Marko had finally arrived and was chatting to a group of guests near the staff exit. I caught his eye and signalled for him to follow me. He made his excuses before we exited through the 'staff only' door and headed for the office.

Miki wasn't there when we arrived, so we took a seat, and I quickly caught him up on the latest events while we waited.

Miki came in about five minutes later.

"So, when are we meeting Glowacki?" I asked.

"Tomorrow night, dinner, eight p.m. at the Estate. Everyone needs to be there."

We both nodded.

"Is he missing his guys yet?" Marko asked.

"Yeah, I told him we would explain everything tomorrow. We need to have all the facts before we talk to Glowacki. Now, what the fuck is happening?" he growled out.

"Don't know for sure yet," Marko replied. "I've got my guys looking into things."

We all knew that no matter what the two Polish guys said, Glowacki was not going to jeopardise our alliance. Certainly not for what only, so far anyway, amounted to around a quarter of a million pounds worth of drugs and about a hundred and fifty thousand cash, which was simply small change for us.

It was always apparent to us it was a setup.

"Gotta have something to do with the Malia Boys," I remarked.

This was the Malia Boys style, for sure. The Somali gang tended to be more brawn than brain, and while they might rule the northeast side of London, they did so through brutality rather than subtlety. These attacks had been low-level stuff, not needing much thought. Nevertheless, something didn't seem quite right.

The attacks by the two Poles were obviously deliberately designed as an attempt to break up our alliance with Glowacki and weaken us. Even so, the Malia Boys alone would be no match for us. There was no way they were working with the

Albanians, though, despite what the Polish traitors told us. So, who then were they working with? Whoever it was wanted to take over our drug operation, and whether we wanted to get rid of it in the future or not, we couldn't let that happen.

These attacks just reinforced the need to have the drugs business gone sooner rather than later. I didn't like the idea of someone trying to set Glowacki up or us. They had only arranged some minor attacks against us so far, which appeared to be an attempt to weaken our alliance, but I was concerned they might up the ante and try to set us up with the law.

When you had a drug operation, drug busts were inevitable, no matter how many cops you had in your pocket. There were several officers in both the Met and the National Crime Agency who would love the prestige of taking down one of the major players, and the level of our operation would carry some serious jail time. Naturally, none of us wanted to end up in prison if we could help it.

When you were in the criminal world, that possibility was always there, but our dad had taught us to be cautious. We kept a low profile and tried hard to ensure that our illegitimate business could not be traced back to us easily. However, there was only so much you could do to control things. And these attacks were out of our control. An unknown enemy with an unknown motive was a threat we couldn't underestimate. It made me angry.

That's why we had to deal with this as quickly as possible. That's also why we had to offload the drugs and arms route and the rest of our drug business as soon as we could after that and everything else that didn't come under the umbrella of white-collar crime. It was becoming way more trouble than it was worth, and I told Miki that. Again. For what was probably the hundredth time this month alone.

He sighed.

"As I keep saying, Sasha, I'm working on it, but it will take time to find someone who can not only afford to buy us out, but whom we can trust not to be an issue for us or our allies in the future. We need to know that they can be trusted in the long term. It is the only way we might ever get to go fully legit. I won't put the family or brotherhood at risk because I make the wrong decision," he growled, sounding pissed.

Uh oh, he called me Sasha; he did that when he was getting fed up with me. He called me Sashenka when he was really pissed, so he wasn't quite there yet, but not far off.

"Okay, okay," I said, raising my hands in surrender. I had pushed Miki enough. I knew better than to poke the bear too much.

"I know it can't be easy; I am just saying, the sooner, the better."

"Let's deal with the current situation first."

He sighed again like the weight of the world was on his shoulders. As Pakhan, maybe it was, I sure as hell wouldn't want that responsibility.

"Yeah, let's deal with one thing at a time," Marko glared at me in annoyance before he turned back to face Miki.

"So, we think it is likely the Malia Boys behind these attacks then?" Marko asked, trying to get back to the business at hand.

"Absolutely, it's their MO," I said, nodding.

"I agree, but we need proof, and we need it before we discuss it with Glowacki tomorrow," Miki growled.

"On it!" Marko and I replied at the same time.

"I'll check with my informants and see what I can dig up, and Marko can get his hackers and spies on it," I said with a straight face.

"I'll have my *research analysts* hack their systems and also speak to my *intelligence officers*," Marko said pointedly, narrowing his eyes at me as he emphasised the names.

As always, I sniggered at him referring to his hackers as *research analysts* and his spies as *intelligence officers*.

He hated them being called hackers and spies. He said what they did was way more than those terms implied. I agreed. However, I also liked getting a rise out of him. The word hacker didn't bother me because, frankly, it was more badass, and I actually preferred the word spy because it conjured up images of James Bond, fast cars, sexy women, and pens with poison darts. That tickled me to no end, and not much else did these days. So, I milked it as often as I could.

He shot me another annoyed look, and I shot him an innocent one right back.

"Enough, go get it done. We don't have time for your annoying brother antics. I want to know who is behind this, and I want the proof now!" Miki said, shaking his head at us both.

As the older brother, he was used to our squabbling and having to keep us both in line, but he knew deep down it was all in fun.

"Sure thing," I said, giving him a mock salute, and he rolled his eyes in exasperation at me before he and Marko headed out.

I called Sergei back and checked that he had adequately dealt with the dealer's body. There was no need for any unwanted police investigation.

Then, I spent the next hour on the phone with my own men and some of our informants, trying to get some more information. I spoke to whomever I could. For the rest, I left messages to get back to me urgently with any relevant information.

I wondered how Glowacki would take the news that he was being set up again and two of his own men were working against him. He'd be livid when he heard he had traitors in his ranks again.

Apart from us, Glowacki and his sons, a few of our closest men, and two of the cops on Glowacki's payroll, nobody else knew that after *the incident*, our alliance, along with our respect for Glowacki, strengthened significantly. They assumed that it was as shaky as it once was. We were happy to let everyone, especially our biggest enemies, think that. It was always best to never fully reveal either your strengths or weaknesses. However, it had obviously meant that, on this occasion, whoever was behind the latest attacks—and I was definitely not convinced it was solely the Malia Boys—saw our apparently shaky alliance as exploitable.

Eventually, having had no luck gaining any additional information, I headed back out to the Main Hall.

I was making my way over to where I saw Romi and Sonia dancing together when I heard an angry woman shouting, "Why, you insolent little madam!"

I immediately turned and headed towards her instead.

I noticed Derrick, Marcie's assistant, was dabbing at the front of a plump woman's dress. He said something, obviously trying to placate her and very obviously failing. Romi and Sonia headed towards the scene, too.

It was time to do some of the schmoozing I hated.

CHAPTER 7
GRACIE

STILL SATURDAY NIGHT - ANOTHER INCIDENT

fter I had run away from the gorgeous Russian guy, I ran straight into Derrick.

"You alright, sweetie?" Derrick asked, seeing my reddened cheeks.

"Sure, just a bit hot and only narrowly managed to avoid a disaster with a tray of drinks," I told him.

"Okay, well, I am going outside where it is quiet to give Marcie a quick call and update her on how everything is going. There are still a few hours to go, so why don't you take a breather and then head back out shortly?"

"Will do," I nodded, thankful that he was too busy to notice my overly flushed state.

My hands were shaking as I downed a glass of water and then splashed a little on my face. I badly needed to calm and cool down. I was always shy around the opposite sex but never quite as bad as this. The Russian guy didn't even speak to me.

I didn't know what I was so embarrassed about. I might have spilt a little drink on a guest, but she had been sweet about it and knew it wasn't my fault. It was his. I might have been caught openly admiring him, but so what? He was gorgeous, and no doubt many women openly admired him. Besides, he hadn't seen me, so really, I had nothing to be embarrassed about.

I needed to get a grip on myself and get back out there before Derrick noticed. I had a job to do and couldn't let a minor incident and a hot guy stop me.

After several deep breaths and a few affirmations, reminding myself that I'd got this, I felt calmer and headed back to the main hall. I decided the best thing to do was to stay away from the hot male—and any others for that matter—and keep focused on the job I had to do. Surely I'd be able to get through the rest of the night without any further upsets or embarrassment?

I walked through the room with a tray of desserts, stopping to offer one to a plump, elderly woman in a long red dress, which was at least two sizes too small for her. As I neared her, someone pinched my bum making me jump in fright, and the whole tray upended. The desserts went flying towards the woman, covering her in cream, strawberry coulis, and small bits of cake and fruit.

"You idiot! Look what you have done!" she screamed.

I groaned. *Oh my god! Not again!*

"I'm sorry about your dress, ma'am, but it wasn't my fault; someone pinched me and made me jump," I said.

"You need to watch where you are going, young lady!" she huffed.

Derrick ran over with a cloth.

"Ma'am, I am very sorry for this unfortunate incident; let me help you get cleaned up," he said as he dabbed at the front of her dress.

"My dress is ruined, and this insolent girl doesn't seem to care! What are you going to do about it?" she shouted loudly.

I noticed that people were staring at us in amusement as we were fast becoming the night's entertainment.

"I'm very sorry, but it wasn't my fault!" I cried.

The attention was making me embarrassed and annoyed.

"Why, you insolent little madam," she huffed angrily.

"I am sure it was an accident, and Gracie didn't mean to make a mess of your dress," Derrick said.

He pushed me behind him while trying valiantly to placate the irate woman who, instead of listening, was continuing to berate me over my so-called clumsiness.

It was unfair, and I fisted my hands in temper. I needed to stand up for myself, but I didn't want to make things worse.

"Now, Mitzie," the man with her, whom I assumed was her husband, said, "I am sure the young lady didn't mean to do it."

He looked at me apologetically.

"It's getting late, and we were just leaving anyway so you can get cleaned up properly at home," he said, attempting to take her arm.

"I want to know what they are going to do about my dress!" she practically screamed at him.

She appeared irate, but I could tell by the gleam in her eye and the way she glanced around that she was thoroughly enjoying the attention from the scene she was causing.

Her eyes lit up further as a male voice drawled, "Mrs Peacock, let me be of assistance."

Oh no, it was him, Mr Sexy Voice!

I never noticed how sexy the Russian accent could be, or maybe it wasn't, and it was just his voice with the slight hint of the accent underpinning his English? Either way, it was making me feel things all the way down to my core, and my face was no longer the only thing that felt hot.

I knew he hadn't looked at me yet, but when he did, he would definitely notice my embarrassment this time. I cringed and tried to hide behind Derrick, wishing for the millionth time in my life that I was not shy with men. I couldn't look at him, but I was aware he was standing to my right side, and someone else was just behind me.

"Why don't you let my cousin Romi here escort you and Mr Peacock home," the Russian gestured to the male behind me.

I peeked over my shoulder and recognised the male as the man who'd been standing with the Russian's sister earlier. In fact, she was standing beside him again, and she grinned at me when she saw me looking. Great, she would be a witness to another embarrassing incident of mine.

"Then you can send me a bill for the cleaning of your beautiful dress. Also, as a special compensation, on Monday evening, if you are free, you and Mr Peacock can enjoy a meal at Tribeca as my guests, of course," the Russian continued speaking to the woman, not taking any notice of me.

I frowned when I realised that instead of being pleased about that, I was actually quite annoyed. Heck, did I want the sexy Russian to notice me?

"Oh, how kind of you, Mr Rominov. That would be lovely, wouldn't it, John?" the woman said, smiling at last. She directed the question at her husband, but I noticed that her gaze never left the sexy Russian as her eyes flickered over him in an appraising manner.

Mr Rominov? Oh dear, the Rominov family were the owners of this club. This guy was obviously one of them. I hoped I wouldn't get in too much trouble over this.

"Indeed, it would be very kind of you, Mr Rominov," Mr Peacock said, smiling broadly, seeming oblivious to his wife's apparent interest in the other male.

"Wonderful; I had hoped to arrange a meeting with you anyway, John, as I have some business to discuss with you. We can have a chat about it then," the Russian said as he gestured towards the exit.

"Super!" John replied as he followed with the Russian's sister and the man called Romi.

"We will look forward to it immensely," the woman simpered and grabbed the Russian's arm.

She chattered at him as they walked away, and my eyes narrowed when I saw how she pressed up against his side. A pang of jealousy hit me like a punch to the gut.

She should take her hands off my Mr Sexy Voice. I felt my anger rising. Wait, what?! No, not my Mr Sexy Voice. No, not mine. Definitely not mine! What the heck was I thinking?

'And why couldn't he be ours? If you weren't such a wimp with men, he could be!' My inner voice chastised me, and I cringed.

I had an inner voice that often tried to get me into trouble. I was sure everyone had one, but mine was out of control at times. I referred to her as my inner devil because while I wouldn't consider myself to be an angel in general, my inner voice was most definitely a devil.

It took quite a bit of effort to keep her in check at times. I often thought that she was the secret sassy side that I kept buried and that maybe I should let her out sometimes. Unfortunately, I was too much of a coward to do that. Although, considering how easily embarrassed I was, that was probably for the best. I wasn't sure I could survive her if I let her loose. So, as always, I simply tried to ignore her.

'Maybe you should listen to me, and you might be able to score an ultra-sexy man like that and have a bit of fun once in a while. Maybe even get laid!' she huffed at me. I groaned. Not only a devil but a horny one, too, it seemed.

"Geez, I need to get a grip on myself," I muttered, shaking my head at my daftness as I stared after the departing figures.

Just then, Mr Sexy Voice turned around and headed back over with his sister. I saw Derrick watching me, trying hard not to laugh. Oh shit, how obvious was I? I was so not going to live this down.

I looked at my feet, cringing and wishing the ground would swallow me up. I avoided looking at the Russian and his sister as they returned to the main hall, afraid I was going to be caught ogling him yet again, and then I just knew I would die of embarrassment for sure.

'You need to go for it, girl! Flirt with him, get his number!' my inner devil said excitedly. I ignored her again.

"Thank you for sorting out that situation, Mr Rominov," I heard Derrick say.

"Never mind, it's fine, forget about it. But it would be better to keep your waitress away from the main hall for the rest of the night. I would rather not have any more dry-cleaning bills or need to take any more annoying women to dinner," he said, sounding irritated.

I glanced at him, but he wasn't even looking at me. He was looking at his phone again and seemed distracted. I huffed. That was how he had bumped into me earlier.

"I will, yes," Derrick agreed.

"Seriously?" I said before I could stop myself. Sexy voice or not, this was unfair.

He looked at me then, his lips pursed in a scowl, and my blood boiled.

There had been two incidents tonight, but I hadn't really been to blame for either. Firstly, the jerk bumped into me, causing me to spill a drink over his sister's hand, and then someone pinched my bottom, making me jump and sending a tray of desserts over that horrid woman's dress. Both times, I apologised, but nobody apologised to me. He hadn't apologised for bumping into me, and nobody had apologised that I had been sexually harassed while working. Yet, I was being punished. Just typical. Well, I wasn't going to take that. Not anymore.

I had vowed to stand up for myself, and it was high time I did. I was pissed.

CHAPTER 8
ASH

STILL SATURDAY NIGHT - SCHMOOZING

After I left poor Romi to deal with the Peacocks, I headed back into the main hall with Sonia. I knew Romi would return for me once he had dropped them off. I smirked at the thought. I was definitely going to get an ear bashing after foisting that hideous woman off on him.

I thought of the way she had pressed herself up against me, squeezing my arm as she batted those over-made-up eyes at me, and I barely suppressed a shudder. I wondered if her attention had moved to Romi now that she didn't have me in her grasp? I snuck a look back over my shoulder and saw her clinging like a limpid to his arm as he escorted her to the car. It was wrong of me, but I couldn't stop the snigger. Sonia looked at me, annoyed.

"What?" I asked innocently.

She just narrowed her eyes and then said evilly, "Just wait until Monday night; you will have a whole evening of dear Mitzie and her simpering and gushing all over you to deal with!"

I paled at the thought.

"Serves you right," she sniggered.

My phone buzzed in my pocket again at that moment, and I checked it. Several messages had arrived. I would read them shortly after I'd spoken with Derrick.

"Thank you for sorting out that situation, Mr Rominov," Derrick said as I approached.

I glanced at the waitress who had been berated by the irate Mrs Peacock, and my breath hitched.

My eyes quickly scanned her up and down, and I gulped.

Just my type, around five foot six inches, slim but curvaceous, with long blond hair in a high ponytail, gorgeous light blue eyes, and the most luscious lips I had ever seen. She was stunning! And blushing madly, obviously embarrassed by the scene.

I couldn't stop staring, and my mouth had suddenly gone dry. I was speechless. I gulped again and tried to pull my eyes away from the gorgeous waitress so nobody would notice I was acting like a fool. Too late! I saw Sonia sniggering at me from behind the waitress's back. That girl missed nothing. I blinked hard and found my voice.

"Never mind, it's fine, forget about it. But it would be better to keep your waitress away from the main hall for the rest of the night. I would rather not have any more dry-cleaning bills or need to take any more annoying women to dinner," I said.

I had intended it to be taken in jest, but it came out gruff, my voice sounding annoyed. Sonia grinned widely. Shit, I was going to get so much stick for this. I quickly looked at my phone again to cover my embarrassment.

"I will, yes," Derrick agreed.

"Seriously?" the waitress said, looking at me aghast.

She was not just a beauty but feisty, too. Yes, she was definitely my type.

"I'm still being blamed for something that was an

accident?" she stated, glaring at me with her hands on her hips and her lips pursed.

Oh, what I would like to do with that mouth. I felt my cock twitch in my pants as blood rushed south. Oh, heck, I needed to get my thoughts out of the gutter before what I was thinking became obvious. I huffed in annoyance. I gave the sexy waitress the once over again and pursed my lips to stop myself from licking them when my mouth dried up.

"If you were being blamed, you would be going home immediately instead of just being kept out of the main hall," I growled at her.

Movement from behind the waitress caught my eye, and I scowled. Sonia was trying hard not to laugh at me and failing dramatically. Her eyes were bright with mirth as she silently chuckled at my plight.

The waitress, on the other hand, looked abashed. All the fight drained from her at my tone, and I knew I was being a jerk.

I didn't understand the effect she was having on me, and it was disconcerting. I wasn't used to such feelings, and I didn't like them. Plus, my sudden inability to control my teenage-like hormones embarrassed me. I had ended up taking the annoyance I felt for myself out on her as if how I reacted to her was her fault. Not good. I felt shame at that realisation. This was unlike me. I wasn't one to blame others for my problems. I knew I should remedy the situation, but I couldn't think how to, so instead, I turned and walked briskly away from her.

I internally berated myself over my behaviour as I walked along the hallway of the staff area. I was angry at my inability to control myself around the waitress. No woman had had such an immediate effect on me, and certainly not such an obvious one. It had knocked me off kilter.

It probably didn't help that I was horny. I hadn't had sex in a few months. The girl I was in a casual relationship with had gone to work abroad when I'd refused to commit to anything more with her. Although I could get a woman if I really wanted to, I hadn't replaced her. Not that I missed her or anything. It was simply because I hadn't been bothered. Nobody had taken my interest until tonight. Obviously, it was way past the time I got laid.

I ran my fingers through my hair and wished I'd been nicer to the hot waitress. I sighed. I couldn't believe I blew my chance. Or had I?

The shock of finding her so attractive had made me act like an untried teenager, but I was a grown man. I could control my emotions. I would get a grip on myself and look for her again later. I'd apologise and do my best to charm her out of her phone number. If I was lucky, I might even be able to charm her out of her panties.

I smirked at that, then cringed when I realised that she was the girl I had bumped into when Sonia had the champagne spilt on her hand. I had been so distracted at the time I hadn't even apologised to her. Now, I'd been rude to her again so as not to show my own embarrassment. I doubted she'd be interested in giving me her number after that. Damn, I could kick myself! There had been too many emotions tonight and too many feelings I was no longer used to. I'd acted like an idiot, but at least I hadn't made too much of a fool of myself. I doubt anyone else would have noticed.

Well, except Sonia.

As if thinking about her had conjured her up, I heard her running along the hall behind me. I cringed. She was she still sniggering. Only, this time, she was not even trying to hide the fact.

"Aw, is my big brother in lurve?" she asked in a silly, babyish voice.

"Don't be ridiculous! I'm just distracted tonight, that's all. We had another situation I am trying to deal with, and I have a lot on my mind," I said, none too convincingly.

"Oh sure, that's the reason your tongue was hanging out as you were ogling the pretty waitress," she laughed.

"It was not!" I said, shocked. I knew I hadn't been quite that bad. Had I?

She smirked at me knowingly. "Ha, maybe not in reality, but definitely metaphorically it was."

"Oh, shut up," I said, but I couldn't stop my mouth from twitching as I tried hard not to smile.

She continued laughing at me as we walked. I scanned the messages on my phone to avoid looking at her.

Miki was on a call when we arrived at his office, so I read my other messages.

Sean had checked in with the other dealers, and they were all accounted for. There hadn't been any further incidents tonight, either. Still, the one with our dead dealer was bad enough.

Once Marko arrived, we ran through some of the information we'd received from our men on the street. Rumour had it that there was an alliance of sorts between the Malia Boys and the Broxley Estate Lads. That was a shock. They were sworn enemies, both constantly fighting over their small areas in the northeast and northwest of London, often attempting to muscle in on each other's territories and business. However, of the two, the Broxley Estate Lads, known locally as the Broxy's, were the more intelligent and better organised, but they also had fewer men at their disposal. The Malia Boys certainly had more men but less brains.

An alliance between them was unexpected. However, it made sense. If they had finally been able to put aside their differences, then together, they would definitely have had a better chance of breaking up our alliance and taking on us and the Polish, which they could never manage alone. Or so they'd think.

Even so, we knew that if the Broxy's had made some sort of alliance with the Malia Boys, it was likely only a temporary arrangement to carry out whatever plan they had. The chances of anything but hate lasting between those two groups was virtually zero. They had no real honour and no loyalty. They didn't care about their families or their brotherhood. That's why they didn't understand us. They didn't get that by killing one of our family; you made an enemy of us for life. Well, they would soon learn their mistake. They assumed we were like them and couldn't form close ties with rival Brotherhoods. We would use that. Their stupidity and assumptions would work in our favour.

It was time we finally taught both the Malia Boys and the Broxy's not to mess with us.

"I'll call Sean and see if he can get a hold of Juana and have her come talk to me now. I'm sure she will have more of an idea if the rumours about the Malia/Broxy alliance are true and maybe exactly what their plan is," I told Miki.

"Great, let me know what you find out," he said.

He and Marko were heading home and taking Sonia with him, since Romi wouldn't be back for a while, and I needed to stay until the end of the event to debrief the security team.

"Have any of you seen Anton?" I asked.

"Last I saw, he was out front making sure all the guests were heading home," Marko replied.

"Cool, I'll catch him later before Luca closes up," I said and kissed Sonia goodbye.

"Night, Romeo," she smirked. "Oh, and by the way, that waitress will probably still be in the kitchen if you are looking for her," she laughed.

"Waitress?" Miki questioned, raising his eyebrows and smirking. I noticed Marko was smirking at me too.

I shot Sonia a warning look, one she totally ignored.

"Yeah, Ash, here, has the hots for a pretty waitress," she said, smiling evilly at me.

"Really?" Miki asked, grinning.

"No, ignore her. She doesn't know what she is talking about." I waved my hand dismissively.

Marko laughed. "Sure, if you say so!"

They all headed out the door, sniggering with a last parting shot from Sonia, "Bye, Romeo."

"Little madam!" I called after her, and she giggled and blew me a kiss before closing the door.

I shook my head and bit back my grin at her behaviour.

As soon as they left, I called Sean and told him to get Juana and bring her to me as quickly as possible. Then, I sat and waited for him to let me know when they had arrived.

Sean was one of our men, and although he had an Irish forename due to his Irish mother, his dad was Russian and Bratva, like him. He was an Orlov, too, though only distantly related to Luca. Sean was our handler. He recruited and handled our primary informants with what he called his *'Irish charm,'* being *'the gift of the gab'* and the *'luck of the Irish,'* which he said made him so great at it. All I knew was that he could charm the pants off most females if he put his mind to it, and likely a good number of males too, if he was that way inclined.

Juana was one of the nicest and the most trustworthy of his informants, and her information was always reliable. If anyone knew for sure if the rumours that the Malia Boys and Broxy's were involved in a temporary alliance were true, it would be her. She was also likely to be fully aware of who else they were in cahoots with because I found it hard to believe these idiots had formed an alliance off their own backs. I was sure someone else was involved.

Juana was Somali herself and one of the only females within the Malia Boys' inner circle. The reason for that was that her father ran the Malia Boys before her cousin Siraaj Farah, who was known as Siri, took over.

Siri and Juana's dad had been close, and when her dad died, Siri stepped up as head. Leadership only went to the males in many of these gangs, and that was the same for the Bratva. In general, we saw women as equals to ourselves, but not where leadership was concerned. We hadn't entirely caught up to the twenty-first century yet. The Malia Boys likely never would, as they viewed women as second-class citizens. If they didn't, they wouldn't run girls and participate in human trafficking.

The fuckers. I fucking hated that. Especially after *the incident*. I couldn't imagine anyone treating women like nothing. I would thoroughly enjoy teaching them a lesson. I took a deep breath and calmed myself before I spiralled.

It was because of their treatment of women that Juana became our informant. She and her sister Jadwa ran their illegal gambling dens and were the croupiers for their higher-stake poker games. They had been doing that for years without any real problems, then one day, some visiting Somali diplomat lost a quarter of a million pounds to a British businessman. He accused Jadwa of cheating and somehow rigging the game.

Siri was in business with the corrupt diplomat, and to keep him onside, he had offered him Jadwa as compensation, which everyone knew meant that she was his sex slave. Jadwa, like her sister Juana, was a beautiful young woman so, naturally, the diplomat accepted. She was then taken back to Somalia, despite her protests, and Juana hadn't heard from her since, though rumour said that she was still being held somewhere by the corrupt politician.

Juana was beaten for attempting to stop this from happening, then watched closely for a while, unable to go anywhere without one of the Malia Boys escorting her. It took some time for Juana to be trusted again. As soon as she was sure that she was no longer being looked at with suspicion, she approached Sean with information about the Malia Boys operations and had acted as an informant ever since.

Juana provided us with whatever information she thought was helpful. It was her way of exacting a little revenge in the only way she could. In return for the information she supplied, we agreed to help her locate where Jadwa was being kept and, if possible, free her. Juana said she could get herself and Jadwa new identities and disappear if we did, but so far, it had proved more difficult than anyone anticipated. The politician had a lot of friends in Somalia, and they'd helped him keep what happened to her hidden. But Miki and I made Juana a promise to help, and we intended to keep it. We still had some mercenaries we knew in Somalia looking for her.

I told Sean to meet me in the back courtyard, as it is the most discreet place here, and we didn't want Juana to be seen. Also, whenever we met, we kept things as brief as possible, so she wasn't missed. If the Malia Boys were to ever find out about her talking to us, she would be dead in minutes, or worse...sent to one of their brothels to be used and abused before they killed her. I wouldn't wish that fate on anybody.

My phone buzzed. "We're here."

CHAPTER 9
GRACIE
LATER THAT NIGHT - THE MESSY KISS

After he left me standing and staring at his retreating back, I stomped into the kitchen, a mixture of embarrassment and anger warring inside at being dismissed by the gorgeous Russian jerk.

"Well, hon, it looks like you made an impression on the sexy Russian, though I am not sure it was a good one," Derrick said, giving me a sympathetic hug.

'Blew it! Again!' my inner devil taunted. Aargh! I screamed silently at her in frustration.

My cheeks burned with shame and humiliation. Why did I always make a mess of things whenever a gorgeous guy was about?

"Of course, I know what kind of impression he made on you by the way you are blushing," he laughed, winking at me in an attempt to cheer me up.

"I am so proud of you for standing up for yourself like that, though," he said, giving me another hug.

"Humph. Well, you didn't," I stated huffily.

I was still pissed at him for not standing up for me earlier.

"You know I needed to placate the woman; it's part of my job," he stated reasonably.

"I know," I admitted grudgingly. "But I was sexually assaulted while doing my job, and nobody cares about that; the only thing anyone took notice of was that woman and her dress!" I said, pursing my lips and frowning dramatically.

"Aw hon, someone pinched your bum? That's nothing. I have had so much worse, believe me," he teased before stating more seriously, "But, just because it happens, doesn't mean it should."

"So, if it ever happens again and you see who it was, you tell me. I will deal with the person. And it won't be by placating him." I saw a glint in his eye that I had never seen before.

Derrick was gay, but before he came out, he was in the army and spent several years in war zones as an army medic. While I knew being a soldier meant he was trained to kill, I'd never really seen that side of him before, but I think I'd just caught a glimpse, and suddenly, I was glad he was my friend.

"Best do what Mr Rominov says and stay here for the rest of the evening, hon," he said.

I opened my mouth to protest, but he stuffed it with a cupcake, laughing as I choked in surprise.

"Stay here and eat," he said before he left.

"Fine," I huffed around a mouthful of cake.

I still wasn't happy about the situation. It still felt like I was being punished, but at least I had cake. Besides, my feet were killing me, so I grabbed a couple more cupcakes and stuffed another in my mouth. By the time I had finished my third, I was feeling happier. There was nothing like a bit of comfort eating to make a person feel better.

Besides, I quickly discovered that being relegated to clean-up duty for the rest of the night wasn't so bad after all. As much as I had enjoyed unboxing the food, I enjoyed boxing the gorgeous leftovers even more.

Of course, I helped myself to another one or two, well actually five or six, as I did it. Everything was just so yummy.

I knew the treats would go down well the next day at the local homeless shelter.

Marcie had close ties with the shelter, having been homeless herself at age eighteen after running away from an abusive father. She had spent several terrifying weeks on the streets in Manchester, where she was from, before coming to London.

Marcie was lucky enough to meet Ben Johnson, who ran the shelter, on her first night here. He had been out with his group dishing out food to the homeless, and she had asked him for help. He directed her to the shelter and helped her from then on by getting her somewhere to stay and encouraging her to go to college.

She volunteered at the shelter while she was at college, but also worked for the student association. That was where she met Claire, and they struck up an immediate friendship. She still volunteered at the shelter on occasion whenever she had time, and since setting up 'Exquisite Events', she made sure that if there were leftovers from the catering, then they would be boxed up and given to the homeless to enjoy the next day. I admired how Marcie had gotten her life together after a horrible start and really wished I could do the same.

So, boxing everything up was fine, but the actual cleaning up afterwards was not as much fun.

I couldn't figure out how to use the stupid dishwashers in the club's kitchen, so I ended up cleaning all the dirty silver platters and glasses myself. It took a while, and my fingers looked like prunes by the end. My feet were killing me again, too, and I was feeling quite hot and sweaty, longing for home by the time the event was over, and the guests had left.

Unfortunately, I was getting a lift home from Derrick, so I needed to wait until the bitter end.

I waved goodbye to the last of the catering staff before I took the trash bags out to the bins. I had to stack the bags beside them near the kitchen exit. They weren't in the way, so I didn't think that would be a problem.

With that done, I started loading the van with the food boxes for the shelter. Derrick planned on dropping them off with Ben on our way home. I was just collecting another box when Derrick popped his head into the kitchen.

"Hey, girl, almost time to go. Can you load up the van with the food boxes while I do a last check of things? Then we can get out of here," Derrick said.

"Already started," I said, picking up another of the large boxes and giving him a wink and grin.

"Good girl," he said, grinning before he ducked out of sight again.

Derrick was a handsome guy, especially when he grinned, and I couldn't help thinking that it was such a shame he wasn't into girls. It seemed like such a tragedy for the females of the species. However, his being gay made it easier for me to be flirty with him, and I enjoyed being able to practise that side of myself on him. If only I was able to be that way with all the hot guys. I sighed.

I was heading through the door to the side alley with another box when I heard a commotion. A fox was tearing open the bin bags, and there was food waste all over the ground outside. Shit!

"Get away from there!" I shouted and chased it away.

I grimaced at the mess.

I turned quickly to go back inside to look for something to clean it up with when something ran smack into me. The force of the impact knocked me sideways, and I slipped on the mess.

"Aargh!" I squealed as I fell forward and landed face-first in the now-open box full of cream cakes.

I was winded for a second before I managed to pull my face out of the box. Lifting my head, I froze when I saw a pair of legs clad in dark grey trousers and highly polished black shoes, now both splattered with cream.

"Are you alright?" an amused voice asked.

Oh no, I cringed, that voice, it was him. There was only a slight trace this time, but the Russian accent was still there, and even if it weren't, I would know it was him by the way the hair on the back of my neck was standing up, making me shiver delightfully.

He leaned down and offered me his hand. I took it but avoided looking directly at him as I knew I would end up getting red with embarrassment again.

"I'm so..." I started to apologise automatically but then thought of my vow from earlier today and cut myself off.

Nope, I was not apologising for something that was not my fault! In fact, it was his, the jerk who kept bumping into me and not apologising!

I felt myself getting angry and let the anger take over. It was better than the constant embarrassment I was becoming accustomed to around this man.

In annoyance, I tried to pull my hand from his grasp, but my hand was slippery and covered with cream, and so were my feet...I ended up slipping again. Backwards this time... and in my frustration, I pulled him with me. He landed on top of me, making my breath come out in a whoosh!

Oh, dear god.

Our faces were very close, and I couldn't help but look into those eyes. They were beautiful. Oh, I could definitely drown in those. They narrowed as he looked at me before I saw recognition dawn.

"Oh, it's you! You do seem to have a penchant for bumping into me, don't you?" He smiled.

Wow, sexy! Eh, *what?* I bumped into him? I shook my head to clear it. No. Nope, the man wasn't sexy at all. He was a jerk!

"Excuse me, I think you will find that you are the one who keeps bumping into me. Twice now, in fact, and you have yet to apologise," I said haughtily, feeling proud of myself.

'You go, girl. Way to stick up for yourself,' my inner devil cried, and I could sense her mentally high-fiving me.

However, my pleasure quickly diminished when she continued.

'He won't even know you are blushing under all that cream. Maybe you should wear a mask more often?'

I cringed. Bloody, annoying voice!

I squirmed as I realised we were both still sprawled on the ground. All that muscle may look great in a suit, but it felt even better lying on top of me. I closed my eyes and relished the sensation for a second. My inner devil was delighted by this. *'Oooh, if only he was on top of us for another reason,'* she taunted.

I felt his shoulders and chest shake, and my eyes flew open again. He was laughing at me. Laughing! What an ass.

Still, his laugh sent little tingles all the way down to my core, and I noticed a little splatter of cream at the corner of his mouth.

'I would love to kiss it right off,' my inner devil purred!

Aargh! No. I pursed my lips in annoyance at both him and her. He was a jerk; it didn't matter how sexy his smile or voice was or how good he felt, he was a jerk.

And he was still staring at me and laughing!

I opened my mouth to tell him to get off me, and suddenly, his lips were on mine.

He obviously had a similar inner devil to me, I thought

absently as he deepened the kiss, and I let him. Yum, fresh cream and Russian male. Nice!

Who said you couldn't have your cake and eat it, too? Did it matter that he was a jerk if he tasted this good?

I moaned in pleasure, dazed with desire.

My whole body reacted to his kiss in a very pleasant way, and I was pretty sure we were grinding against each other. Oh my, we definitely were, and his body was definitely reacting to mine, too. I felt rather triumphant at that discovery.

My inner devil couldn't have been more pleased.

CHAPTER 10

ASH

As soon as I got the text from Sean, I rushed out of the office and down the hall, but instead of taking the emergency exit, I found myself in the kitchen, disappointed to see it was empty. Damn! I must have been subconsciously looking for the hot waitress after all. I guessed Sonia knew me better than I'd realised.

I had just thought what a shame it was that she wasn't there and hoped I might still run into her again sometime soon, when I did just that. I hadn't realised the woman lying face down in cake and cream was her, though, until I had offered her a hand up and ended up sprawled on top of her instead.

I had said something, trying to sound amusing and charming at the same time, but failed dramatically, sounding yet again like a complete jerk. Not my usual MO around hot women whose pants I wanted to charm off, but it seemed to be a pattern whenever she was near.

This woman seemed to have me reacting totally out of character. I suddenly felt embarrassed again, like I had earlier, and that made me uncomfortable.

I knew that she was right; I really should apologise for

bumping into her. Twice. But I was way too distracted by her curves while lying on top of her to formulate a coherent sentence. And what nice curves they were, too. I couldn't stop staring at her.

She was covered with cream and bits of cake, and her eyes were closed. She looked utterly tasty. Like a big cupcake buffet, all for me! I chuckled at that, and her beautiful blue eyes flew open again. I could drown in those eyes. She was a beauty, and I wondered if she would taste as good as she looked. She was covered in cream, but I bet even without it, my hot waitress would still taste sweet.

My inner voice told me to go ahead and have a taste. The woman probably thought I was a jerk anyway, so I might not get another chance. I decided he was no doubt right and quickly leaned down and captured her lips just as she was about to say something.

Yum. Who said you couldn't have your cake and eat it, too?

I was pleasantly surprised when, instead of pushing me off and slapping my face as I expected, she kissed me back. Wow! I deepened the kiss, enjoying the way her tongue danced with mine in perfect sync. Bloody hell, she tasted good. My cock was already semi-hard, and I couldn't stop from grinding it against her.

I was entirely lost in the moment, when someone cleared their throat loudly and I reluctantly broke the kiss off.

"Sweet," I said, licking my lips for a final taste before grinning at her. "Knew you would be!"

Just then, my phone buzzed, bringing me fully back to reality. It was Sean again telling me to get my arse out there as Juana needed to get back before she was missed. I berated myself for messing around when I should have been taking care of business. Damn it!

"Shit, need to go," I said, quickly jumping off her.

I pulled her up off the ground, reached back into the kitchen, and grabbed some paper towels. I thrust several into her hands and ran off towards the back courtyard, quickly cleaning myself up the best I could.

"Hi, Juana. Hi, Sean," I said as I greeted them both. "Sorry, I got held up," I apologised, feeling guilty for keeping them waiting.

"What have you got for us?" I asked her.

They both looked at me a bit oddly but said nothing. Neither did I. I was no doubt still covered in cream, but I wasn't going to explain why.

"Not much yet regarding what the plan is, but I can confirm that the Malia Boys and the Broxy's have indeed formed an alliance."

"I knew it! Those assholes!" I shouted.

"There is a big meeting on Tuesday night. I'm not sure where yet, but I know I am going to find out because I will be there. I've been told to *'act as a hostess!'* Siri wants me to serve drinks and ensure that there are at least a dozen of our hottest girls there to entertain his guests. The bloody bastard. He knows I hate that sort of thing, especially after what happened with Jadwa. Fucker!" she ranted.

"He isn't planning on passing you on to someone like he did her, is he?" Sean asked angrily.

I noticed the way he was looking at her and thought that he and Juana might have a thing.

"Nah, he can't afford to lose me. I'm too useful now and know too much. Made sure of it! He wouldn't want my loyalties to be divided," she said, and I saw her brush his hand with her own.

Yeah, they definitely had a thing going on. That could end up being a problem. If anyone discovered it, one or both were liable to be killed. I didn't want to see that happen to either of them. Perhaps dealing with Siri and his Malia Boys sooner rather than later would be best for everyone.

"So are the Broxy's the only guests?" I asked.

"Not quite sure, but I expect so. I don't think anyone else is involved in this alliance. Also, both seem to want to keep the whole thing a secret, so I doubt there will be anyone else there except us girls. However, if I find out otherwise, you guys will be the first to know."

I nodded.

"Anything on Jadwa?" she asked, and I could see the hope mixed with despair as she looked me in the eye.

"Sorry, sweetheart, nothing yet. But our guys are still working on it and will keep doing so until we find her," I promised.

"What if she is dead?" she whispered.

"If she is, we will kill the bloody politician and any other person who may have harmed her," I swore, hugging her.

She nodded and smiled sadly.

"I know you will."

"Don't give up hope, Juana," I said.

"Jadwa needs you to have faith that we will find her, and we will," I told her.

She nodded again and squared her shoulders.

"I'll see what I can find out at the meeting and let you know as soon as I get the chance," she stated before giving us both a quick hug and running off.

"You really think we will find Jadwa alive?" Sean asked.

"I think if she were dead, we would have heard by now. Someone would have talked to one of our guys in Somalia. The fact that nobody has, means they are still scared of possible repercussions from the politician and his friends, and that would suggest to me that she is indeed still alive. Nevertheless, whether she is or not, like I said to Juana, we will keep pushing with this until we find out, one way or another, and then we will make the politician pay. Bastard deserves to die, and he will sooner or later," I vowed.

"Let me know if you hear anything else," I told Sean, clapping him on the back before we parted ways.

I checked my watch. It was two a.m., and likely the hot waitress would have gone home already. Pity, I could have offered to help her clean off more of that cream from her body. My mind started wandering, thinking of all the ways I could lick her clean, and I felt myself getting hard again. Geez, I definitely needed to get laid. Maybe I would just check the kitchen, just in case.

I headed down the side alley towards the kitchen and noticed the mess had gone. The door was still open, but the kitchen was definitely empty this time. Heck, getting Little Miss Hot Mess's number now would be difficult. However, I was a resourceful guy, and when I wanted something… it happened.

Romi returned to collect me, so I said a quick goodbye to Anton and met Romi outside. On the way back to the Estate, all I could think about was long blond hair, blue eyes, and that kiss. What a kiss!

When we got home, Miki was still up, and we joined him for a vodka nightcap. After filling Romi in on the information we'd discovered tonight about the Malia boys and Broxy alliance, I filled them both in on what Juana had said before we all finally headed off to bed.

CHAPTER 11
GRACIE

THE FOLLOWING WEEK - TRYING TO FORGET MR SEXY VOICE

After Derrick dropped me home that night, and true to form, I replayed the evening over and over in my mind, especially my interaction with the gorgeous Russian with the sexy voice. Oh, and that kiss!

I had been left wishing the ground would open up and swallow me yet again when the sexy Russian ran off, leaving me a mess. Not to mention thoroughly embarrassed and annoyed at the audacity of the man who had kissed me and then ran. If I thought he was a jerk before, I knew it now.

Derrick had helped me clean up, interrogating me in the process.

"And just what were you and the delightful Mr Rominov doing rolling around in the garbage, young lady?" he asked, with his eyebrows raised and his hands on his hips as if he was my dad or something.

"Nothing, he just bumped into me, and we, eh, we slipped," I stuttered, embarrassed at being caught in such a compromising position with that jerk.

"And landed on each other's faces lip-locked? Yeah, I could see that," he laughed.

"You have got the hots for the sexy Russian, and I guess you made a better impression on him than we first thought, huh?" he said, nudging me and wiggling his eyebrows suggestively.

"I have not got the hots for him," I denied.

"Anyway, he kissed me. What a jerk! Who does he think he is?" I said, trying to sound outraged when, in fact, the only thing raging about me was my hormones. It had been the hottest I had ever been over a guy in, well, forever, and all we did was kiss.

"It wasn't even very good anyway," I lied, not very convincingly.

"Oh, I could tell by the flames coming from your panties!"

"Derrick Reid!" I exclaimed, shocked.

"Don't deny it, girl! Anyway, it is about time you got some action, so if you get the chance, you should definitely go for it!"

"He isn't even that attractive!" I lied again, patting myself as I tried to get the cream and crumbs off me and hide my embarrassment.

"Girl, he is gorgeous, and you know it. And that accent…. Who knew the Russian accent could sound so sexy?" he gushed.

"I know, right?" I agreed with enthusiasm before I could stop myself.

"Ha, busted!" he simpered, wiggling his eyebrows again.

"He is still a jerk, though," I pouted in annoyance.

"Yeah, maybe, but a gorgeous jerk, and it's about time you got yourself laid anyway, so if the opportunity arises, take it!"

"Derrick Reid, I do not need to get laid!" I stated indignantly.

"Oh, you so do!" he replied.

My inner devil shouted *Yep!* in agreement.

Geez! I guessed they were both right, but despite how hot

our kiss was, the guy had run off and never returned. He hadn't even asked for my name or number. So, if I was going to get laid anytime soon, it wasn't likely to be by him. Damn!

That had been four days ago, and thoughts of my few encounters with the sexy Russian continued to bombard me on a regular basis.

Jerk or not, I secretly wished he had asked for my number. But he hadn't even asked for my name, so I needed to accept that and forget him. However, it was not proving an easy task.

I was glad that I had convinced Derrick not to tell Marcie or Claire about my encounters with the sexy Mr Rominov. I didn't think I could stand the embarrassment. Also, since I hadn't had a boyfriend or even a date in ages, they'd be dying to know all the juicy details. I knew I would never hear the end of it if they knew about the kiss, so I thought it best to keep it from them.

Of course, I had to agree to go shopping with him as the price for his secrecy. I wasn't the biggest fan of shopping, but Derrick loved it and was a fashion addict, he especially loved shoes. Whenever the latest in shoes or trainers hit the shops, Derrick would be first in the queue.

He was off for a few days, and so here I was on Wednesday, being dragged around London's trendiest boutiques before my evening shift at my new job. Derrick was shopping for a birthday gift for his new boyfriend. They'd only been dating for about four months, but I could already tell by the way Derrick spoke about him that he was head over heels. He was seriously loved up.

He chatted away about his new love with great enthusiasm, and I couldn't suppress a pang of envy. It didn't help that he kept mentioning what a great kisser the guy was. Naturally, that conjured up memories of the great kiss of my own, and at one point, I must have sighed as he tilted his head, studying me.

"I'm sorry, sweetie. I know you said the sexy Mr Rominov was a jerk, and you weren't interested, but I know you liked him really. Are you really disappointed that he didn't ask for your number?" he asked, raising his brow in question.

"A little," I told him truthfully. "But he was a jerk, and so it's probably for the best," I said, not quite believing that.

In reality, I had been pining over the situation for the last few days. I had been convinced that he had been just as into the kiss as I had been. He initiated it after all and had been grinding his hips against me in such a way that I couldn't miss his desire. And his words '*Sweet. Knew you would be*,' suggested he'd liked my taste as much as I'd enjoyed his.

So, why hadn't he asked for my name and number? I questioned for the millionth time in the last few days. I must have misunderstood the situation. He couldn't have been that into it after all. Or maybe he was happy to have a quick kiss with a waitress but wasn't interested in anything further with one. I couldn't help feeling hurt and confused over the whole thing. Yet, I also couldn't get the annoying male out of my head.

If I was as confident as Marcie, I could try to look up the guy's number myself to contact him and see if he wanted to hook up, but I was nowhere near her level of confidence. The thought of doing such a thing made me nauseous.

He had likely already forgotten all about me anyway. A rich, sexy man like that would have women lined up to kiss him. He was hardly likely to remember me, the clumsy waitress who caused trouble and sassed him one minute and then rolled around on the messy ground with him the next. It hardly made for a good impression. I cringed in embarrassment.

"Besides, he's a rich Russian businessman. Probably way out of my league," I told Derrick, unable to shake off my feelings of inadequacy and disappointment.

"Nonsense. That guy would have been lucky to have you," Derrick huffed, sounding outraged at my comment.

"But you're right. If the sexy Russian couldn't see that, then that's his problem, and he doesn't deserve you. You need to forget him and move on," he agreed.

"Maybe you'll meet a nice young man at the Bell Tavern," he said, smirking.

"Oh, ha ha. You know I'm not into Daddy Dom's," I replied, unable to hold back a grin.

"Well, maybe you should give it a try. Works for me," Derrick winked and waggled his brows suggestively.

I groaned. Derrick's new boyfriend was only a couple of years older than his own thirty years, but I guessed that still counted.

"We can't all be as lucky in love as you," I said, laughing.

I couldn't help but hope that, one day soon, I would meet someone nice and manage to speak to the guy long enough to at least get a date and perhaps another kiss… or even something more. I sighed. What a pity that it wouldn't be with the sexy Russian.

Once again, I lamented my luck that the first guy I'd literally fallen for had to be a Russian jerk who could so easily run off after that sinfully delicious kiss. The rejection of that stung. I huffed; the arrogant, annoying male could keep his sexy Russian accent and those gorgeous grey eyes and that tall, muscular body and that thick dark hair.

But he's just so dreamy. You need to find a way to see him again, my inner devil moaned. I completely ignored her!

"Gotta go, sweetie, things to do, people to see. You enjoy work," Derrick said, hugging me goodbye.

"Bye," I shouted and waved as he sauntered off, heading for the tube home with all his purchases, including a lovely Rolex for his 'daddy'.

I wasn't sure I could understand the whole daddy thing, but if it worked for him, who was I to judge? Derrick was right about one thing, though: I needed to forget the Russian and move on. The kiss we had may have blown my mind, but it was apparent it hadn't had quite the same effect on him. So, I needed to put the whole sorry affair of last weekend and one Russian male behind me.

I walked into the Old Bell Tavern and took up my position behind the bar, determined to do just that.

Having made somewhat of a disaster of my waitressing gig, I'd decided to try my hand at bartending again. My old college buddy, Gina, managed a quaint little pub in the centre of London, and I asked me to fill in while they were short-staffed.

It was a good fit for me as I did a bit of bartending during college, so I knew all the basics and didn't need any training. Also, Marcie, Claire, and I had a regular at-home cocktail night once a month, where Marcie taught us how to make different cocktails, and I was becoming really proficient at making them. Even though the Old Bell Tavern was more of an old man's type pub and anyone ordering a cocktail was few and far between, bartending was an excellent stop-gap job while I decided what else I was going to do. And, of course, it paid the bills in the meantime.

I'd only started work at the Old Bell Tavern on Monday night but was already getting into the swing of things. I hadn't had a single incident yet, and as the night wore on, I started to relax into my role. I even found that I was managing to flirt a little with some of the male customers, all in good fun, not seriously of course.

It helped that they were all middle-aged or older, and as I'd already told Derrick, I was definitely not into daddy-dom, so I didn't get too embarrassed. I sniggered, thinking again about my conversation with Derrick earlier.

"Looking beautiful tonight," one of the elderly regulars said as I poured him his pint.

"Why thank you, kind sir," I said, batting my eyelids and doing a pretend curtsey, making him chuckle in response.

If I kept this up, I just might manage to speak to a guy without dying of embarrassment by the time I was fifty! By then, the guys I would be flirting with would be about the same age as those I was practising with now, so I should be adept at it.

So, between working at the pub and the banter with the staff and regulars, I was pretty busy, which prevented me from totally obsessing about the sexy Russian. Nevertheless, whenever it was quiet, I couldn't seem to stop my thoughts from straying to the man I had secretly named Mr Sexy Voice. It seemed the more determined I was not to think of him, the more I did.

It pissed me off. I wasn't sure if I was more annoyed at the Russian or myself. He because he hadn't apologised or asked for my name and number after kissing me, or me because I refused to forget the jerk.

Then don't. Tell Marcie to give him your number, my inner devil purred.

Absolutely not! I told her.

Coward! She replied.

Shut up! I cut her off, annoyed.

Seriously, I was arguing with myself now?

Holy heck, if I kept this shit up, I would need to go to a shrink! I shook my head at my silliness. Perhaps Derrick was right, and I needed to get laid. I could ask Claire or Marcie if they could set me up on a date with someone. They were always saying they would if I wanted them to, but so far, I hadn't taken them up on the offer. It may be time I should.

I gulped. Just the thought of that had me feeling sick. No, I would rather track down Mr Sexy Voice and ask him out than go on a blind date. I was so not doing either. I sighed, feeling deflated. I would simply have to work harder at forgetting him, no matter how long it took.

Thankfully, one of my favourite regulars arrived and distracted me from my inner musings.

CHAPTER 12

ASH

THE FOLLOWING WEEK - LOOKING FOR LITTLE MISS HOT MESS

All night and throughout the morning on Sunday, I thought about my encounter with the hot, sexy waitress that I had dubbed my Little Miss Hot Mess. I couldn't get that kiss out of my head and was determined to track her down. Unfortunately, it had to wait because I had other things to focus on.

My brothers and I met with Glowacki and his sons on Sunday afternoon to discuss the situation.

We sat at the meeting table in his office while I updated him on everything Juana had told me. Miki added the rest of the information we had and, to his credit, Glowacki kept his temper in check as he sat and listened until he'd finished.

Needless to say, Glowacki was furious at the thought of being linked in any way with the Albanians, set up or not.

"Fuck," Glowacki shouted slamming his fist down on the table, finally letting loose.

His fury burned bright in his eyes as he struggled to regain his control.

No wonder, even if it weren't for our mutual hatred of them

due to past events, neither we nor Glowacki would ever want to work with the Albanians; they were totally crazy.

They had no sense of family and no loyalty to anything but their code, which was the law they lived by. From what I'd heard, it consisted of about seventeen different rules, and anyone who broke them forfeited their life, usually in a very gruesome way. The rules seemed pretty screwed up, too. For example, one of them was that they were not allowed to marry, another was to forsake family in favour of the Albanian mafia and other stuff that was equally as dumb.

Their code made no sense to my family or Glowacki's. I couldn't understand how it made sense to anyone. I doubted even the Malia Boys or Broxy's would understand it, even with their own lack of morality. Anyway, living by such a strict code meant they didn't work well with others. I couldn't think how whoever was behind these attacks believed we would fall for their trick.

"Any idea who the boss of that fucking lawyer is?" Glowacki asked.

"Not yet," I answered.

"We'll find out, soon," Marko chipped in.

Miki and I nodded. Whoever he was, we would find him.

It was infuriating to think that someone was behind the scenes, orchestrating these attacks and playing us for fools.

Glowacki was especially furious that two of his own men were involved. We didn't know who recruited the pair or why they had decided to betray their Brotherhood. Nor did we know if there were any others. So, Glowacki needed to clean his house. He would need to test the loyalty of the rest of his men and ensure that if there were any other traitors, they were taken care of efficiently yet discreetly enough that we didn't alert the enemy that we were on to them.

We had decided to let our enemies continue to think that our alliance was shaky and use that to our advantage. To aid with that, we arranged for a few of our men to spread the rumour that we were suspicious about the attacks, thought they were by the Albanians, and that Glowacki might even be involved. Further to our rumours, Glowacki arranged to get one of his own out that two of his men were missing, and he was suspicious we might be involved. We wanted our enemies to believe their scheme was working until we understood the full extent of their plans and could decide how to deal with it.

The meeting had been intense but at least it had helped keep my mind off a certain someone for a while. However, by the time we got back home, my mind was back to obsessing over her. I decided to call Marcie first thing in the morning at her office and get her to give me the waitress's number. I didn't like having to wait, but since I didn't have Marcie's personal number, there was nothing I could do about it.

First thing the following morning I hurried to my office and called Exquisite Events. Unfortunately, Marcie's secretary told me she was on holiday, and Derrick was out of the office on business for a few days. Damn it! I really wanted to see my Little Miss Hot Mess again.

All I could think about was our rather messy but delicious roll around in the trash. In fact, that kiss had been replaying in my mind on a loop, as evidenced by the almost constant semi I had sported for the last few days, much to the chagrin of my trousers! She really was becoming an obsession.

I couldn't get the woman out of my head. It didn't help that everyone kept teasing me about her, either. Derrick hadn't been the only one who'd caught our cream-covered romp. Anton had apparently stuck his head in the kitchen and saw what had happened, too, and told Luca, who then told Miki, who took great delight in telling everyone else.

So, now all my family and friends knew what a fool I'd

made of myself over my Little Miss Hot Mess, as they all now referred to her too, ever since I'd let the little nickname slip to Sonia. They were having way too much fun at my expense. Funny, though, I didn't really mind. I actually enjoyed it. It was nice having a laugh with my family again, even if it was at my expense.

Nevertheless, not knowing when I might see her again was torture.

I ran my hands through my hair and blew out a breath in frustration. There was nothing for it. I would just have to wait a bit longer, but I was a patient man; I would wait another few days if I had to. In the meantime, I had responsibilities to deal with.

One of which was my business dinner with John Peacock and his oh-so-delightful wife, Mitzie. God, that was a blast! I spent most of the dinner fending off her wandering hands under the table while she sat way too close to me in the booth I had stupidly reserved for us. I made a note to never sit in a booth if I ever had the unfortunate pleasure of dining again with the Peacocks. I felt nauseous at the thought.

I would much rather have had dinner with my Little Miss Hot Mess and have her get all handy with me. Now, there was a female I wouldn't have wanted to fight off. As soon as I found out who she was and contacted her, I planned on inviting her out on a date and hoped like hell she agreed. No, that wouldn't be a problem. I would pull out all the stops to ensure that she did. I went to bed that night imagining all the ways I could do that.

———

I tried hard to keep myself busy on Tuesday. I had plenty to do. Romi and I met with Dariusz Glowacki. We were working hard to set things up so that outwardly it appeared that cracks were forming in our alliance, while we worked together behind the scenes to both pull that off and help the Glowacki's route out their traitors.

I did my best to keep my mind focused on the business at hand, but it wasn't an easy task. Since our kiss, I just couldn't get the sexy waitress out of my mind. No matter how hard I tried not to think about her, my thoughts strayed to her, and every time they did, my cock reacted.

So, by Wednesday, I was chapping at the bit to locate her. I could have asked Marko to get her number for me. He could have hacked into the files at Exquisite Events and found it for me in no time. However, we used Marcie's company a lot and planned on continuing to do so; plus, I liked her and so didn't want to do anything which would breach our relationship. Also, to be honest, I didn't want my family to know just how obsessed I was becoming. They worried about me enough.

I had business to attend to that morning, but afterwards, I returned to the Estate for lunch. It turned out to be only Sonia and me; everyone else was busy. I kissed her on the cheek before sitting down.

While we ate, we chatted about the family businesses, and then Sonia asked if I'd managed to get the number of the pretty waitress.

"Not yet," I told her.

"What? The great Saschenka Rominov can't get the number of a pretty waitress he's obsessed with?" she exclaimed in mock shock.

"Ha, you're losing it!" she taunted.

So, I threw a roast potato at her, shocking her and hitting her chest, leaving a greasy stain on her pretty cream top. Her eyes widened then narrowed, and she grinned evilly and threw it back at me. I ducked, and it missed. I quickly picked up a forkful of peas and pinged them towards her. A full-on food fight ensued, and we laughed our heads off until the table, floor, and we were a mess.

"Oh my god, I can't believe we did that!" she said, still laughing.

"Obviously, Little Miss Hot Mess has made even more of an impact on you than I'd thought!"

"What are you talking about?" I asked, frowning.

"She's obviously got you longing for food games," she winked and wiggled her eyebrows at me.

"Very funny!" I rolled my eyes.

"I think I like this girl already," she smirked.

"Seriously, you need to get with that girl!" she stated.

I tutted and rolled my eyes again at her comment, and she chuckled then sobered.

"Ash, you haven't been this playful in years. Then you meet her, and your fun side has come out twice already."

"After only one kiss! Imagine how much nicer you'll be to live with if you actually got laid," she smirked.

"Ha, ha," I laughed, picked up a potato off the floor and chucked it at her again as she burst into giggles.

"That's enough nonsense for today; I have more work to do," I said.

"And, as a punishment for all of your teasing, you can clean this mess up for Nonna," I chuckled as I took in the mess we'd made.

"Typical!" she shouted as I headed towards the door. Another potato whizzed past my head and hit the wall, making me laugh louder.

"Oh, and her name is Gracie, by the way!" she shouted after me, and I immediately did an about-turn!

I quirked an eyebrow at her. "Say what?"

"Her name is Gracie," she repeated, "I heard Derrick call her that a few times."

"Anything else you know about her that you haven't told me?" I questioned, giving her a hard stare, annoyed it had taken her so long to mention this.

She shook her head, looking contrite. "Sorry."

I huffed and left the room, a mixture of annoyance and elation warring inside. Elation won, and I smiled widely. I finally had a name for Little Miss Hot Mess. Gracie! I liked it, but I still couldn't help thinking of her as my Little Miss Hot Mess.

Armed with her name, I called Exquisite Events again, hoping to speak to Derrick. But my elation was short-lived when I found out that not only was Marcie still on holiday, but Derrick was also off for a few more days. Seriously? It should not be this hard to get a number for my Little Miss Hot Mess. It was as if fate was conspiring against me.

There had to be another way. I mulled it over for a few minutes then smiled. I lifted the phone and called Anton. One of his men was Derrick's boyfriend. I asked him to find out form him all he could about Gracie, and he promised to call me back with whatever information he could get.

Finally on Friday morning Anton called me back. He'd come through for me and managed to find out where Gracie worked.

Yes! I cried in triumph after putting the phone down.

Finally, I knew where to find Little Miss Hot Mess. The sexy little waitress and that cream-covered kiss had haunted my dreams all week, and I was determined to get another taste of those luscious lips again. Tonight. I wouldn't wait any longer.

Anton had said that Gracie would be working at a pub called the Old Bell Tavern this evening, which was perfect as I was due to meet with another Somali informant at a location that was not far from there.

I planned on popping into the pub afterwards. If it went to plan, I could apologise for my behaviour, blame it on being distracted with important family business, charm her phone number out of her, and grab another kiss. Hopefully, if I was really fortunate, I'd even get to take her home. I liked that part of the plan, and so did my semi, who made an appearance again at the thought.

The rest of the day went by in a flash, and before I knew it, I was headed to the meeting. Romi scowled as I drove off, leaving him standing at the door. He wasn't happy that I was going to the meeting alone, but I was adamant, and he knew how stubborn I could be, so after a brief argument, he finally gave in.

"You'd better bloody check in as soon as it's over!" he shouted, his words ringing in my ears as I turned the music up and headed down the drive.

I parked near the meeting location and jumped out, feeling that strange sense of excitement again. Just like I'd felt on Saturday night when I met my Little Miss Hot Mess. Since nothing else of note had happened that evening, it had to be because of her. I wasn't quite sure what that meant, but I was looking forward to finding out.

I saw Mohammed the moment I walked into the alley. Good, he was on time. I wanted to get this meeting over with so I could head to the Old Bell Tavern.

I couldn't wait to see how a certain blue-eyed blonde would react when I walked up to her bar and ordered a drink. My heart sped up at the thought of seeing her again. That's when I heard someone behind me. Shit! I was distracted and not paying proper attention. A stupid mistake. I felt him getting closer. I reacted, but just a little too late and I got sucker punched. I fell to the ground as the world went black.

———

After being knocked out, I'd finally come round only to find that not only were my hands and feet tied, but I was hanging from a hook in the ceiling of a small room which looked like the basement of an abandoned building. I hadn't had time to process much apart from the excruciating pain in my arms before I was hit in the face by a big black dude I didn't know.

He must have been the one who managed to sneak up behind me. Shit, I really felt like an idiot.

Firstly, I had told Romi not to come with me to the meeting because I wanted to sweet-talk Little Miss Hot Mess afterwards without him tagging along. Secondly, I'd allowed myself to be distracted by thoughts of her and let my guard down. I never did that. I knew better than to do that. Well, now I was reaping the benefits of my stupidity. I berated myself as the asshole hit me again.

"Where is your lab located?"

"What lab?" I asked, feigning innocence.

"Don't play dumb with me, you Russian piece of shit!" he shouted, then punched me in the stomach. I grunted. Fuck, that was a sore one!

"Where the fuck is it?" he screamed at me.

I didn't answer. If he thought beating me would make me talk, then he was a bloody fool. I wouldn't talk, no matter what they did. No matter how much pain I endured. There was nothing I couldn't bear to keep my family and our business safe, so I was prepared to take a lot of pain. In fact, I expected it. This was only the beginning. I would take whatever the assholes had to dish out. If they tortured me right, that might mean days of pain.

My family would come for me. I only hoped they would find me before I died. I could deal with the thought of death, but I prayed my family wouldn't end up suffering further because of my thoughtless actions. They'd suffered enough. I should never have gone to the meeting alone.

I grunted as the air was slammed out of me by a fist to the stomach.

I was hit a few more times by the bigger guy and must have passed out briefly because now my informant Mohammed was having a turn. I hadn't even seen them switch over. He had two sovereign-type rings on his right hand, which were acting as a cross between a knuckle duster and a small chib, bruising and cutting me at the same time.

My head lulled forward as I spat out some blood. Sweat dripped down my brow. I screwed up my eyes against the burn as several drops ran into my eyes. I blinked rapidly, trying to clear my vision.

"Tell us where the lab is, and we will let you go!" the double-crossing bastard said. I snorted. *As if!*

His fist connected with my face again, snapping my head to the side. The metallic taste of blood filled my mouth as I bit down hard on the inside of my cheek.

"You guys are going to pay for this!" I smirked, or at least I tried to, but my face was swelling up fast, so it was probably a more grotesque-looking grimace than anything.

"You think this is funny, huh?" he shouted, nodding to the big guy to take over.

He punched me in the stomach. Then punched me again and again.

Oof! The air whooshed out of me. That last one not only winded me but hurt like hell. I was sure I'd felt one of my ribs crack. I tried to drag air back into my lungs, but it was a struggle. I couldn't breathe deeply, so I took several shallow breaths and tried to concentrate on calming down my racing heart.

They'd taken a breather themselves, and I was glad of the short reprieve. It didn't last long.

"You stupid Russian asshole. You are going to tell us what we want to know, and then we are going to kill you and your family."

That really pissed me off. Fuck! When I got the chance, I was so going to kill these motherfuckers! I sniggered.

"You stupid motherfuckers are dead. My brothers are going to torture you two fuckers for days for this, then when you finally beg for death, I'm going to slit your goddamn throats," I said.

My mouth was swollen, and my words slurred, but the coldness in my tone was enough to make them pause. Mohammad gulped loudly. He knew me and my brothers and our reputations. He was scared. Good.

"Call off your dog and tell me who's behind the attacks on my family, and I might let you live," I told Mohammad.

The big guy growled in rage before striking me again.

Fuck, I needed another breather. I pretended to pass out and waited. The second Mohammed stepped close enough, I brought my knees up, ignoring the excruciating sharp pain in my ribs, and kicked out with my tied feet, catching him in the balls. The pain took him to his knees, and I kicked him in the head, knocking him down, but unfortunately not out.

The big guy ran at me before I could do any more damage to Mohammad. His big, meaty fist slammed into the side of my head, and my vision swam. Several more blows rained down on me as I hovered on the verge of unconsciousness. Eventually, Mohammad pulled him off me.

"Calm it!" he shouted, holding the asshole back.

The big guy was losing control. Shit, I was relying on them not wanting to kill me too quickly so that my family could find me. I needed to stop goading them, no matter how much that grated. I had to be sensible and stay alive. Soon, Romi would wonder why I hadn't checked in with him. He would know something had gone wrong and would start looking for me. It would take a while, but I'd be found eventually. My family would get me out of this. I just had to stay alive. Then, I would take great pleasure in killing these two.

I took another blow to the gut. Shit, I swung wildly with the impact. Mohammad was in front of me again, his hits to my stomach keeping me winded and ensuring I didn't have the opportunity to kick out again.

My arms strained under the weight of holding up my bulky frame, and if they stayed that way much longer, my shoulders were liable to dislocate, especially with all this swinging about.

The big guy was over in the corner, breathing heavily and trying to compose himself while Mohammad got in another few blows, alternating between my body and head. I hovered on the fringes of consciousness again, barely registering as a phone rang and the blows stopped.

I lifted my dropping head as Mohammad left the room. The big guy stood watching from the corner, saying nothing, seemingly back in control. I had to admit I was thankful for another reprieve.

My breaths were coming quick and shallow. My whole body screamed in pain, and I could barely see out of one eye. The last punch had been to my head, and it felt fuzzy. My eyes grew heavy. I fought waves of dizziness and nausea as I tried hard to keep them open, but it was just too hard, and I succumbed to blackness and oblivion.

CHAPTER 13
GRACIE

By Friday night, I was becoming so proficient at my job that Gina had given me a set of keys and was entrusting me to lock up at the end of the night.

I was so proud of myself. It had been a week since I had been sacked, and despite the events of Saturday night and the annoying obsession with the Russian jerk, I was feeling lighter than I had for months. I still hadn't decided what I wanted to do with my life, but it had only been a week, so I had time.

Meanwhile, I was enjoying feeling competent again. The last few days had given me a badly needed confidence boost, and while I had a long way to go, I felt pleased with the progress I had made.

Gina had left earlier to head to a family event, so it was just myself and the other bartender, Thomas, who remained to finish up.

Thomas cashed up because he was meeting his girlfriend at a local club and planned on dropping off the night's takings in the bank's overnight deposit on the way. We had already agreed that I would close things up by myself, so I locked the front door after him and hit the button on the shutters at the front, leaving just the back door open.

I spent the next half hour or so finishing the cleaning. After that, I replaced the kegs of beer in the basement, as they were running low. They were heavy, but luckily, we stored them near the systems so we could shuffle them along the ground and get them close enough to replace them without too much trouble. One of the couplers was a bit stiff and difficult to turn, but I managed to get it off and then attached the new keg without any sort of accident. Yay for me!

Immensely pleased with myself, I headed back upstairs. It was nearly one in the morning, and I was tired and glad that Marcie had let me borrow one of her vans to drive while she was away. My feet were killing me, so I was looking forward to getting home to bed. I just needed to wash the kitchen floor and take the rubbish out first.

My mind naturally flashed back to last Saturday night and rolling around in the trash with a sexy man on top, but I slammed those thoughts right back down where they'd come from, determined to forget all about him.

I put on some music to keep me distracted while I worked. I sang along as usual and messed around with the mop, pretending it was a microphone. Charlie Puth came on, and I ran around using an apron as a cape while I laughed and sang, "Superman's got nothing on me!" and pretended to fly.

Eventually, I was done. I set the alarm, turned off the lights, and closed the back door. I double-checked it was locked and then dumped the bag of rubbish in the bin before turning to head out of the alley towards where I'd parked the van in the street.

Although it was the end of June, there was a chill in the air and a slight drizzle, so I zipped up my black hoodie and pulled up the hood.

I rummaged in my bag for the van keys, dropping my phone in the process. I crouched down to get it just as a black SUV with tinted windows came screeching into the alley in front of me. The hair on the back of my neck stood up, and I felt danger. I stayed crouched low and shuffled myself back to hide behind the largest of the bins.

Peering out, I watched as two black guys got out of the SUV. One of them opened the door of the building on the other side of the alley. I wasn't quite sure what that building was used for; I thought it was vacant. It certainly looked like it.

I watched as the men reached into the back of the SUV and pulled another guy out. He looked unconscious as they half dragged, half carried him inside. Then, the SUV quickly backed out of the alley and headed off down the road.

I huffed out a breath I hadn't even realised I'd been holding. That did not look good. I should probably call the police. But what if I was wrong and all I'd seen were simply two guys helping their drunk friend home after a hard night of drinking? Hmm, while that might be the case, I wasn't convinced.

I yawned. I was tired. I supposed I could just go home and forget about it. No, I dismissed that thought as soon as it emerged. If something bad was happening, I couldn't simply ignore it. I might not be very confident, but I wasn't a complete coward. I wouldn't let something awful happen and not do anything about it. Yet, I would look foolish if I called the police and it was nothing. Besides, I didn't want to waste their time.

I bit my lip as I looked at the building. *You could just check things out*, my inner devil said. I huffed, but she was right. I could sneak over and find out what was happening before I decided what to do. I shifted on my feet, unable to decide what to do.

Finally, I let my curiosity get the better of me, crossed the lane, and crept over to the door I'd seen the men enter. I noticed that it hadn't been closed properly and was ajar. I stood very still, not even daring to breathe as I listened for any sounds from inside. I couldn't hear anything at first, but then I heard some talking and what sounded like a smack and a grunt.

I bit my lip again and grimaced. I was sure that sounded like someone was in pain. I strained to hear more. The sounds that emerged made me gasp. Somebody was being beaten up. Shit!

I noticed a small, barred window near the bottom of the wall a few feet away. There was light coming from it. It looked like a basement.

I knew I needed to call the police, but instead, I felt myself move towards the window. I stopped at the side and crouched down. Keeping my body out of the way, I peeked inside.

Years' worth of grime covered the window, but a small area was clean enough for me to see inside. The room was small and sparse, with a desk and chair in one corner. Faded wallpaper hung partly off the wall. A single bulb gave the room a dull glow. The place looked like it hadn't been used in a long time. Well, until now.

I moved my head so I could get a better look. A mainly naked man was tied with his hands above his head to what looked like a hook hanging from the ceiling a few feet to the left of the light. A closed door was on the right. The two black guys were standing in front of it.

One of the men said something to their captive and then hit him. I quickly scooted back from the window and pressed my hands over my mouth to stop crying out at the sound of flesh meeting flesh.

I took a steadying breath, then forced myself to look again as the sounds continued. The bigger of the two guys hit him in the face again, and his head drooped.

I couldn't help feeling sympathy for the guy whose face was already bloody and swollen. I peered hard at him. Something about him seemed familiar as if I should know him, but I didn't know why. I was caught up in my thoughts and must have missed them asking him something.

"Answer the question, you fucking Russian," the smaller guy shouted.

Russian?

Their captive dragged his head up and spat out some blood. Then he laughed. He actually laughed and said, "You guys are going to pay for this!"

I froze. No, it couldn't be!

But it was. The men had called him Russian, and even though his words were slurred due to his swollen mouth, I would recognise the sound of that voice anywhere.

We've got to help him, my inner devil shouted at me, and for once, our thoughts were in alignment.

I winced as the bigger of the two black guys hit him again. I knew I should call the police, but who knew how long the police would take to get here? He could be dead by then. I needed to help him, and fast!

Before I could think better of it, I ran to the van and grabbed the box cutter from the glove compartment, then reached under the driver's seat and pulled out a baseball bat. Derrick had insisted Marcie kept a bat under the seat of all the company vans ever since she was attacked after an event a few months ago when a guy had tried to grab her.

Derrick was a big fan of baseball after living in the States for a couple of years after he came out of the army and literally "came out." He played on a small local team in London now. Luckily, on that night, Derrick's own bat was in the van. So, Marcie grabbed the bat and hit the fucker on the side of the head. He had run off, leaving her a bit shaken, though thankfully not hurt.

After that, Derrick insisted each van had a bat. If the

police asked, we were to say that it belonged to Derrick and he had left it there after playing a game, along with the ball and glove he also put in the vans, for authenticity and deniability! *No, your honour, the baseball bat was never intended to be used as a weapon; it was just in the right place at the right time*!

I was really glad to have it now. I pocketed the box cutter and, with my weapon in hand, ran back to the open door. I didn't have a plan, but I was glad I was dressed in dark clothing with a hood to hide my hair and some of my face.

I hesitated; I really should call the police. *No! No time! They're hurting him, and by the time the police get here, he could be dead!* My inner devil screamed, and I knew she was right.

I was going to have to pull up my big girl panties and rescue him myself.

I shouldn't have listened to Charlie Puth earlier. Obviously, the lyrics *Superman's got nothing on me!* had gone to my head, and I now thought I was some sort of bloody superhero in a movie. Shit!

This was so unlike me. I was not a person who ran into things head-on without thinking. I was not just a shy person; I was a scaredy cat too, to be honest, and what I was contemplating doing was way out of my comfort zone. However, I had been promising myself I would be more confident and assertive. This wasn't exactly what I had meant at the time, but hey, ho!

Suck it up, girl! My inner devil said, and I wanted to strangle her as I took a deep breath and entered the building. I crept down the stairway, which faced the outer door, with the bat held up and to the side as if I was waiting for someone to throw a pitch.

It had gone quiet when I first entered the building, and I

held my breath, wondering if somehow they knew I was there. I exhaled when the sound of a punch and an '*oof*' rang out.

What the hell was I doing? I was shaking and terrified. I needed to turn around and go hide and call the police. I turned to leave but stopped and closed my eyes at the sounds of heavy breathing, grunts, and flesh pounding on flesh. The sounds sent shivers down my spine.

"Stupid, mother fuckers!" I heard Mr Sexy Voice shout.

His voice was still sexy despite the pain in it, but his words were slurred, making my heart lurch and my stomach churn. He was hurt, and I needed to stop them from hurting him more.

I tiptoed down the steps. I was halfway down when a phone rang, and the other noises stopped. There was another door at the bottom of the stairs, and I dashed to the side of it just as it opened.

One of the black guys came out, yapping away frantically in some foreign language I didn't understand. The door closed behind him, and he spit out what sounded like a curse in whatever language it was, then turned to go back inside, and that's when I swung. He was taller than me but only by a few inches and slim built, so he went down like a sack of potatoes, out cold! Yay, I mentally high-fived myself. Gosh, that was strangely exciting. One down, one to go!

I remembered a movie I saw once where the hero knocked on the door, and when the bad guy opened it, he punched him right in the face. I decided to try the same tactic. I used the bat to knock lightly on the door and took up position off to the side again. It opened quicker than I had anticipated, but the guy clearly didn't expect to see me in front of him and didn't have time to react before I swung my bat again and whacked him.

Unfortunately, he was a lot bigger than the other guy it didn't knock him out. Instead, he staggered back. I followed quickly and hit him again on the other side of his head. That did it. He fell into the room, definitely out cold this time. I played a lot of tennis at high school, and I had a great swing and a mean backhand; thank God for that. He was still breathing, too. I sent up a silent prayer of thanks for that one! I might want to get my Mr Sexy Voice out of here, but I didn't want to kill anyone in the process.

I stepped towards Mr Sexy Voice and stopped dead for a minute and just stared at his almost naked form. I couldn't help it. I had never seen a man who looked that good before. He had strong shoulders and such well-defined arse cheeks. He was only wearing boxer briefs, which showed them off so well I could barely refrain from grabbing them just to give them a squeeze and feel how hard they were.

His head was hanging down, and it bobbed slightly as if he was trying to stay awake, but even though he was barely conscious and strung up like he was, he still looked powerful. What a body. I could definitely climb that like a tree.

Oh, and he had a tattoo on his right shoulder; it looked like a giant spider's web, but instead of a spider, he had an eight-point star within it. I wasn't sure what that signified, but it was sexy as hell. I did like a guy with tattoos.

He groaned again, bringing me out of my thoughts. My cheeks reddened in shame. Seriously, this was not the time to be ogling the poor guy. I needed to move my arse before the men woke up. I ran towards him and took out the boxcutter, but I couldn't reach his hands. I grabbed the chair from the corner of the room and quickly climbed up to cut him free. He dropped down and fell to his knees with a loud groan. He was still conscious, but barely. Hooking my arms under his, I helped him to sit.

"We need to get out of here," I said, grabbing his trousers and helping him put them on.

He needed to be decent, but we didn't have time for the rest of this clothing, which looked shredded anyway. The black guys were still out cold, but I doubted they'd remain that way for much longer. I didn't know how we were going to make it out of here, but we had to.

With a great deal of effort, we made it out of the room and up the stairs with him half walking, half leaning on me. My nerves were fraught as, at any time, I expected one of the guys to come chasing after us.

I stopped at the front door and peered out, checking to see if the black SUV had returned. I didn't want to escape the guys downstairs only to run into more outside. Poor Mr Sexy Voice was valiantly holding on to his consciousness, but I didn't know how long for.

Everything seemed quiet, so we stumbled through the door and made our way down the alley, doing our half-leaning, half-dragging thing again. It was a strain to hold the bat in one hand and help take his weight with the other, but he needed the help, and I was not letting go of that bat. Not for anything.

After what seemed like an eternity but was probably only a few minutes, we reached Marcie's van, and I opened the passenger door. It took a bit of pushing and shoving, but I finally got him inside. Did I get a squeeze of his ass as I did it? You better believe I did. But it was only because there was no other way to get him inside, of course, and nothing to do with me wanting to cop a feel of his body. Yeah right!

I secured his seatbelt and then ran around to the driver's side. As I climbed into the van, I checked the door of the building, but there was still no sign of the two black guys. I breathed a sigh of relief as I started the engine. We needed to get out of there as fast as possible.

"Where to?" I asked.

He didn't reply. I looked over at him and he was

unconscious. Oh shit, what was I going to do now? I didn't know where to take him.

"Mr Rominov, can you hear me?"

Yes, I called him Mr Rominov because I didn't know his first name, and Mr Sexy Voice or Jerk seemed highly inappropriate right now.

He didn't make a sound. I tried again, shaking his shoulder lightly. "Mr Rominov?"

Still nothing.

"Hey, wake up!" I shouted, shaking him harder.

No response. The guy was out cold. Shit, what was I supposed to do with him now? *I can think of a few things,* was the inappropriate comment from my inner devil. I shook my head and completely ignored her. This was not the time to be stupid. I needed to keep it together and figure out what to do.

I huffed as I drove out of the alley frantically trying to weigh up my options. I couldn't call the cops now, not after I had charged in there like a vengeful siren and smashed two guys over the skull. I had a feeling that wouldn't go down too well with the police. They didn't like vigilante's in the UK. I could end up in real trouble. I didn't even know Mr Rominov's full name or anything else about him, so I had no idea where to take him or who to call to come get him.

I thought of the club where we'd first met, but it would be closed now. Anyway, I doubted the guy would want me taking him there, not in the state he was in. Also, it might not be safe. It could be where the black guys kidnapped him from.

The hospital was an option. I could drop the unconscious Russian off at a hospital anonymously and let them deal with him. I didn't think he had recognised me, he'd been barely conscious while I rescued him, so I might get away with that.

I didn't know who those guys were or why they had kidnapped him and were beating him up. Maybe he had been a jerk to them too, I thought snarkily, then felt burning shame. That was so unfair. Even if he had been a bit of a jerk to me, he didn't deserve to be beaten up! Besides, it seemed as if they were trying to get information out of him for something. If that was the case, they could be looking for him again, and the hospital was an obvious place to look. Damn. I couldn't take him there. No, there was nothing for it but to take him back to my place. I would look after him until he woke up and I could get him proper help.

A short while later, I parked in the driveway at the rear of my home. It was dark and silent. Claire and Marcie had gone away for a Spa break. Thank goodness. I didn't know how I would explain all this to them. However, as I sat there deliberating how to get the guy out of the van and into the house, I wondered if perhaps I should call them. Maybe Marcie could help.

I took my phone out but hesitated and bit my lip. Marcie worked for the Rominov family occasionally, but as far as I was aware, the relationship was solely of a professional nature. It was unlikely that she would have any way of contacting someone who could help him out with business hours. It was better not to call her. It would only worry her and Claire. They would want to call the police, and after what I had done, I was hoping to avoid that unless absolutely necessary.

No, I would keep to my plan. I would look after Mr Sexy Voice until he woke and told me who to call. With my decision made, I gave him a shake. This time, he roused enough for me to get him out of the car and into the house, but it was a struggle for him to remain awake.

Nevertheless, with a great deal of effort and some stopping to catch our breath, we did our half walk, half carry technique again to get him up the stairs before he fell awkwardly onto my bed and passed out again.

I sighed with relief as I slid to the floor next to him, pulling in great lungfuls of air. Geez, I needed to get to the gym more.

I looked at him sprawled face down on the bed. I'd have to turn him over, get him into a better position and deal with his injuries. I might even have to strip him. I blushed, feeling overwhelmed at the thought.

Ha, at last, we have a man in our bed! My inner devil shouted with glee! My face flamed at my thoughts. Geez, I needed to get a grip on my silliness. All this internal battling between my good and bad sides had to stop. I was acting nuts.

I needed to make the guy comfortable. It was time to act like a grown-up and not some silly little girl. I just rescued a man. I was badass. My chest swelled with pride. My confidence was growing, and I liked how that felt. My inner devil was a part of me that I had kept down for too long. She might be inappropriate at times, but usually, she just encouraged me to embrace my true self and not hide behind my shyness. I had to let her out more and stop reigning her in.

I had done that tonight. I'd pulled my big girl panties on, and it had worked out. There was no reason why I couldn't keep doing that. All I had to do was believe in myself. Just like Claire and Marcie always said. From now on, I was going to own being an adult. I was going to be more confident, and I was going to become the kind of woman I wanted to be.

I mentally rolled up my sleeves and got to work. I grunted as I pulled the heavy Russian up the bed and then rolled him over so I could assess just how bad his injuries were.

As I already knew, his face was severely bruised and swollen, and his wrists were red and grazed from the rope he'd been tied up with. I hadn't really had time to notice his front as we escaped after spending too much time ogling his ass. I did now, though. He had a well-defined torso and an obvious six-pack underneath a hell of a lot of blood and bruises and red patches where more bruising was likely to form. There were several gashes, too, probably from the large sovereign-type rings one of the guys had been wearing. Gosh, they looked terrible, but not too deep, thankfully.

I gingerly touched his ribs, and he groaned in pain but didn't wake up. I bit my lip. What if the guy had internal bleeding or something? I should have taken him to the hospital, I berated myself.

No, maybe not. That would mean the police might be informed, or at the very least, there would be a lot of questions to be answered at the hospital. Questions I didn't have answers to or didn't want to give answers to. Besides something about the whole situation made me think that the Russian wouldn't want either the hospital or the police involved.

However, I needed some other help with this. And then it dawned on me. Derrick! I needed Derrick. Derrick had been in the military for years and had trained as a medic. He would know exactly how to deal with My Sexy Voice's injuries.

I grabbed the phone, called Derrick, and told him to get over here pronto as his medical experience was required.

"You okay? What the hell's going on?" he asked, sounding frantic.

"It's not for me, it's for a friend, he got himself beaten up," I told him.

"What? He who?" he asked, louder this time.

"You'll see when you get here. Please just come," I pleaded in response.

I heard another sleepy-sounding male voice in the background and then some whispering before he said, "Be right over!" and hung up.

I paced around, unsure what to do while I waited for him to show. I kept glancing at Mr Sexy Voice to check if he was still breathing correctly, and thankfully, he was. Thirty minutes later,

Derrick stood over him with what looked like a medical kit in his hand.

"What the hell happened? And what the hell is Mr Rominov doing in your house and in your bed in this state?" he asked in a voice that made me think of a headmaster.

"He was kidnapped! And then beaten up by a couple of guys, and I rescued him and brought him home," I replied in a rush.

"You did what? Wait, what?" he asked, shaking his head in confusion.

I took a deep breath before explaining everything a bit more calmly and in more length. While I did so, Derrick systematically assessed the injuries.

"Well, apart from the obvious cuts and bruises, I would say he has two broken ribs, but luckily, nothing else is broken, and I don't think the ribs are too bad. They certainly haven't punctured any lungs."

I sighed in relief.

Derrick removed Mr Sexy Voice's trousers and boxers, which were now covered in blood. I blushed and forced myself to turn away and not ogle the poor man again.

After removing his clothes, Derrick wiped him down with disinfectant wipes and put antiseptic cream on his cuts. Once that was done, Derrick dressed Mr Sexy Voice in a pair of shorts which he had in his bag. I tried not to look but felt my blush deepening as I caught a glimpse of something I shouldn't. Oh my!

Together, we settled him against the pillows and under the covers before heading downstairs.

Derrick was concerned that Mr Sexy Voice might have a concussion and told me to keep an eye on him throughout the night. He also left some strong pain medication for him to take when he woke up.

As he left, he warned, "When he wakes, get a number for someone to call to come collect him. Then get rid of him and keep away from him. He is obviously in trouble, and you don't need to be dragged into any more of it. He is dangerous!"

His blue eyes glinted as cold as ice as he spoke. I gulped. This was not my usual flighty, happy-go-lucky friend; this was the side of Derrick who had been a soldier. This was a powerful and dangerous man, and if he was telling me that the one asleep upstairs was another dangerous man, I really should listen.

I nodded and closed the door behind him.

Derrick was right, and yet I knew that I had never felt as alive as I had tonight, nor had I ever had as much excitement. So, I would try to heed his warning, but I wasn't sure how easily that would be.

I made a coffee and trudged upstairs. I spent the rest of the night sitting in a chair next to my bed, watching over my patient. It brought back unhappy memories, and it was exhausting, but strangely, it also made me feel needed again. I hadn't felt needed since my mum passed away, and it was nice.

CHAPTER 14
ASH

SATURDAY MORNING - SAVED BY LITTLE
MISS HOT MESS

woke with a start. My whole body felt like it had been hit by a train. Shit, what happened? I tried to open both of my eyes but couldn't, and it took some effort to crack even one open. I realised then that the left was swollen shut.

"Hey, you're awake," a female voice said.

I looked towards it, and my breath caught. It was her! Little Miss Hot Mess! What the heck? How the hell was she here? And where the hell was here?

I glanced around, my head pounding. I noticed that I was in a room on a bed that I didn't recognise at all.

She smiled at me, and I suddenly didn't care where I was; I was just glad to have her smile at me. It was such a gorgeous smile.

"Little Miss Hot Mess," I said, but it came out like an incoherent mumble. I tried to smile back at her but ended up grimacing in pain instead. My lips were swollen, and my cheeks ached.

Memories rushed back. Mohammad, the bigger guy, getting beaten up, and then vague images of someone who had helped me escape. It was a bit of a blur. Things didn't make complete sense.

More questions bombarded me. How did I get here? What was she doing here? Where was I, and who had helped me escape? I wanted to ask them, but my brain couldn't seem to focus on what to say. I was sweating with the effort.

She leaned over me and wiped my brow with a cloth. My heart stuttered at her closeness. It was all I had been dreaming of for the last week. I tried to smile again but couldn't. Shit, I must look terrible. Just typical, I was finally getting to see Little Miss Hot Mess again, and I was in this state. *Fuck! What a way to make an impression, Ash!* I chastised myself.

It seemed I was destined to make a lousy impression where she was concerned. First, I was a complete jerk, then kissed her and ran off without even getting her number, and second, I was beaten up and looked a bloody fright. I had no idea what she must think of me, but if she didn't run in the opposite direction after this, she must be crazy!

I sighed. I would worry about changing her opinion of me later. In the meantime, I needed to find out where I was and how I was rescued and ended up here. I tried to sit up and groaned at the pain in my side. I guessed I had a broken rib or two, after all.

"Are you in pain?" she asked, and I groaned again in answer. My head spun, and I felt disorientated.

"Here, take these," she held up some pills and a glass of water in front of me.

"They are for the pain; Derrick left them for you last night when he checked you over. You have two broken ribs and some minor cuts from that asshole's ring, but otherwise, you only have a lot of bruises. I guess you're lucky, considering the beating you were getting."

She sat on the bed beside me. I put the pills in my mouth,

and she helped me sip some water before asking, "Do you remember what happened?"

She was still sitting close to me on the bed. I shook my head. I couldn't speak, not simply because of my swollen mouth but more because of the effect she had on me. When she was near, my usually cool, unaffected nature was the complete opposite; hot and very much affected. It was disconcerting, and yet I found I liked it. Also, I wanted to find out what she knew before I said anything.

"You were attacked, and some guys were beating you up. Do you remember any of that?" she asked, her eyes searching mine as she waited for me to answer.

I nodded slowly. More images flashed through my mind as the memories came flooding back, memories of a tiny figure in black and a woman's voice telling me, *"We need to get out of here."* I could vaguely remember catching a glimpse of blonde hair as my rescuer helped me up some stairs, and I remembered thinking that the hair reminded me of Little Miss Hot Mess but dismissing the idea at the time.

I looked at the woman before me in awe as I realised that it was, in fact, her. Somehow, I was rescued by the woman I had been fantasising about for the last week. How was that for a weird coincidence? And how the hell did that happen?

I really needed to ask her, but my head was still so fuzzy, and I still couldn't seem to think clearly enough to form the question.

"Do you remember me?" she asked.

I nodded, "Little Miss Hot Mess!"

"Huh?" she asked, looking at me as if my brain was addled, "What are you talking about?"

"You," I pointed at her, "The waitress from Glitz, my Little Miss Hot Mess!" I explained, forcing the words out.

"You were a real mess covered in cream and cake but also

really hot," I told her. The words were coming a bit easier now. "I didn't know your name, so I gave you one," I said, making a show of checking her out.

I gulped. My waitress was even hotter than I remembered.

"I'm Ash, by the way," I added, realising I still hadn't introduced myself. My words were coming a bit more easily now.

"Gracie," she said quickly, "My name is Gracie!"

"I know. Now. Nice to meet you properly, Gracie," I nodded my head more vigorously this time and grimaced at the sharp pain in my head.

"Wait, we need to talk, but I'm getting you an ice pack first, so stay there, and I will be back in a minute," she said, rushing from the room.

She returned a short while later with an ice pack and held it to my face over my left eye. I leaned into her and smelled her wrist. She smelled good. I wanted to lick her. Instead, I took the ice pack and pulled away from her slightly before I could do something stupid like try to kiss her again. *Now was not the time!* I reminded myself sternly. Besides, I wasn't in any fit state to do that. Not that my cock was convinced. It took that moment to decide to jerk, and I moved my legs to cover the motion. Geez, I must have lost quite a bit of blood during the beating, but it obviously wasn't enough to affect that part of my anatomy.

Despite my pain, I really wanted to re-enact last week's kiss. Maybe if I asked, my Little Miss Hot Mess would take pity on me and kiss me. Although, the way I looked right now, I'd probably scare her off for good. I had to behave myself and make a better impression than I had.

"So, what was that all about last night?" she questioned, oblivious to my internal musings.

I hesitated. I was not sure what I should say, so I decided to keep it as simple as possible, but first, I needed to know what she knew.

"How about you tell me what you saw and heard and how you got me out? Then I will tell you how I got there in the first place?"

She told me, and I couldn't believe what I was hearing. This beautiful woman had rushed into a basement, risking her life to face two men and help a virtual stranger who had acted like a jerk to her only days before. Not only that, but she also actually managed to rescue me. On her own. Wow! I looked at her with a mix of awe and lust. This girl was a badass, and it was hot!

"I can't believe you not only went in there to help me after I had been such a jerk to you the other night, but you also beat the two guys up and then rescued me!" I said incredulously.

She blushed but grinned at me and admitted, "It was kind of cool!"

Cool? Wow. I was grinning inside because my face wouldn't allow me to do it for real. This girl was amazing!

She told me how we got back to her place and that it was Derrick who had fixed me up. I was grateful for that. The pain medication was starting to kick in, but even with it, my broken ribs ached like fuck.

"So, is he the one who put the shorts on me then?" I asked.

"I had been hoping that was you," I said, with wicked thoughts running through my mind.

She blushed a deeper red, and it was so cute and made her look angelic.

Then she stunned me by saying, "If I ever take your clothes off, it won't be to put others back on and definitely not when you're unconscious. You will be fully awake and begging me to!"

And just like that, I caught a glimpse of her inner devil!

The combination of her angelic looks and her inner devil set me on fire, and I groaned and squirmed as the semi-hard-on I had been sporting jerked in response.

"I just might hold you to that, Little Miss Hot Mess!" I said, chuckling when she squirmed in embarrassment.

"So, your turn to talk!" she said, sounding all prim again. I loved the contradiction in her.

I took a sip of the water she held for me while I tried to decide what to say.

"Someone jumped me on the way to a meeting," I said, deciding to be as vague as possible.

"Who were they, and why were they asking about a lab?" she asked.

I looked away from her. Shit, she heard them questioning me about the lab; damn, she hadn't said that.

Still, I stuck to the story I'd started, "I have no idea, a case of mistaken identity probably."

"So, you are telling me you didn't know these guys or anything about a lab?" I could tell she was a bit suspicious now.

"That's what I'm saying, yes," I confirmed, hoping she would let it drop.

I didn't know why, but I didn't like lying to her. It was better for her that I didn't drag her into my family's business any more than I had already. Nevertheless, it felt wrong.

I wanted to tell her everything, which was out of character for me. I was secretive by nature but also through necessity. I wanted to tell her everything, but I wouldn't. I didn't know her. I couldn't trust a stranger with my family secrets. Yet somehow, she didn't feel like a stranger to me. It was odd. That shocked me, so I bit my tongue before I could blurt out the truth.

"Uh huh!" obviously, she was not at all convinced.

"Well, now you are awake and can give a statement. Do you want me to call the police?" Gracie asked, sounding hesitant.

"No!" I said quickly. I couldn't help but notice how her body relaxed a bit at that.

"I'm from a prominent family, as you've probably guessed, and this will cause publicity that we don't need. My family and I will deal with it privately. Plus, it is a bit embarrassing that I found myself in such a position," I added on for good measure, hoping she would think that was the reason I didn't want police involvement and nothing else. I don't think she did, though.

"These were bad guys, so you shouldn't feel bad about them jumping you. I mean, it is not something you would expect," she consoled me, obviously deciding not to call me out on my lies, which I was sure she could see right through.

She was observant, intelligent, and super sexy, with just a little bit of sass that had me intrigued. I really had to see this girl again.

"Well, I'm sure it isn't really any of my business, and since I didn't call the police at the time and went all vigilante on their asses, I guess sticking with the no police idea suits me too," she said with a nervous smile.

Yep, she definitely knew there was more to the story than I was telling her. I just hoped it wasn't going to scare her off. Nah, I wouldn't let it! It took me a week to find her again, and I wasn't letting her get away from me that easily. I would just have to pour on some more charm.

"So, is there someone I can call to come collect you? Or can I drive you somewhere?" she hurried on, stating, "You didn't have a jacket or phone when I rescued you, so I couldn't look for any contacts then."

I guessed the bastards must have smashed my phone at the scene, so we couldn't be tracked.

"May I borrow your phone, and I'll call someone?" I asked because I really did need to let my family know where I was and that I was safe. They were liable to be frantic by now.

"Oh, you might want to get them to bring you some more clothes, too; yours were covered in blood. I'll give you some privacy to make your call," Gracie said, handing me her mobile and heading for the door.

"Will do, and Gracie?" I called after her, "Thanks for rescuing me and thanks for this," I waved her phone at her.

"You're welcome!" she smiled, and my heart skipped a beat.

When this was sorted out, I was taking that girl out! Then, back to my place if all went well. I felt pleased at the thought as I dialled Romi's number.

CHAPTER 15
GRACIE

SATURDAY MORNING - SAVED BY MR
SEXY VOICE

"Will do, and Gracie? Thanks for rescuing me, and thanks for this," Ash waved my phone at me.

My breath hitched. Even beaten to a pulp, there was something about the sexy Russian that took my breath away. I was glad to see that he was looking a little better than he had a few hours ago. I kept a cold cloth pressed to the right side of his face most of the night to help reduce the swelling. It had done the trick. The right side of his face had been the most swollen last night, but today, his left eye was. It looked sore, but the ice pack he was now holding against it would hopefully help. The painkillers were easing his pain, and he was talking better. All in all, I was pleased with the outcome of my overnight nursing skills.

"You're welcome!" I smiled, leaving the room just as he began talking rapidly in Russian.

I was exhausted after being up all night and was getting sleepier by the minute, so I headed downstairs, intent on making some coffee to keep myself awake.

As I made a cup with some toast for breakfast, my mind

kept returning to our conversation. I couldn't help but notice the hesitation in Ash's voice or the way he paused before answering my questions. It definitely got my Spidey senses tingling, and not in a good way.

I wondered if I should sneak back upstairs and listen in to what he was saying, but I dismissed the idea immediately. It was better not to know whatever it was that he was so reluctant to tell me. Besides, I didn't speak Russian, so it would be pointless anyway.

I was intrigued, though. There was definitely more to my Mr Sexy Voice than he wanted to admit.

I smirked to myself because I couldn't believe that not only had I created a nickname for him, but he had created one for me, too! "My Little Miss Hot Mess," he'd called me. "You were a real mess covered in cream and bits of cake, but you were also really hot." *Ooh la la*, my inner devil purred.

He called me his and thought I was hot? I felt giddy with pleasure at that. He'd been flirting with me, and I liked it. I wanted him to do it more. I felt my cheeks heating with the very idea, but for once, I didn't care. I was determined not to let my shyness stop me from enjoying Ash's flirtations or, in fact, returning them.

I remembered telling him, *"If I ever take your clothes off, it won't be to put others back on and definitely not when you're unconscious. You will be fully awake and begging me to!"*

I giggled. Oh my god, I couldn't believe I'd actually said that! Maybe all that practice with the older men at the pub had helped after all.

I thought about his reply, *"I think I just might hold you to that, Little Miss Hot Mess!"* Oh my, I so hoped he did! The sooner, the better! Maybe I'd be getting laid by Mr Sexy Voice after all. I felt like I might burst with excitement from the prospect. He was so very hot.

Last night, I'd finally let my sassy side out, and it had been freeing. I had kicked the ass of two big black guys and freed my sexy Russian. I'd brought him home and looked after him. It had all been terrifying but also the most exciting thing I had ever done. Apart from kissing the hot Russian while we rolled around in creamy stuff, of course. If I could pull off a rescue like that, I could surely handle a bit of flirting. Oh, and maybe plenty more if I was lucky and didn't stuff it up through shyness. I was a real badass, and from now on, I was going to act like one. I couldn't wait to flirt with him again.

I finished my breakfast and decided to make some for my sexy guest. As I buttered his toast, I wondered if he had finished his phone call yet, and who it was he had called. I knew he had a sister. I wondered if it had been her or maybe the man she had been with at the Glitz opening. I wondered how he and his family would deal with what had happened.

I frowned, remembering his reluctance when answering my questions. I felt my cautious nature taking over once more. I needed to rein myself in. I was getting carried away. The guy was indeed hot, and I liked his flirting, but there were things he wasn't telling me, and I wasn't sure what to think about that.

Who was he really? Why were those guys hurting him? Why had they been questioning him?

I had a lot of questions, but I wasn't sure I really wanted to know the answers.

I hadn't wanted to go to the police for obvious reasons, but I didn't buy his reasons for not wanting to contact them. Although I was happy he didn't want the police involved, it still seemed strange. I wondered what he was hiding.

Derrick's warning came to mind. He was right. Ash Rominov was trouble, and not just because of how well he kissed me or how my body reacted to him. The question was, how much trouble? And was it something I wanted to get more involved in or not?

I didn't know the Rominov family at all but if they were the type of family that people kidnapped and tortured, maybe I should steer clear, regardless of how hot Mr Sexy Voice was. It wasn't something that happened to average, everyday families after all.

I bit my lip, suddenly wondering precisely what I had gotten myself involved in. I'd rushed into things last night with little thought, and yes, I had even enjoyed it, but it could have gone so wrong. I was lucky that I had pulled the rescue off. I was just now beginning to realise that I could have been in serious trouble if I hadn't been so lucky. I gulped, no longer feeling quite such a badass after all.

Flirting with Ash was fun, and the prospect of sex with him was exciting, but I wasn't sure if either was worth putting myself in more danger for. It was probably better to keep my distance and end things now before I got myself into any further trouble. Maybe this was as far as I should let things go.

Yes, I nodded, confirming my decision. That was probably for the best. I would play the gracious host until someone came for him, and then I would say goodbye. So why did the very thought of saying goodbye to him tug at my heart?

I shook my head and took a deep breath, garnering my resolve before I picked up his breakfast tray and headed upstairs.

I just reached the top stair when the back door burst open. My heart sped up. *What the hell?*

I peered over the banister and saw one of the black guys from last night run in. Shit! I dropped the tray in fright and bolted into my bedroom, shouting, "Ash!"

Luckily, he had already managed to get himself up and was standing beside the bed when I darted into the room.

"The black guys are here, or one of them is," I said while running to the side of my bed.

Thanks to Derrick, I'd started keeping a large Maglite torch there for safety purposes. As he explained, it was helpful if the power went out, or if I needed to break a window to get out if there was a housefire. He also said, *'No, your honour, it was not intended to be used as a weapon when the man broke into my house, but I panicked and hit him over the head in self-defence!'* which told me the real reason he wanted me to put it there.

When he said these things as if he were talking to a Sheriff in court, it always made me snigger. Unlike in the USA, we regular folks in the UK couldn't legally carry any kind of weapon, so if the need arose where we needed a weapon, we had to make do with whatever was nearby.

Derrick was an advocate for self-defence training for all women and gay men, and he ran several courses. I'd taken part in his beginners one and was signed up for the advanced. Thank goodness I had a friend like Derrick.

I grabbed the torch just as the big guy came rushing into the room. He had a large machete in his hand. Oh shit! I didn't have time to react, but luckily, Ash had already positioned himself behind the door. As the guy ran towards me, Ash jumped on his back, taking him down.

"Ooof!" they both said as the air whooshed out of them, and the machete flew from the black guy's hand as they hit the floor.

I winced at the sound, imagining how much that must have hurt Ash with his broken ribs.

I rushed over to help. I was about to wallop the guy on the head when his friend ran in, distracting me, and I missed. Luckily, Ash had managed to grab the guy's head and banged it on the ground several times.

I left them struggling and set my sights on the smaller dude with the sovereign-type rings who'd just arrived. He was brandishing a smaller knife in his hand and charged at me. I dodged him, stepping to the side the way Derrick had shown me, and grabbed his arm. In a slight variation to the move, I used the Maglite to batter his hand, loosening his grip on the knife, which fell to the floor.

He wasn't expecting that and looked as surprised as I was that I'd done it. We stared at each other for a few seconds in shock before he drew a gun from the back of his waistband. Oh, hell no, was all I could think as I watched him bring it up towards me!

CHAPTER 16

ASH

struggled hard with the big guy. He kept trying to get up, but I held him down, pinning his arms with mine, not wanting him to be able to turn around or get a chance to use that bloody machete.

It wasn't an easy task. The guy was huge. I wasn't small myself, but he was bigger, and I was weak after the beating I'd had.

I wondered where that double-crossing bastard, Mohammad, was. As if conjured up by my thoughts, he appeared in the doorway. After taking in the scene, he charged straight for Gracie.

Shit. He had a knife. She didn't have a baseball bat now, and I doubted her torch was going to prove helpful against his knife.

I pounded the big guy's head on the ground. I needed to get to her, but the big fucker just wouldn't pass out. My ribs screamed in agony and sweat ran down my face as I continued to try to pound his head into the floor, but I was losing the battle. If I didn't get to Gracie soon, she might be injured or worse, and I couldn't let that happen.

Out of my peripheral vision, I saw Gracie side-step Mohammad. I watched in awe when, in a smooth action, she grabbed his arm and then brought her large torch down on his hand, making him drop the knife. Wow! Badass! And so hot! I wasn't expecting that. He obviously wasn't either because he stopped his attack and stared in shock. It didn't last, though. A second later, he pulled a gun from his waistband. Oh, hell no!

As soon as I saw him raise that gun towards Gracie, I saw red. My fury at Mohammad and concern for Gracie gave me the extra strength I needed. I cracked the big guy's skull hard, and he went limp in my arms. I immediately sprang to my feet, all thoughts of pain and tiredness gone.

"Gracie!" I shouted in warning.

I ran towards them and threw myself at the bastard who dared to threaten her, tackling him side-on. "Oof!" the air whooshed out of me with the force of the impact as I brought him to the ground.

Fuck, that hurt. My ribs screamed in pain again. If they hadn't already been broken, they sure as hell were now. Mohammad was going to pay for this. He was a dead man. If he hadn't been already for kidnapping and beating me, then he certainly was now for threatening my Little Miss Hot Mess.

As we struggled, the gun went off, barely missing her and lodging in the wall. That was close. Too close.

Gracie moved behind us and out of the line of fire as Mohammad and I grappled for control of the weapon. I kept myself pressed close to his body, with one hand tightly around his wrist and the other holding him to me so that he couldn't bring that gun up again.

We struggled like that for a few seconds. Mohammad was smaller than me and much smaller than the other guy, but I was too weak to get the better of him in this position. No matter how I tried,

I couldn't get him to drop the gun. My strength was waning again. I didn't know how long I could keep this up. So, I did the only thing I could in the position we were in and head-butted the little fuck.

That was something I learned from a friend up in Glasgow. It's called a *"Glasgow kiss"* there. They've got a sick sense of humour that way, I guess.

It didn't knock him out, but it dazed him enough for me to grab the gun and pull the trigger. He hit the floor hard. Under normal circumstances, I'd have been annoyed at killing him so easily after what he'd done. But these weren't normal circumstances, and I was too damn exhausted and worried about Gracie to care.

I struggled to stand, feeling dizzy. I swayed slightly on my feet, but luckily, Gracie was there. I put my arm around her as she helped me to the bed. I pulled her down beside me. That was when I heard Miki shouting, "Sashenka!"

Oh, oh! He was using my full name, so I guessed he was pissed at me for going off on my own to meet the informant. Shit! "Up here!" I shouted back, and a second later, he and Romi ran into the room.

I still had my arm around Gracie and kept it there. They ignored her and started firing off questions to me in Russian, asking what the heck was going on. I did my best to answer.

Gracie started to move away, but I pulled her closer. *Uh uh, you are staying right here, baby, you are mine now.*

"Miki, Romi, this is my Little Miss Hot Mess, Gracie," I said proudly.

"Gracie, sweetheart, this is my brother Miki and cousin Romi," I introduced. Both guys grinned.

"Nice to meet you, Gracie; we have heard a lot about you," they said almost in unison, then laughed and smirked when she blushed.

"So, you are not only hot and sassy but brave too!" Miki stated with a wink.

"Yes, she is!" I growled at him, "And she is mine!" I stated possessively.

He could keep his bloody smiles and winks to himself. This girl was mine! Miki and Romi laughed, and I scowled at them.

"Got it, bro!" Miki chuckled.

Gracie was looking at me in shock. I winked at her.

"If you think I'm letting you go easily after you saved my life and then fought those guys a second time with me, you are so wrong!" I told her.

"Erm, what?" she asked, blinking rapidly as if she was trying hard to process my words.

"You heard me. You are mine now, Little Miss Hot Mess, and I won't be letting you go!" I informed her.

She gasped, looking outraged. Hmmm, obviously, we were not on the same page yet. Guess I needed to change that.

"I don't belong to anyone, and I'm certainly not yours!" she declared, standing up to face me with her hands on her hips, looking pissed.

"Ha, good luck, little brother," Miki said before he and Romi left the room, chuckling.

"We'll see!" I grinned at her. God, she was so hot! I eyed her up and down, wicked thoughts of all the things I wanted to do to her running through my mind.

"You're nuts!" she cried, shaking her head at me.

"Over you!" I agreed, nodding, and smiling.

"If I wasn't already before, I certainly would be after that little display of bravery, hon," I stated and then pulled her back down and onto my lap for a kiss.

She squealed, and I took the opportunity to plant my lips on hers the way I'd been dreaming of doing for the last week. She tasted so good; even without the cream, she tasted sweet and like sin. I could kiss her for hours, even with my sore mouth. I was very pleased that she was kissing me back just as deeply. Hmm, I groaned against her lips as she moaned into mine.

I was so lost in her that I didn't hear Miki and Romi entering the room again until one of them cleared their throat. I very reluctantly broke our kiss but kept my arms around her. I didn't seem to want to let her go, and thankfully, she didn't fight me on it. We stared at each other, panting hard. That kiss had taken our breath away.

I looked into her gorgeous blue eyes, and it hit me like a punch to the gut. She was the one. At that very moment, I knew it. Woah! That thought should worry me; we had only just met, after all, yet it didn't.

I marvelled at how, just a week ago, I'd thought it would be difficult for me to find a woman who could fit into my life and believed that love was unlikely to be in my future. Yet here she stood. Not only could I imagine her standing beside me as my equal, taking the dangers of my life in her stride, but I could imagine falling deeply in love with her. I didn't think it would take much. I felt like I was already halfway there. She was staring at me, too, with a shy look on her face, and I wondered if she was thinking something similar.

"We need to go. Cleaners are on their way," Miki said, pulling me from my musings.

I nodded as he and Romi lifted the big guy between them and hoisted him out of the room.

Miki was right. We needed to get out of here. Our cleaners would take care of everything for us. Yet, I didn't move and kept her sitting on my lap. Her breath hitched and she gulped loudly as I pressed little kisses to her jaw and nibbled her neck. We really should move, but I wanted another minute to savour the feel of her in my arms. Besides, although the cleaners were on their way, thankfully, the police weren't.

Miki would have had Marko check. So, we had a few minutes.

Luckily, the gun Mohammed used had been fitted with a silencer. That was unusual for a weapon used by the Malia Boys, but it was probably all part of the plan to frame the Albanians with the attacks against us.

The UK wasn't a place where the average citizen carried a gun, so when one was fired, it was especially noticeable and attracted a lot of unwanted attention. The Malia Boys were not too bright and viewed going to jail as some sort of badge of honour, so they didn't really seem to care about keeping a low profile or being caught, but the Albanians did. They were brutal buggers and lived by their crazy code of rules, that was true, but they were generally intelligent enough to prefer not to get caught or end up in gun fights with the police. So, they tended to use silencers on their guns. We did, too, on the rare occasions we used them.

The use of a silencer here saved us from having to worry about police involvement. As prominent London businessmen, we had friends in high places, including several top lawyers, judges, and the head of the Metropolitan Police, and we wanted to keep it that way. We had to if we were ever going to become legit in the future. The police we had on our payroll were there for use in emergencies only. Like Glowacki, we tended to keep any contact with them to a bare minimum and only utilised our more corrupt resources if we absolutely needed to. The less we needed to use them, the less likely anyone would become suspicious of them or us.

"Pack a bag, enough for a few days," I told Gracie, grinning at her.

She was coming home with me, just like I had hoped for last night. If I played my cards right, that was where she would stay because now, I was thinking of something way more than the casual relationship I'd planned. If I had my way, she'd become a permanent fixture in my life. And I very much intended on having my way!

"Wait, what?!" she asked confused.

"You can't stay here in case more guys come looking for us, and this place needs to be cleaned up anyway," I explained.

"Okay, I'll call Derrick," she said.

No fucking way!

"No need, you are coming home with me," I said, trying to keep calm.

No way was she staying with anyone but me.

"Oh no, I am not!" she protested, standing up again and moving away from me.

"Oh yes, you are," I declared, standing up and stalking her.

She took a step back, and I followed her, backing her up against the wall.

"You are in trouble because of me, Gracie, and I will be the one to protect you until it is safe," I told her firmly.

She looked like she was about to protest further, but I took the opportunity to kiss her deeply again. She resisted for a second before melting into my embrace. When all her resistance disappeared, I pulled back. I stared at her and licked my lips. Her eyes tracked my tongue, and she gulped but didn't say anything. I smiled and moved away.

"Get your bag, honey. You're coming home with me," I said again.

She huffed, not ready to give in to me as completely as I'd thought.

"No. I don't know you, Ash. If I'm in danger, I should go and stay with Derrick," she replied, glaring at me.

My spine went rigid. The only person who would be protecting her was me. I was the reason she was in danger, and I would be the one to protect her.

Besides, we needed time to properly explore this thing between us, and I had a feeling that if I let her go just now, she might not give me the opportunity to do that in the future. But it looked like I was going to need to convince her of how good we could be together, and I knew just where to begin. I licked my lips and grinned wickedly as I crowded her again, pressing her back against the wall once more.

Leaning down I whispered in her ear, "Tell me you are mine to protect and keep safe, sweetheart!"

She shivered, and my cock twitched in my pants.

I smiled inwardly at her reaction, brushed my lips against hers and said it again.

CHAPTER 17
GRACIE

STILL SATURDAY MORNING - GOING HOME WITH ASH

Ash pressed me against the wall again, and it should have annoyed me. His predatory actions and possessive looks should have made me afraid of him, but I found they had completely the opposite effect. I didn't feel threatened by his behaviour at all. Instead, I was getting more turned on by the minute.

He was dangerous. I'd be a fool not to be aware of that. Yet, I didn't feel any aggression from him. I wasn't scared of him being violent towards me. In fact, somewhere deep down, I knew he would never be. No, the danger I sensed from this guy wasn't anything physical. Ash was dangerous to me in other ways because the power and strength I felt in him had me weak at the knees.

I couldn't help my shiver of desire when he whispered in my ear, "Tell me you are mine to protect and keep safe, sweetheart."

It would be so simple to give in and say those words, but I held off despite how much I longed to. This man could turn my mind to mush and make me do practically anything for him with just that voice of his.

I needed to hold my own with him, or he would walk all over me, and I didn't want to be that type of woman. Somehow, I didn't think that deep down he would wish me to be either.

Whoever Ash was, I felt that he would need a strong woman to stand at his side. As I thought back to the words he had said about me fighting beside him, I knew that to be the truth. Besides, I might still be a bit shy and awkward, but I was done allowing it to make me weak. I had found my strength the night before, and I was determined not to lose it.

"I can take care of myself. Last night and even this morning should have proved that," I replied. I was glad to hear my voice come out steady and strong, even though my knees felt weak at our closeness.

"You're amazing, Gracie. Don't think I don't know that. You did great last night and this morning, but you don't know my world like I do. You don't know the danger you could be in," he stated.

I processed his words. *His world?* Hmm, I wondered what exactly that meant but couldn't ponder it further as he continued.

"You're my responsibility now. Nobody else will protect you except for me. From now on, that's my job."

He was staring into my eyes so intently. My heart raced, and my breath was shallow as I gazed back at him. Was it wrong that I was thrilled by that? I wanted him to protect me. I wanted whatever it was he was offering. Oh, I had it bad! I gulped loudly, and he smirked, knowing he was affecting me in exactly the way he wanted to and pleased with the fact.

"Say the words, sweetheart," he mumbled, nibbling my ear.

His Russian accent was more pronounced again, and it sent waves of pleasure straight to my core. I felt my panties getting wet and I blushed. Oh, my holy hell! What this man could do to me with just his voice, eyes, or kiss was unbelievable. I couldn't begin to imagine what he could do to me if things went any further than that.

He looked up at me expectantly. I bit my lips, undecisive. I wanted to get to know the man in front of me, and I definitely hoped to have an intimate relationship with him. But was going home with him now the right thing to do? I really wasn't sure. I knew I felt safe with him, but was I really?

I sighed and nibbled on my lip again.

"You can trust me, Gracie," he said in earnest, and I saw the truth in his eyes. They were beautiful eyes. I could easily get lost in them. His hand cupped my cheek. I leaned into it, unable to stop myself. My core clenched when his lips brushed lightly over mine as he repeated the words he wanted me to say.

"Tell me you are mine to protect and keep safe, sweetheart."

I whimpered. Actually whimpered. Oh no! I could have cringed. My embarrassment quickly turned to passion, however, as he brushed light kisses all over my face and neck. His hands ran all over me. Shivers of electricity lit up my veins at his touch. He sucked on the sensitive part of my neck near my collarbone, and I moaned in pleasure.

"Say the words, sweetheart; I need to hear them from you," he demanded.

He wanted me to talk? He had to be kidding. I couldn't even think straight, let alone form a coherent sentence. I didn't want to talk. Talking wasn't important. Kissing was. I pulled his head down and tried to press his lips back on mine.

He pulled away again.

"You want me to kiss you, Gracie?" he asked.

I nodded and leaned towards him again, but he stopped me.

"Then you need to say what I want to hear," he replied, his lips close to mine but held just out of reach.

I pouted and tried for his lips again, but he held me off.

"Tell me, sweetheart!" he demanded again.

Damn that man! He was manipulating me and I knew it, but all I could think of at that moment was getting his lips back on mine. How he managed to make me want him so badly, I didn't know, but in that second, I realised that I would say the words. I would agree to go home with him. In fact, I would likely agree to anything he wanted just so he would keep kissing me. I was so lost in him.

"*I'm yours to protect and keep safe!* Say it, sweetheart, and I will," he murmured insistently.

And so, I did.

"I'm yours to protect and keep safe," I said in a rush, making him grin widely

"Good girl!" he said, rewarding me by kissing me deeply. We kissed for what felt like hours, but it was likely only a minute or two. Finally, he pulled away again, leaving us both panting hard.

We stared at each other with huge grins on our faces as we tried to catch our breath.

Whatever was happening between us affected us both in the same way. I couldn't help the feeling of happiness that bubbled inside me at that thought.

"You're mine, Gracie. Now go pack quickly," he said, turning me towards my wardrobe and patting me on the ass before leaving the room.

I was still a bit dazed from his kisses and his proclamation that I was now his to react. I probably should have protested, but I had enjoyed it, so I was glad he left, and I didn't need to.

I stuffed things into a small suitcase as I tried to process everything that happened and the jumble of emotions that were spinning inside me.

My hands shook, and I was aware that it wasn't just from kissing Ash. I was still feeling the effects of my nerves from our earlier confrontation with the black guys, and I hadn't even begun to process the fact that they had found us and attacked us in my home. Or the fact that one of them was now dead.

I was only beginning to realise the danger I'd been in, and I knew when the adrenaline wore off entirely, I'd need to deal with the fear I could feel buried away. Yet, despite the nerves and hidden fear, I was wildly excited at the same time. I had never felt anything like I did when I was with this guy. Who knew what lay in store for us in the future? I longed to find out.

This guy was special, and what was between us was special, and I knew that that kind of special didn't come along often. So, no matter how dangerous this guy and his world might be, I was ready to meet that danger head-on. That should have scared me. Yet, as soon as I realised it, I felt a sense of calmness, of rightness settle over me, and I quickly finished packing.

A short while later, I was sitting in the back of an SUV with Ash. He was holding my hand and smiling at me. Wow!

I tore my gaze away from his lips and forced myself to look out of the window instead so I wouldn't give in to my urge to straddle him and kiss him like a woman possessed. We weren't alone, and I wasn't ready for any more public displays of affection. My cheeks heated at the thought.

This all seemed so surreal I could hardly believe any of this had happened. A week ago, I had been annoyed at Ash for being a jerk and running off after kissing me, thinking I would never see his sexy self again. Now, here I was, heading to his home to stay with him.

It couldn't be real. Surely, it was a dream? Maybe I was still in a drunken stupor after getting fired and had dreamed the whole week up. Yet Ash's warm hand clasped in mine felt very real. I snuck a peek at him. He was still looking at me. He smirked and winked as if he knew my thoughts. Considering the heat, my face was probably bright red again, so he no doubt did.

I closed my eyes in embarrassment, and he gave my hand a little squeeze as he chuckled quietly.

That chuckle had the same effect on me as his eyes, his lips, his hands, and his voice. Oh my. If he kept that up, I wasn't going to be able to refrain from jumping his bones much longer.

I turned my head and stared unseeingly out of the window again. This was definitely no dream. I felt a thrill of excitement ran through me. I really had rescued him last night, and this morning, we were attacked and nearly shot.

I should probably be running as far away from this guy as possible, all things considered, but in the last week since we first met, my life had become pretty exciting! It was like I was on some sort of adventure which was both thrilling and dangerous.

I couldn't wait to see what else was ahead. Especially if it involved more kissing! I definitely wanted it to involve more kissing and maybe a lot more than that. *Oh yes, please!* I smirked, glad that my inner devil and I were once again in total agreement.

I watched the countryside fly by as we sped towards Ash's home. He had told me it was called Rominov Strana (literally Rominov land or country) and was located in the small town of Harpendon, near St. Albans, Hertfordshire. I was looking forward to seeing it. We couldn't be far away now.

I bit my lip. I needed to tell Derrick where I was going.

It wasn't as if I felt that Ash would hurt me. After all, he had insisted on protecting me, but nevertheless, we'd been attacked in my home, and I wasn't sure if my friends and family could be in any danger. Also, I couldn't just disappear. Derrick would be frantic and probably imagine the worst.

My concern was more about what I could tell Derrick without causing any issues for him or Ash and his family. I wasn't a fool. I knew there was more to Ash and his family than met the eye. I have read enough mafia-style romances not to believe they might even be Bratva. If so, then I needed to be careful what I said to others. I'd have to subtly check with him what he wanted me to say.

Claire and Marcie were away for a few days at the spa, so I didn't need to worry about telling them anything yet. I was glad about that. It meant they would be safe in case anybody else did try to kill us. That was something else I needed to talk to Ash about.

Hopefully, the cleaners, whoever they were, would fix and secure the house.

That expression alone had told me so much about who I was likely dealing with. I yawned. The adrenaline was finally wearing off, and I was left with an overwhelming tiredness.

"Will your clean-up crew fix the door?" I asked Ash just to be clear.

"Yes, sweetheart, don't worry about a thing; they will get everything sorted," he reassured me.

"What about the trouble?" I asked.

"My brothers and I will sort that out, hon; we will keep you safe, I promise," he said, and I could hear the sincerity in his voice.

"How did they find us?" I asked. It had only just dawned on me that I might have been followed home after all.

"No idea yet, hon, but I will find out."

I didn't press him any further on that but would later. At some point soon, we would need to have an honest talk about what he had gotten me into. In the meantime, I was too tired to deal with it.

"I need to call Derrick and let them know where I am," I said.

He assessed me before replying.

"Okay, you can do that later, but let me talk to him first and explain things. You were due to be off work today, so that is fine, but tomorrow, you will need to call the pub and tell them you're sick and won't be in for a few days as you can't go to work until we sort this out," he told me.

How did he know my work schedule? Another question for later. I realised I was starting to rack them up. Ever since Ash had kissed me in my bedroom and manipulated me into agreeing to let him take care of me, I hadn't really been thinking properly at all. Manipulating devil! *Oh, but what a way to manipulate* my inner devil purred! Oh, hell yeah! I couldn't be angry at him for that. Not at all.

"Fine," I agreed, "But you will need to tell me a bit more about what is actually going on here if it is going to affect my life like this. And I'll want the truth," I said, narrowing my eyes at him so he was aware that I knew there was way more going on here than a case of mistaken identity.

I hadn't wanted to know before when I thought I could simply send him off without another thought, keeping myself out of trouble. However, as soon as he kissed me again, I quickly realised that I was already in way too deep for that. Now that my life had obviously become entwined with his, I needed to know exactly what I was getting myself into.

I knew involving myself with this man was going to change my life dramatically. It already had. I had definitely grown as a person since I had first laid eyes on him, and I wanted that to continue. I wanted to be the sort of woman who could stand at the side of a man like Ash. Whoever and whatever that was.

"We're here!" Ash said as we pulled up to a set of huge gates surrounded by a high wall.

Romi said something in Russian into the intercom before the gates opened, and we drove through. Oh my gosh!

I leaned forward, straining for a better view. There was a long driveway lined with trees, and at the bottom, I could see a massive country manor. There were too many windows to count and a large porch with steps leading up to a big white door between two white columns. It was gorgeous. Absolutely breath taking!

The front door opened, and I saw the woman from the Glitz event, Ash's sister, standing there. Ash helped me out, and a second later, she ran over and grabbed him in a tight hug.

He wheezed, "Bloody hell, Sonia, I already have broken ribs. Can you please not break any more?"

"Sorry," she said, looking a bit contrite before her expression turned to annoyance.

"At least you only got some broken ribs and a beating; you could have been killed!" she said, punching him in the arm.

"Hey!" he shouted.

"Next time, don't go meeting folk alone!" she cried.

"Even if it is because you don't want a chaperone when you go courting!" she laughed mischievously and looked pointedly at me.

"Quiet, Sonia!" Ash said. She looked between us and smirked.

"Ah, I take it Gracie doesn't know you put yourself in danger so you could go see her and ask her out without an audience then? Oh, and I guess you haven't apologised yet, either? Huh?" she asked, innocently batting her eyes.

I turned to him and smirked as I saw how uncomfortable he looked. So, Mr Sexy Voice, with his cool act and dominant persona, could get a bit uncomfortable sometimes, too, huh? That made me feel a lot better about my own continual embarrassment.

"I hadn't gotten around to telling her yet," he stated.

My insides did a little jig, or maybe that was my inner devil or both. Either way, I was really pleased to hear him confirm he was coming to find me to ask me out.

"No time like the present!" she said, smirking wickedly at him. He shot her a look that I was sure could kill.

"Fine," he said, turning to me.

"Gracie, after last weekend, I felt I owed you an apology for my behaviour. I had stuff on my mind, and I acted like a jerk…"

"You can say that again!" she butted in, obviously enjoying herself.

He shot her another annoyed look. I had to agree with her and was pleased he was finally apologising.

"Anyway, I'm sorry," he said to me, smiling sheepishly.

His expression was so cute I wanted to melt.

"That's okay," I said, smiling shyly.

He grinned with obvious relief. Sonia nodded in approval before turning to me.

"He has also been obsessed with you since your cream-covered kiss, which we all heard a lot about, by the way, and tracked you down to work in the Old Bell Tavern so he could ask you out."

"Oh, I'm flattered," I said, and I meant it. I looked up at him under my eyelashes, blushing madly at the thought of them all discussing our kiss.

"Good," she said, looking at me intently.

"Ash needs someone who can bring out the fun in him again and give his life a bit of excitement!" she laughed and winked at him.

He grinned widely at me.

"I'm not so sure about that," I laughed, "I think it is more a case that your brother has brought quite a lot of excitement to mine!"

"And I intend to bring a lot more!" Ash whispered in my ear, making me shiver and bite my lower lip while thinking some very wicked thoughts.

Sonia was looking between us again with an odd look on her face. She turned to me and suddenly hugged me.

"Thank you so much for rescuing my brother." And I had a strange feeling she wasn't just talking about last night.

I guessed news travelled fast in the Rominov family.

"You're welcome," I said, my face flaming with all this attention.

"Come on, let's get you inside," Ash said, taking my hand and leading me into a very grand entrance hall.

I stared around in awe. There was a long hall on the left with several doors leading off it and a staircase leading up on the right with marble flooring and the requisite chandelier, as expected, for such a wonderful space. Oh my!

Ash showed me up to a guest room, which was large and decorated like something you would expect to see in a luxury hotel. I could definitely get used to this.

He showed me the bathroom. The bath was huge, as was the shower. Both could easily fit two, and I found my mind going to places it shouldn't when I looked at them. His mind must have been going there, too, because he came up behind me and wrapped his arms around me.

"I could use a shower; want to join me?" he murmured.

I gulped and stepped out of his arms, feeling a cross between the desire to embrace my new sassy warrior woman side and make my inner devil happy by saying yes, please, and the desire to run and hide as would be my usual reaction. I wanted him, but things were moving a little too fast for me right now. He smirked.

"Maybe another time, sweetheart?" he said, winking, and it wasn't quite a statement and not quite a question, but more like a promise for the future.

I desperately held back a yawn, not wanting him to think I was bored by the thought. Far from it, my insides were going crazy at the idea, but I was exhausted and really needed to get some sleep.

"Okay, sweetheart, I need a shower, so I'm heading to my room. It's opposite, along the hall, the last door on the right if you need me. Why don't you get settled in and maybe take a nap, as I guess you didn't get any sleep last night? Lunch is served at 1 p.m. in the dining room. I'll see you there," he said before leaning in and kissing me on the forehead.

He headed to the door, then suddenly turned and strode back, took my face between his hands, and kissed me quickly and deeply on the lips before leaving the room with the parting shot, "Sweet dreams, Gracie!"

Wow, oh wow! I suddenly felt damp down below, and I was sure any dreams I had would definitely be sweet and very definitely filled with him and his kisses! In fact, after that kiss, that was the sort of dream I absolutely needed. I quickly unpacked and then threw back the quilt, jumped into the bed, and snuggled down, hugging the pillow, wishing it were Ash! Oh, I definitely had it bad!

CHAPTER 18
ASH

STILL SATURDAY MORNING - TAKING
GRACIE HOME

walked to my room deep in thought, my steps lighter than they had been in a long time. Although Sonia had embarrassed me by making me apologise to Gracie in front of her, I was glad that she had because now that it was over, we could move on.

Also, now Gracie knew that I had been planning on asking her out and that I already liked her way before the events of the last few hours. I wanted her to know that I had been thinking of her since our first kiss. I was secretly hoping she had been thinking of me since then, too. The way she had reacted to me, I believed she just might have been, and that thought had me elated.

I hadn't been able to stop touching Gracie all the way back to the Estate and had kept a tight hold of her hand. She hadn't protested, and I could tell from her shy smile and blush that she liked it.

She was such a contradiction. She had a certain shy innocence about her, yet she also had a fiery side. When we first met, her sass and kiss had made me hot; the thought of her rescuing me had made me hotter, but this latest act of bravery had me burning for her in a way I'd never felt before.

When I'd shown her the bathroom, I had teased her with the suggestion that we shower together. I was delighted when I noticed the flare of interest in her eyes. She was definitely interested, but she was also shy, and the way she had bitten down on her lip had been utterly adorable. My cock had jerked in response, but her nervous reaction told me her feelings on the subject were mixed.

So, I left her to get some well-deserved rest. That was for the best because despite my unruly member making its ire known by throbbing like mad, I really wasn't up to doing anything more than sleeping, and neither was she. We were both exhausted from all we had been through.

Exhaustion didn't seem to bother my cock, though. I adjusted myself to take the pressure off as I paused just outside my bedroom. I threw a look back along the hall to her door. I longed to return to Gracie's room and sink my cock into her, but instead, I resolutely turned, walked into my own room, and closed the door firmly behind me. There would be plenty of time for slacking my desire and giving my cock exactly what it wanted later, I consoled myself. Of course, the bugger still refused to be appeased and maintained its erect state as I read the text from Anton confirming his men were on their way.

I'd spoken to him while Gracie was packing and filled him in on the events of the last twenty-four hours. He had agreed to send a few of his men over to guard the outside of the Estate. We had our own security, but it didn't hurt to get some extra help under the circumstances, especially since Sonia and Nonna were here, and now Gracie would be staying with us, too. I couldn't let anything happen to any of them.

After everything that had occurred over the last couple of

years, especially the most recent events, my protective instincts had already been in overdrive. My growing feelings for Gracie seemed to have ramped those feelings up even more. I wanted to go and check on her just to make sure she was safe. I knew it was irrational, so I stopped myself yet again from returning to her room.

Instead, I forced myself to undress and get into the shower. My broken ribs throbbed worse than my cock, and my energy levels were crashing now that the adrenaline from this morning's fight had completely worn off. I turned the spray on as high as possible and let the warm water pound over my tired, aching body.

My cock still refused to go down. I huffed. I gave myself some quick hand relief, wishing it were Gracie. Since I couldn't yet enjoy the real thing, I settled for picturing her face and remembering her curves pressed against me as I'd lain on top of her during our cream-covered kiss. I came quickly, even though I knew that my fantasy was a poor substitute for the real thing.

I groaned in pain as I stepped out of the shower and reached for a towel. I really was bloody exhausted. My thoughts strayed back to Gracie once more. My mind had never seemed to be off her for long this past week, and I had a feeling that was the way things would remain in the future.

I couldn't help moaning as I thought of her luscious lips on mine while I towelled off. I wondered if she was taking a shower herself or maybe napping in bed. My active imagination provided me with sexy images of both scenarios. Whatever she was doing, I would love to be there with her instead of here alone. My cock jerked in agreement. Shit, I was hard again!

Damn, that girl made me hot. I liked her. I liked her a lot. I reached for my shaft and felt it pulse in my hand. I needed to sleep, but there was no way I would get any sleep with a raging hard-on like this. So, I dealt with myself again, coming even quicker this time. The sensations were too much for my weakened body, and I swayed as my release coated my hand. I clutched the sink for support and waited for the wave of dizziness and nausea to subside before cleaning myself up again.

I staggered naked to my bed. I went to pick my trousers up off the floor so I could retrieve the medication from their pocket and cursed as a sharp pain seared my torso. Sweat coated my skin, and my whole body tensed in agony as another wave of nausea assaulted me. I quickly swallowed a couple of painkillers. God, I needed them. My head pounded, and everywhere ached.

I was ready to crash. I needed to nap. I had things to do later and needed to rest and regain my strength. Not to mention that when I finally fucked Gracie, it would not be over quickly. I planned on taking my time and savouring every inch of her, and while I looked forward to that immensely, as the pain in my body testified, I was in no real state to do her justice.

I needed to heal and regain my stamina and preferably a bit more upper body movement before I could get properly down and dirty with Little Miss Hot Mess again. It might take a few days to get my strength back and get over the initial pain, but in the meantime, I would work on wowing her. I winced from pain in my mouth caused by the very wide grin I was sporting.

I realised with shock that I smiled, grinned, and even laughed a lot over the last few hours. It had been a long time since I was happy enough to grin at anything, never mind grinning this big at just the thought of a woman. It was odd; we barely knew one another, and yet her presence in my life had already made me feel lighter than I had felt in years.

I also realised that even in my fury at the big black guy and Mohammad, I hadn't spiralled out of control. I had been enraged and used that to fight the guys, but I had been aware of everything while I did so. I didn't get out of control and lose sight of my surroundings as I had been doing recently. I had been aware of everything at all times, especially where Gracie was and what was happening to her. It seemed that her presence didn't just make me happier; it also calmed me.

I had doubted that I would ever find someone like her, loyal, brave, passionate, good at heart, and sexy as hell. Gracie was all of these things. I couldn't believe my luck. I was going to make that woman mine. I had no doubt about that. I was never letting her go.

I eased myself under the covers, groaning as my body settled on the bed. I closed my eyes and let out a long breath. Gracie would be mine completely. I just needed to remember not to push her too hard and give her time to get to know me. That wouldn't be an easy task for me. I was impulsive and impatient, and when I decided I wanted something, I tended to go all out to get it. However, I didn't want to scare Gracie off, so I would take things at her pace. *I just hoped her pace was fast. That* was my last thought before I sunk into blissful oblivion.

A few hours later, I woke feeling sore but much more refreshed.

I grabbed another quick shower. I had things to do, and then I wanted to meet Gracie for lunch. I'd told her I'd see her there because I needed to talk with Miki beforehand. We had arrangements to make.

I was so busy thinking these thoughts that I didn't realise I was standing outside Gracie's door with my fist poised, ready to knock. What the fuck? I stopped myself. I was being way too intense again. It had only been a few hours since I had left her, and lunchtime was still some time away. She was likely still sleeping. I'd told myself earlier I needed to take things slower. Rushing to her side again the minute I woke up wasn't taking things slower.

I hadn't even realised I'd approached her room with the intent of seeing her again. I needed to get a grip! She was a total distraction, a beautiful one, but a distraction, nevertheless. I had things to do that needed focus. *She will still be here when I get back, and I can look forward to tasting her luscious lips again then,* I reminded myself.

Although now I was here, maybe I should just check on her, just in case she needed anything. I could steal another kiss. *Back off!* I told myself sternly and forced myself to turn and head downstairs. Pursuing Little Miss Hot Mess could wait; right now, I had more pressing matters to attend to.

I made my way towards the offices in search of Miki. I expected him to have returned home and be waiting to discuss things with me. After he chewed me out a bit first, of course.

Our Cleaners should have fixed up Gracie's home by now and gotten rid of Mohammad's body. That was what they were for. We would deal with the other guy ourselves. Once we had gotten all the information out of him, we could, of course.

When Miki and Romi had come to collect me from Gracie's earlier, Vlad had been with them. He'd waited outside and arranged for the Cleaners to come. Then, while Romi drove us home, Miki and Vlad took the unconscious black guy to the C. Miki had arranged for Luca to meet him there and stay with Vlad to watch the guy until he returned with me later.

The C was our code for The Smithson Crematorium in South London, which was privately owned by us via one of our shell companies and was untraceable back to us. It was run on our behalf by a distant cousin loyal to the Bratva, Jonathan

Reston and his family. The security was taken care of by another of our companies, RomCore Security, which specialised in setting up and monitoring security cameras. This company was also one that couldn't be traced back to us.

The C was the place where we took people whom we needed to question and most often kill. We had a large basement area underneath, which was soundproof and kitted out to make torture and disposal easy.

Our dad had made it when he took over the crematorium not long after he came to London. He'd needed a safe place to carry out all of our unpleasant business, of which, when we first came to London, there was a lot. He'd needed somewhere private yet easily accessible that could allow us to safely dispose of bodies. So, when the Smithson Crematorium came up for sale, he had our shell company buy it, and we have used it ever since.

Being in London itself meant that we never had to travel far with a prisoner, and since we could interrogate and then dispose of the person in the same place, there was less chance of us being caught. So, it was a perfect place for such nefarious purposes. The only people who knew about the C and its less-than-legitimate purpose were the Reston family, us, and a select few of our most loyal men.

That was the same with our drug lab; only a few people knew of its location, too. It made everything a whole lot safer.

Of course, that was why I'd been beaten. Mohammad and the other guy had wanted the location of the lab. Whatever the Malia Boys and Broxy's had planned, it obviously involved the lab.

The lab was where we cut our coke and made our Molly. It was also a part of our current drug supply route. All the drugs that passed along the route passed through the Lab location for one reason or another.

In fact, the Lab was located close to the C on a

neighbouring farm linked by a private road. It was hidden well underground, with various farm buildings above helping to disguise it.

The farm itself was run by our elderly friend Dimitri Molinov and his family. They were also Bratva, and Dimitri was our dad's bodyguard for a while before he retired. The Bratva link, though, had been well hidden by my brother Marko and his team of IT wizards, so nobody outside of the brotherhood knew about it.

We shifted the drugs when required via the private road linking the farm and the crematorium. Our RomCore security firm helped ensure that the route from the farm to the nearby motorway was clear. That aided us greatly in the movement of the drugs as we could ensure that we avoided the police and any possible ambush by our enemies while making shipments. The security in place would also be a great help to us if our enemies did find out where the Lab was, and it seemed like they were intent on doing so.

I knocked on Miki's door and entered when he called.

"Well?" he asked, raising his eyebrows at me, obviously expecting an apology for my stupidity.

"Yeah, yeah, I know! I shouldn't have gone off alone to meet Mohammed," I said.

"No, you shouldn't have, Sashenka!"

Uh oh, he was using my full name again, and his accent was really thick. He was definitely still seriously pissed off at me!

"It was bloody stupid! You should have taken Romi or me, and then we could have left you to go on your amorous adventures. If Gracie hadn't found you and had the nerve to go in and rescue your sorry ass, who knows what the hell would have happened!" he fumed.

"I know, it was stupid. I admit it, and it won't happen again!"

"It better not!" he leaned forward and narrowed his eyes at me,

"Or next time, the Malia Boys won't be the only ones beating up your stupid ass!" he shouted.

Yep, definitely pissed!

He shifted back in his chair and took a deep breath, obviously trying to calm himself before he spoke again.

"Ash, since we lost Krissa, you keep taking stupid chances. You have been lucky so far, but one day, your luck will run out. This family have lost enough; we can't afford to lose anyone else!"

He sighed and ran his fingers through his hair.

"You have got to stop blaming yourself for what happened. The ones responsible were the ones who hurt Krissa, and we have killed two of them and will kill the other one soon, I swear it."

This was something I'd heard so often before. My head was swimming! I couldn't think of this right now; otherwise, I'd be spiralling out of control when I went to question that Malia asshole, and we wouldn't get the information I needed. I breathed deeply, needing to get away. I couldn't talk about this.

"I know," I ground the words out, "And I won't take any more stupid chances. I promise."

"Good. We will head over to the C after lunch," he said, dismissing me.

"Oh, and Ash," he called after me.

I turned around.

"That's one heck of a woman you've got there, brave, beautiful, and can stand up to your sorry self! She's a keeper, so don't blow it!" he said, and if I hadn't known better, I'd have said the look on his face was envious, almost wistful.

"I'll try my best not to," I stated with a nod and smirk.

I certainly would, and I agreed she was definitely a keeper.

Thinking about Gracie helped stop the spiralling. The moment my mind went to her, I felt myself calm. Thank fuck. I really didn't need that right now.

I headed to my own office to catch up on some work, looking forward to seeing my Little Miss Hot Mess at lunch very soon.

CHAPTER 19
GRACIE

woke up from my nap and stretched, feeling quite giddy. I had drifted off to sleep replaying Ash's kisses in my head, and although I was as horny as hell, I had never felt so happy. It was crazy to think that this gorgeous, rich, and obviously dangerous man wanted me.

I still needed to call Derrick. I had to let him know where I was. If he hadn't heard from me soon, I thought he might turn up at my house, and if I wasn't there, he'd be frantic.

I wasn't sure yet how I was going to explain where, in fact, I was; however, I would figure it out. I took a shower and got dressed while I wondered what the rest of the day would bring. My bedroom was beautiful, and I couldn't wait to explore the rest of the house and the gorgeous gardens that had lined the driveway.

That wasn't all I wanted to explore, of course. Whatever this was between Ash and me, I really wanted to explore it and, despite the danger, or maybe because of it, I had never had so much fun. My inner devil was revelling in the idea that Ash liked me, and I had to admit, the rest of me was too.

I pushed my thoughts away before they could take me to

places that would make me blush. I was so looking forward to seeing Ash again I could hardly contain my excitement as I hurried downstairs in time for lunch. As I got to the bottom, I noticed Sonia entering a door up ahead. I followed her, guessing it must lead to the dining room. It did, indeed.

When I entered, Sonia beckoned me to sit next to her. I was a bit nervous when I saw Ash wasn't there yet.

"Hi," she said, and her friendly smile made me relax as she asked me how I liked my room.

"It's lovely, thank you. And very kind of you all to look after me here. I hope it isn't too much trouble?"

"Nonsense, it's no trouble at all." she insisted.

"Anyhow, you are only in trouble because of us, and you saved my brother's life, so that makes you practically family in our eyes. Besides," she smirked, "Ash is totally enamoured with you, and so you may actually be family soon anyway," she remarked matter of factly.

Wow! Woah! Really? Bit fast! I was not sure what to think about that declaration. The man was gorgeous, and there was a definite connection between us, but it was still early days; we hadn't even done anything but kiss yet. It was a bit soon to be thinking of becoming part of their family.

As if thinking about him conjured him up, Ash walked in. He kissed Sonia on the cheek and did the same to me.

I turned to look at him, and he took that as an invitation to kiss me again on the lips this time.

"Nice nap?" he asked.

I flushed as my mind flashed back to my dreamy and rather naughty thoughts about him, and I realised I must look a bit guilty when a knowing look entered his eyes, and he grinned seductively.

"I certainly did!" he said, wiggling his eyebrows

suggestively, making me blush again before taking a seat next to me and pulling it so close that our legs were touching.

All the while, Sonia grinned knowingly at us.

It was all very disconcerting and overwhelming. I was about to move my chair away from Ash when his brothers and Romi came in. Deciding that moving now might create a scene and embarrass me further, I stayed where I was and tried to ignore the feeling of his leg against mine. It wasn't easy; the warmth seeping from his body was heating me up in all the right places. Oh my!

Ash introduced me to his younger brother Marko, who shook my hand and winked, then laughed as Ash made a growling sound under his breath.

My eyes flicked towards him, and the sound immediately stopped, but I noticed he'd moved his chair even closer to me.

My cheeks heated, but I ignored them and concentrated instead on listening to the men as they chatted quietly.

A short while later, an elderly woman came in carrying a big serving dish with what looked like Spaghetti Frutti di Mare. It smelled delicious. She exited and returned quickly with a platter of garlic ciabatta and a large bowl of salad. Oh, yum was all I could think as my stomach rumbled quietly.

While we waited for whatever else she was bringing, Sonia told me that the woman was called Maria. Apparently, she had been their mother's nanny when she was a child in Italy and had then followed her out to Russia when she married their father. Maria had become their housekeeper. However, she was always more like a member of the family, and they thought of her as a grandmother, called her Nonna, and loved her to bits. I thought that was sweet. I'd never known my own grandparents, so I thought it was nice that they all had their Nonna.

When Maria joined us to eat, Ash introduced us.

"Beautiful as well as brave!" Nonna stated, looking at me, then she turned to Ash, nodding at him approvingly.

"You must call me Nonna too, dear," she said to me in a thick Italian accent.

I smiled warmly at the woman I knew I was going to like.

Ash beamed, and I noticed the others did, too. I guess I met with the family's approval then. I smiled inwardly at the warm fuzzy feeling that thought invoked.

Nonna's cooking was as amazing as it looked. We all ate heartily. I hadn't eaten much since yesterday, so I was very hungry and stuffed myself.

I didn't think I could eat another thing, until she brought in dessert. I did love my dessert.

There was a plateful of delicate sugar-coated pastries and another with cannoli crepes. I loved sugary desserts, and they looked terrific, decadent actually, and I couldn't decide what to have. As I sat pondering over them, Ash took matters into his own hands and put several small pastries and a crepe onto my plate.

I blushed and raised my eyebrows at his forward behaviour in front of his family, but a quick glance around told me that nobody else seemed to care. It was as if they had already accepted me as his, and so his overt displays of possession and entitlement were expected. Normal even. I thought briefly that I should be bothered by his display, but I wasn't. I liked that he was taking care of me. I liked it a lot, in fact.

"You'll love them!" he declared before loading up his own plate in a similar way.

They did look so good. I was not sure where to start when Ash leaned over, cut a bit of crepe with his fork, and held it to my mouth. I felt myself blushing again at this open display of familiarity. I wasn't used to this kind of behaviour, but I found that I was happy to get used to it.

"Try it; it is filled with cream, and I know how much you like cream!" he practically purred, obviously thinking about our cream-covered kiss.

Everyone around the table sniggered.

Thankfully, I hadn't been eating it at the time, or I would have choked. I wasn't quite sure if I wanted to kill him or kiss him at that moment.

"Go on!" he encouraged, and all thought of killing him went straight out of my head because, oh my gosh, that voice!

I was pretty sure this guy was trying to seduce me. It was not going to be hard, I realised, as his words alone had me shifting uncomfortably in my seat, my panties wet. He smirked wickedly, noticing his teasing behaviour was having the desired effect.

Okay, Mr Sexy Voice, you want to play dirty, do you? You are on. Challenge accepted. Two could play at that game. If he wasn't embarrassed to behave like this in front of his family, I wouldn't be either. Besides, nobody else was looking. They were all too engrossed in a story Nonna was telling them.

I felt deliciously wicked as I leaned towards the fork, looking him in the eye, and slowly, very slowly, took the food off the prongs. The room around us melted away, my sole focus on the man in front of me. I held his gaze while I chewed and swallowed, then ran my tongue seductively over my lips. I licked off the little bit of cream left there, moaning in delight. He gulped, and I smirked. Gotcha!

"Nonna, you are an amazing cook. Your pasta was lovely, but I must say that your desserts are even more exquisite!" I told her before slowly dragging my gaze from Ash, who was staring at me open-mouthed.

"Thank you, dear," she said, with silent laughter in her eyes.

I noticed then that everyone was staring at us in amusement, too. Oops. Busted! Normally, I would be bright red and praying the ground would open up and swallow me right about now, but not today. Today, I just gave a little giggle instead, and thankfully, everyone went back to making small talk as I finished off my desserts without any additional help.

Ash had turned a little in his seat after my tease, but not before I saw a decidedly large bulge in his pants. He was stuffing his face with his dessert, and I noticed that he seemed as hyper-aware of me as I was of him, yet he deliberately avoided my gaze. Oh yeah! It was good to see that I could turn the tables on Ash when I wanted to and show him that he was not the only one in control of this relationship. I had to fight hard to keep the smirk off my face.

A little while later, and seemingly recovered from my teasing, Ash gave me a tour of the house.

It really was very beautiful, but my favourite place was the library on the top floor. It was huge, with floor-to-ceiling bookcases all around three walls attached with ladders so you could climb right up to the top shelf and move along it. I bubbled with excitement. I had to try that later.

In one corner was a desk and chair, which would be a great spot for a writing corner.

A real fireplace was the focal point in the centre of the room, with a very comfy-looking sofa and oversized chairs facing it, and several other high-backed old-fashioned style reading chairs were dotted around the room. It was amazing, and I could lose myself there for hours.

Ash was talking, I realised, but I had been so distracted I missed what he had said.

Not wanting him to know that I hadn't been paying attention, I nodded and smiled, hoping that was the right response. He looked pleased enough, so I guessed it must have been.

I walked over to one of the shelves, unable to stay away from the books any longer.

I noticed a section which appeared to be dedicated to the romance genre. Oh my, I scanned the titles and saw so many were books by my favourite authors. Geez, I must have died and gone to heaven!

I picked up a Maggie Cole book and smiled. I had this on my Kindle, but I really loved the smell and the feel of a real paper book. I touched it lovingly. I guessed someone here liked their romantic novels, too. Probably Sonia. Something we would have in common then. I wondered who her favourite book boyfriend was? I could never choose just one. I loved them all!

Oh my god, there was a whole collection of Sophie Lark's books! And the latest from Eden Summers, too! This was definitely my favourite room, and I would definitely be spending as much time as possible here from now on. Maybe I shouldn't bother with the other room and just take up residence here instead? I could easily live in here. It was every book lover's fantasy, a library of their own.

"So, what type of romance is your favourite?" Ash asked.

I heard myself saying, "Dark mafia romance," without thinking.

Suddenly, he moved closer, and I looked up at him.

"You wanted to know what those guys wanted with me?"

I blinked, confused for a minute. What was he talking about? Oh, right, the black dudes! This was important, I reminded myself. I'd better pay attention, I guessed. I could gush over the books later.

"You are a clever woman, Gracie, and I am sure you have already figured out that this situation is not about a case of mistaken identity. My brothers and I are known as Oligarchs, which simply means Russian businessmen, and we do indeed own numerous businesses both here in the UK and abroad. However, as you know, sometimes in business, you make enemies. People want what you have, and the men who kidnapped me, beat me, then attacked us this morning, want to take some of our business away."

I nodded.

"Anyway, they wanted the location of one of our businesses, and they didn't get it. It also seems that this attack is linked to a larger plan against us being formulated by two of our smaller competitors. As such, they will likely continue with their attacks unless we do something about it. Unfortunately, you have been dragged into this little business war of ours and are therefore also a target now, so, in order to keep you safe, you will remain here with us until we have dealt with things." He looked at me intently as if trying to gauge my reaction.

"Those guys were ready to kill you; that is more than just your usual business take-over attempt," I said, frowning. I was pretty sure that this was about something other than legitimate business. Maybe I was reading way too many dark contemporary romances, but I really thought this family might be Bratva.

"Are you Bratva?" The words popped out before I could stop them.

"Yes," he replied with only the tiniest hesitation. Oh my gosh! I didn't know whether to be scared or excited. Yep, I was definitely reading way too many dark romances!

"That's what I thought! I have to admit I have read too many dark mafia romance books for that not to have crossed my mind."

"Thought so," he said, smirking and stepping closer to me, "Do you think that's hot, sweetheart?"

I gulped.

"Do you like the idea that I have a dark side?" he questioned.

Oh, hell yeah! Both me and my inner devil shouted together.

I should have been scared, but I wasn't. Instead, I was excited and quite a bit turned on.

I stared at him and licked my lips. This guy could definitely be one of my book boyfriends come to life with his good looks and bulging muscles, and cocky dominant air.

"Do you?" he asked again, using his tactics from earlier and whispering in my ear.

I gulped, opening my mouth to speak, but no words would come.

He raised his eyebrows in question. Oh, he actually wanted an answer. He was crowding me again, doing that book-boyfriend thing, pushing me up against the wall. I shivered. Oh my! It was getting hot in here. I could feel his cock getting hard against my belly. I guessed he liked the idea of me finding him hot!

"Well, Gracie?" he asked, and my girly parts gushed.

He was making it very hard to think with him being so close. But he wanted an answer, and I knew he wouldn't be satisfied until he had one. I opened my mouth again, and this time, I found my voice, but only barely.

"Yes," I whispered.

He grinned triumphantly and captured my lips in a demanding kiss, thrusting his tongue deep inside my mouth.

Trapped between him and the bookcase, I felt every inch of him. His kiss was becoming frantic as he held me tightly. It was as if he couldn't get enough of me. I knew the feeling! The taste of him was intoxicating, and I was addicted!

He shifted enough to allow his hand to snake between us. He cupped my sex through my leggings and started to rub. It felt good, really, really good. I moaned into his mouth and couldn't help from grinding against his hand. My core clenched, and I felt myself getting wetter.

Just as suddenly as he'd started, he pulled away. I was about to protest, but he was soon back, this time slipping his hand inside my leggings and down into my knickers. He rubbed my clit gently at first, then increased the speed until I was panting and bucking against him. *Oh god, please don't let him stop,* I prayed.

Thankfully, he didn't. He continued to rub me before slipping two fingers inside my channel. I tensed for a few seconds as the stretch nipped uncomfortably, but I was so wet and slick that I adjusted quickly and soon, it felt bloody amazing. This guy knew his stuff. I was no virgin, but I might as well have been.

My prior sexual encounters with the only two boyfriends I had had were pretty mundane if I was honest, and nothing like what I had read about in my romance books, and certainly nothing like this. This was already on another level, and I was pretty sure this was just the start. A little taste of things to come, you might say! I was so very close to coming. I couldn't believe it. I had never come with a guy before, but I was about to come with my Mr Sexy Voice.

He thrust a few times more times, and I bucked my hips and groaned in pleasure, teetering on the edge.

"Come for me, sweetheart!" he demanded, and that was all it took. Yep, he was definitely a real-life book boyfriend! How lucky was I?

I cried out and clenched tightly around his fingers as he continued to pump them in and out until my body shook with pleasure and my legs buckled. I clung desperately to him to stop him from falling, although I knew he would never let me. Oh my god! That was utterly amazing!

I looked at him in shock as he brought his fingers to his mouth and licked my juices off them, murmuring, "Hmmm."

Fuck! That was so hot!

"Just a little something to remember me by while I am away taking care of business," he told me cockily.

I felt that I should say something sassy in return, but I was still too dazed by the whole experience to even form a sentence. If that was just a little taste, I couldn't wait for a full-on gluttony experience!

He reminded me to remain in the house with Sonia while he was gone before giving me a quick peck on the lips.

"I'll be back either later tonight or tomorrow. See you soon, Little Miss Hot Mess!" he winked, turned, and walked out of the library, leaving me staring after him awestruck.

If I thought I was in trouble before, I now knew without a doubt that I definitely was. In fact, I thought I could already be falling for Ash. I smiled. I didn't think that was such a bad thing. Not at all. I should be terrified of that idea. Ash was Bratva, a mafia man with a dark side he had admitted to.

I might have only known him for a week, but he was certainly bringing out a more confident, sassy, warrior-woman side of me that both my inner devil and I loved. I felt like a heroine in my very own dark mafia romance, and I liked it!

I giggled as I picked up the nearest Sophie Lark novel and settled into the comfy sofa. Well, I had better start reading up on how to handle my hot alpha mafia man then, and where better to start than here, I thought, grinning, and opening up *Brutal Prince*.

CHAPTER 20

ASH

SATURDAY AFTERNOON - THE C

'll be back either later tonight or tomorrow. See you soon, Little Miss Hot Mess!" I winked, turned, and walked out of the library, trying desperately to walk normally and ignore my throbbing dick!

As soon as I took Gracie into the library, I knew it was a good idea. Her face had lit up the moment she saw all the books.

I understood. It was actually one of my favourite places, too. Only my family were aware that I liked to read and often went there to escape when things got a bit too overwhelming. It could get quite crowded here when we were all at home, especially if we had guests, and I couldn't always endure crowds.

Sonia spent a lot of time here, too, hence all the romance books. The minute Gracie picked one up and I saw it was a dark contemporary romance, it gave me a very wicked idea!

"So, what type of romance is your favourite?" I'd asked, trying to sound innocent. Her answer, "Dark mafia romance, I guess," had me doing a mental high-five! All I could think about was how I planned on making her fantasy of a mafia book boyfriend into a reality.

I told her a bit more about my family's situation, avoiding anything illegal, as I tried to gauge her reaction. I needn't have worried. My Little Miss Hot Mess was a smart cookie, and she guessed my family's connections immediately. I knew she would.

Gracie had come straight out and asked me if I was Bratva! I shook my head; she never failed to surprise me. She didn't seem bothered when I confirmed it. In fact, I had a feeling my dark side turned her on. I'd pushed her against the bookshelf and made her come.

I'd wanted to lift her up, free my cock, and push into her, but my aching ribs protested the thought even though the rest of me was longing to. I hated the fact that I wasn't fit enough to do justice to worshipping Gracie the way I wanted to. So, instead, I had a little taste and gave her something to think about while I was away.

I smirked as I headed towards Miki's office, feeling thoroughly pleased with our little encounter. The look on her face when I left told me that it was definitely worthy of one of these book boyfriends Sonia liked to talk about. In fact, it had better have bloody well surpassed them. Gracie had loved it, I was sure, and I hadn't even brought my A-game. Just wait until I did! I grinned like a fool.

I couldn't wait for our next encounter. I intended to ensure that Gracie was so sated afterwards that she'd fall for me the way I knew I was falling for her. Let's just say that as soon as my body healed a bit more, I didn't plan on letting her out of my bed until I was sure she was as lost to me as I was to her.

I pushed open Miki's door, happier than I had felt in years. That was Gracie's doing. I loved being in her presence and wasn't happy that I had to leave her now. I missed her already.

I shook my head and stretched my neck. Even with the pain medication, I was aching all over. I wanted nothing more than to curl up in bed with Gracie, take another taste of her, and then fall asleep with her in my arms.

I sighed. Unfortunately, duty called. I forced myself to push aside thoughts of my Little Miss Hot Mess. There were things I had to do, and I needed to get my head in the game. There was an enemy to deal with. It was time to focus.

———

Miki, Marko, and I headed to the C to meet Vlad and Luca, leaving Romi in the house to look after the females.

With the rest of our security staff and a few of Anton's men manning the perimeter of the Estate, they would be safe. If anyone even tried to cause trouble for us, they would get more than they bargained for.

Once we reached the C, we fell into our usual routine.

Our dad had taught us to be extra careful when we were at the C to ensure we didn't leave behind any forensic evidence. It was so much easier to get caught now than it was back in my dad's youth. Even so, Dad had always been cautious. He had quickly developed a routine and a set of eight rules, which he taught us, and we strictly adhered to even though he was gone.

Rule One - Ensure that whoever was brought to the C was either blindfolded or unconscious going in, and—either dead or very rarely for those who actually lived through the experience —blindfolded or unconscious going out. That way, they couldn't identify the location.

Rule Two - Strip everything off. All clothes, jewellery, and watches were removed and left with our other belongings, including phones, in the changing room. No personal items were allowed in the main room.

Rule Three – Wear one of the disposable suits and a washable toolbelt to carry our favourite weapons before entering the main room.

Rule Four - Always have more than one person at the C; never be there alone, whether in the main room or not.

Rule Five - Know your game plan before you go in so you don't end up killing someone if there is a better way of dealing with them that suits the family. Stay in control.

Rule Six - Never leave a weapon in the room. Always carry them with you and keep them with you.

Rule Seven - Dispose of the body in a body bag and get it incinerated in the crematorium as soon as possible, along with the disposable suits, the person's clothes and other personal belongings. Never keep a souvenir.

Rule Eight - Thoroughly clean everything, including the toolbelts and weapons, afterwards before showering in the separate wet room and then changing back into normal clothing.

These rules had kept us safe and out of jail and, hopefully, would continue to do so.

The big guy was hanging up in the main room when we entered, in a very similar position to the one I was in last night. His eyes widened when he saw us. I smirked. He wasn't so sure of himself now.

We were a pretty scary sight, I guessed, because it was obvious from our outfits what we had planned. The guy was going to die here today; that was a foregone conclusion, and he knew it. The only thing for him now was to decide how much pain he was willing to suffer first because we wanted information from him, and unlike him and the little fucker Mohammed, we were very good at extracting information.

Luca and Vlad had already started by the look of things.

The guy's mouth was bloody, and there was an obvious swelling appearing on the right side of his face.

"Guy was mouthing off about beating you up, Ash, so we gave him a taste of Bratva justice," Vlad said.

I smirked again, nodding in approval.

"Fucker," Miki said, pulling a knife from his tool belt and, within minutes, the big guy was screaming for him to stop. Yet the asshole had only answered a couple of our questions.

My dad had taught us how to make shallow cuts so that they caused a great deal of pain but didn't actually hit anything vital. Just in case we wanted the guys to live. Also, because, to tell the truth, none of us were into blood and guts, nor was it some sort of power trip for us. We simply wanted to get the information we needed as quickly as possible and then put an end to things.

If someone ended up here, it was because they were a real threat to our family or our allies and not someone we could deal with legitimately. Never anyone who was innocent or who could be otherwise persuaded to talk, and only ever men! No women. If we ever found ourselves needing information from a woman, there were other methods of persuasion that didn't include direct violence.

We tended to go for maximum pain with little effort, but we could and would get far more brutal if the need arose. That tended to be determined by how resistant the person was to our brand of persuasion or the reason they ended up here in the first place.

We gave the asshole a short breather before my turn.

This guy had beaten me and was probably going to kill me so that in itself had signed his death warrant. However, his actions had also put Gracie in danger, and that made me absolutely furious with the bastard. Also, considering he and Mohammed were the reason I was in no fit state to slake my lust with Gracie tonight, I was going to make sure he suffered a bit extra for that.

I planned on getting a few punches in and then continuing with the questions. However, as I approached the asshole, he decided to taunt me.

"That is one cute little blond bitch you have there, Ash; bet she's a great fuck. I bet she tastes really good, too," he said, and that was it. The red mist descended, and I spiralled.

I punched his stomach. My body ached with the effort, but I paid it no attention. I punched him again and again, enjoying his grunts of pain.

I kept hitting him. The sound of blood rushed in my ears as my whole body shook with rage. *How dare the fucker talk about Gracie like that. I was going to fucking kill him!*

I was vaguely aware of voices shouting, but I was too far gone for the words to penetrate. At some point, I became aware of hands on me, pulling at me. I fought against them, but eventually, I was pulled off the asshole.

I continued to fight for a minute as bodies pressed me to the wall. Finally, the red mist faded, and when I saw that Marko and Miki were the ones holding me, I stopped fighting.

Miki was talking, but I was panting hard and couldn't hear. I concentrated on bringing my breathing back under control, and eventually, his words penetrated the fog in my brain.

"Calm down, Ash!"

"Fuck, you were playing into his hands. The asshole wants us to kill him before he gives us the information we need, and you nearly gave him his wish. You know better than that!" he cried.

He was right. We needed information, and I needed to get myself under control. I held my hands up in surrender, and my brothers let me go. Still shaking with fury but more in control again, I managed to step away from the wall. I walked further away from the asshole so I wouldn't be tempted to turn around and finish the job anyway. I dragged air into my lungs, taking deep breaths to calm myself.

A few minutes later, when Miki was sure I was calmer, he nodded to Marko. It was time for baby brother to do his thing. Out of all of us, our little brother Marko was the most vicious when he wanted to be.

After a few minutes with Marko, the guy was ready to talk.

His name was Abshir. It turned out that he was the brother of Leyla, who was Mohammed's girlfriend. Apparently, Mohammed had been planted as our informant by the Malia Boys' boss, Siri, over a year ago. He had been feeding us information that Siri wanted us to know, although Abshir had no idea why.

Kidnapping and torturing me had been Mohammed's idea. It had been an attempt to impress their boss. Siri wanted the location of the Lab, and they wanted to be the ones to provide it. They'd hoped for a slice of the pie when the Malia Boys' plan came to fruition.

Leyla had been driving the SUV when I was kidnapped. She was ambitious and had egged Mohammad and her brother on. She had left them to take me to the basement while she went to tell Siri that they had captured me.

Initially, he hadn't been pleased as it wasn't part of whatever plan he had, but since it had been done, he decided to use the situation to his benefit. He'd called Mohammed and ordered him to kill me and frame the Albanians. Thankfully, Gracie had come to my rescue first.

However, Leyla had been returning to pick them up when she saw me leaving with Gracie. She had followed us, which is how they knew where to find us the following morning.

As for what Siri's overall plan was, the guy didn't know, except that it involved raiding the lab once the location was known. The guy did say that Siri already had the location, and that was why he had ordered me killed immediately. He also confirmed that the alliance with the Broxy's was tenuous at best and definitely a temporary thing, and that the Malia Boys had only agreed to it because the payoff was good.

Apparently, it had been agreed between them that the Malia Boys would get our lab and drugs side of things and be in control of the drug route, which would expand their own operations.

The Broxy's would take over our money laundering businesses and those of Glowacki for their own use. They would also get Glowacki's drug business. However, the Broxy's also wanted to take over our hackers to create a large-scale fraud business.

Unfortunately, they guy didn't know how they planned on doing all of this. He did, however, confirm that the alliance had the backing of someone powerful with a lot of money. That was obviously whoever the lawyer's boss was. Something we had yet to find out.

Once we got all the information we could, Miki stepped forward and quickly cut the guy's throat. Then we double-bagged the body like always. After that, we texted Jonathan to tell him there was a body to be disposed of first thing in the morning before we put it in the lift and sent it upstairs.

The lift worked like a dumb waiter but was big enough to hold several bodies lying down. When it was here, it came directly into the main basement room and made it easier to drag the body or bodies inside. When it went upstairs, it appeared to simply be a cold storage room for holding bodies for cremation and looked like a normal part of the crematorium. The lift mechanisms and buttons were all cleverly disguised, so they were not easily noticed by anyone who didn't know of their existence.

The lift was another idea of my dad's. He was a brilliant planner and a brilliant strategist. We all learned a lot from him and were good at these things, too, although Miki was definitely the best. He was so very like our dad, not only in looks but in personality. That's why even if he hadn't been the oldest, he would always have made the best pakhan out of us all.

We cleaned up and then finally headed home. After punching the guy so much while still being injured, I ached like mad again. The pills I'd taken had worn off, and I needed more. Thinking of the medication reminded me that I had promised Gracie we would contact Derrick.

I knew a lot about him. He had been Marcie's assistant at Exquisite Events for some time now. I always checked out the owners and high-up employees of all the businesses I worked with, whether on the legitimate side of things or not.

However, I had been looking further into him for a very specific reason. I knew about his medical training in the military before Gracie told me, and it was that which interested me. Our doctor was old and ready to retire soon, and while we found a good replacement, we needed someone else with medical training that we could rely on.

We wanted someone trustworthy and discreet yet able to work with us and who wouldn't baulk at our lifestyle. Derrick seemed a decent guy overall, but I was also aware that he was happy to break a few rules now and then, so I hoped he might be that person.

He was a good friend of Marcie's, and it seemed he was a good friend of Gracie's, too. So, knowing what I did about him, I knew that he would be worried about her. However, it was the early hours of the morning by the time we got home, which was too late to call. I was shattered anyway. The events of the last couple of days were catching up with me, and the nap I'd had earlier hadn't been enough.

The phone call would wait until the morning, I decided as I grabbed another shower and took some more medication.

Even though we always cleaned up at the C before we left, I always seemed to want another shower as soon as I got home, too. I wasn't sure why, but it was as if I felt that a second shower helped cleanse me of the sins committed there. Who knew, but I never felt really clean unless I showered twice.

I wanted to go and see Gracie, but I was frankly too exhausted, and I didn't want to wake her, so I forced myself to climb into bed alone. The minute my head hit the pillow; I was out cold.

CHAPTER 21
GRACIE
SUNDAY - FALLING FOR THE BRATVA
SECOND!

While Ash was away, I lost myself in my book, only forcing myself to leave the library when my stomach growled. Realising it must be near dinner time, I headed off to find Sonia. She was in her room, and we went down to dinner together. It was another lovely meal cooked by Nonna.

I really liked Nonna. She was funny and told us stories about her life in Italy when she looked after Ash's mother as she grew up. Nonna really made these stories come to life. I could almost picture the young Marissa and the palazzo where she lived as a child. It made me long to visit Italy someday.

Romi was also a good conversationalist and was really quite charming. Sonia certainly seemed to agree. I couldn't help noticing how she tried to keep him talking all the time. He did have a lovely accent, although personally, I happened to think it was not quite as lovely as that of my own Mr Sexy Voice.

I saw that he was always glancing at her, too, when he thought she wasn't looking. Hmmm, cousins or not, I was sure something was going on there. Or at least both parties secretly wished as much.

My phone vibrated, and I glanced at it, hoping it might be from Ash. Unfortunately, It was another text from Derrick.

Derrick had sent me numerous texts, but I didn't reply right away, hoping to wait until Ash returned so I could check with him what he was comfortable with me telling Derrick.

I knew what this family was now, and that made me cautious. They were obviously dangerous people, yet I liked them, and I thought they liked me. They seemed to have assumed that I was now Ash's girlfriend and had taken me under their wing. They had been very welcoming, and I was flattered by their attention.

Nevertheless, I was aware that their life was one where they needed to be careful about who knew about their activities and exactly how much they knew. The family obviously worked hard to maintain their outward appearance of being simply Russian oligarchs, and I would never do anything to jeopardise that. Therefore, I wasn't going to tell Derrick anything more about the recent events without talking to Ash first.

Derrick was relentless, however, and as the day wore on and I hadn't answered, his texts became more frantic. Eventually, I succumbed to texting him back. I simply told him that I was safe and had gone to stay with friends for a few days. He wasn't so easily mollified, though, and demanded to speak to me in person to ensure I was alright.

Ash had said he wouldn't be back until late. I knew that Derrick was worried, but I had to wait until I knew what to say before we talked, so I took the coward's way out and turned my phone off. I knew I was only delaying the inevitable. I would definitely need to call him in the morning. Otherwise, he was likely to turn up at the Estate demanding entry.

Thankfully, Derrick hadn't mentioned anything to Claire or Marcie. He likely hadn't wanted to worry them while they were on their much-needed short break, but I was glad of the reprieve. I'd need to tell them something eventually, but not yet.

I'd actually had a text from the girls earlier, too. They'd told me all about the various spa treatments they'd indulged in, including getting massages from hunky male masseurs. Marcie was especially happy about that! Personally, I would find that excruciating and not in the least bit relaxing or enjoyable. Well, maybe if it was Ash, I might feel differently. I grinned wickedly at the thought.

It was weird how quickly I had come to crave my sexy Russian's company. We barely knew each other, and yet I couldn't stop thinking about him. I missed him terribly and hoped he was safe. I knew he was with his brothers, but I was still worried.

After dinner, Nonna retired to watch her soap operas. Romi had business to deal with in the office, so Sonia and I went to the cinema room to binge on some Netflix and kill a few hours.

By the time 11 p.m. came, I was tired and ready for bed but wanted to wait up for Ash. I was anxious to see him again. The men had been gone for hours, and it bothered me that they weren't back yet.

Sonia assured me that they were fine and would have everything under control, but I couldn't help but worry about what trouble Ash might get himself into without me there to get him out of it.

I laughed inwardly at the very thought. I might have helped Ash yesterday and this morning, but I knew that he wasn't the type of man who would normally need anyone to protect him.

In fact, I expected he was usually the one doing the protecting. Still, I found that as much as he had stated that I was now his to protect, I felt the same about him. Nevertheless, I reminded myself that he wasn't alone and that his family would have his back. There was nothing I could do but wait.

Eventually, Sonia convinced me to go to bed, and I dragged myself up to my room. While I undressed, I thought about the events of the last two days and how much my life had changed since meeting Ash a week ago. I realised that I wasn't the same girl who went to the Glitz event. I already felt more confident, sassy, and sexy. I knew the catalyst had been my sacking, but I put the majority of the changes down to meeting Ash. I'd come such a long way in just a week, and I was excited to see how much more I would develop and grow with Ash in my life.

Wow. It all seemed crazy and fast, but it also felt so right. I felt alive and excited about the future. I couldn't wait to explore this thing between us. I was amazed at how easily I had accepted that he and his family were Bratva, but I put that down to my romance novels. Had the books I read romanticised that life too much, I wondered? Could I truly handle the real thing, and did I want to? Those were some of the questions going through my head as I climbed under the covers. I guessed only time would tell.

In the meantime, I planned on getting some sleep and dreaming about Ash and some of the sexual encounters we might have in the future. The taste in the library whetted my appetite, and I couldn't wait to have another.

I drifted off to sleep with a smile on my face, and my thoughts filled with intense grey eyes and a sexy Russian accent.

CHAPTER 22
ASH

As soon as it was light, I was awake with a raging hard-on. I needed to see Gracie, but I knew that my body was still not quite healed enough to do our first-time justice, so I needed to get my shit under control.

I took a cold shower, which helped, but I was still sporting a semi as I walked to her room a short while later. I knocked on the door, but there was no response. I tried again, but still no response, so I entered the room.

Gracie lay on her side, sleeping. I took a moment to observe her at rest. She was absolutely the most beautiful woman I had ever seen, with her long golden locks framing her face. Her pale skin was flawless, and her lips were full and pink. I knew I should probably leave or wake her, but I couldn't seem to do either. Instead, I stood there staring at her, feeling a bit like a creep, unable to pull my gaze from her.

Her eyes moved beneath her eyelids, and she appeared to be dreaming. I wondered what she was dreaming of, and when she turned onto her back and moaned, I hoped it was me. She moaned again, stretching her body, and I licked my lips at the sensuous picture she posed. She looked so sexy. I vaguely registered the thought that I really should go. Yet still, I didn't move.

I scanned her body, noticing a small foot sticking out of the cover. It was the cutest thing I'd ever seen. I'd never had a foot fetish before, but all of a sudden, I couldn't get the image of sucking on her toes out of my head.

She stretched languidly and moaned again, and my gaze was drawn back to her lips. Another moan. My cock jerked at the sound.

I was pretty sure that her dream was of the ex-rated kind, and I smirked as a wicked thought entered my mind. Was this a situation I was going to take full advantage of? Damn, right.

I leaned down to kiss her lightly on those luscious lips. I was delighted when she responded in her sleep, and I smiled against her lips and then deepened the kiss.

I removed my clothes, slipped under the covers, and pulled her close. Kissing her again, my hand slipped inside her pyjama shorts. I started working my fingers over her hard little nub, and I was rewarded when she moaned into my mouth and moved against me. My Little Miss Hot Mess was a sensual creature, and I liked it.

My cock liked it too. In fact, it liked it so bloody much it was throbbing so hard that it physically hurt, but I ignored it. It wanted to bury itself into Gracie and ride her hard, but I wasn't up to the kind of sex it wanted, so it would have to wait. When I took her, I wanted to blow her mind, and for that, I needed to be at full strength. Currently, I ached all over, and my ribs throbbed even worse than my cock.

Still, I fully intended on having another taste of my Little Miss Hot Mess right now, and neither my ribs nor my cock nor any other part of me was about to stop me,

So, I willed my cock to calm down; it wasn't at all happy with that, but tough. Besides, I told it, delayed gratification could make great sex even better. It didn't go down any and continued to throb angrily as I worked Gracie's little nub between my fingers, so I didn't think it believed me.

She was still sleeping and moaning and bucking against my fingers as I slid down her body and pulled her shorts down before replacing my fingers with my mouth. I licked and sucked deeply on her clit and was rewarded when her whole body shuddered. Spurred on by her reaction, I continued with this for a while, enjoying how she squirmed beneath me, her hips bucking up into my mouth. She was getting close; I could feel it.

I grazed her clit with my teeth, then gave her a slight nip, and that's when I felt her come awake with a jolt. I looked up at her, and our gazes locked. I smirked as I inserted two fingers inside her and thrust them in and out gently.

"Morning, sweetheart!" I murmured.

She looked a bit shocked to see me but didn't protest. Her cheeks flamed, and her eyelids fluttered as I continued my assault on her pussy.

"Do you like that, sweetheart?" I asked. Even though I could tell by her reaction that she did, my ego still wanted to hear her confirm it.

She nodded, and I grinned.

"You're back! I was worried," she said, and I froze, looking deeply into her eyes.

She'd been worried about me. That thought had me elated. I was happy I realised Sonia was right; Gracie was bringing me back to life again. Her presence was opening me up, making me feel emotions I'd long since thought dead, and I couldn't be more pleased. I loved that she had been worried about me because that meant that she cared.

"That is nice, sweetheart. I like that you were worried about me, but you didn't need to worry. Everything was under control.

Besides, now you are here, and I have a reason to come back safe." I told her, meaning every word.

She smiled shyly again as I crawled up the bed, ignoring my aches and pains, and took her lips in a tender kiss. I looked her in the eye as I began thrusting my fingers inside her again.

She was blushing, and it was so cute. I pulled her top off and pecked her on the lips before pressing light kisses to her neck and jaw.

Slowly, I made my way down to her breasts, alternating between kissing and licking her skin. I took one breast in my mouth and sucked her nipple, then the other. She thrust her torso towards me, and I took that as an invitation to continue enjoying her tits.

While I licked and suckled on them, I slid one hand back down to her pussy and pressed my thumb to her clit, circling it gently. She was so wet for me. I thrust two fingers inside while my thumb continued to press against her clit. She felt so good.

I was thoroughly enjoying the feel of her bucking against me. My cock really wanted in on the action and was pressing between us so hard that I was frightened it would bruise her hip. Seriously, I couldn't ever remember being this hard before in my life. *Soon*! I told it, *Patience*!

I pulled back and to the side a little to ease the pressure. I continued to ignore the throbbing between my legs and concentrate on the throbbing I could feel between hers. Gracie's pussy was soaking wet and open for me now. She was so close. I added another finger and curled them slightly, hitting just the right spot, and she came undone, clenching tightly around me. Fuck, it felt good!

"Oh god," she cried.

I cockily responded, "Not God, baby, Ash! I am real and can make you come; God can't!"

I looked at her and winked.

"What a way to be woken up," she chuckled.

"Stick with me, sweetheart, and I will wake you up like that every morning," I said and meant it. She blushed, looking a bit awkward.

I lay beside her, unable to stop staring and grinning at her. My attention must have embarrassed her further, though, because she shifted uncomfortably under my gaze. She was just so cute. I couldn't resist leaning down for another kiss. Unfortunately, she didn't let me capture her lips in the way I'd hoped.

"I need to brush my teeth!" she cried as her hand flew to cover her mouth, and she darted out of the bed.

Realising, she had nothing covering her ass, she squealed. She bent down to pick my t-shirt up off the floor and held it up in an attempt to cover her bum, but not before she gave me a show first. Realising her mistake, she squeaked and ran into the bathroom, slamming the door shut behind her.

I doubled over, laughing hard.

"No point in hiding from me now, sweetheart. I've already seen what you've got!"

"Oh my god!" she groaned, and I cracked up again.

One minute, my Little Miss Hot Mess was as sassy as hell, and the next, she was just as shy. She was a mix that intrigued me and turned me on at the same time. I could hear the shower running now, so I tried the bathroom door, intent on joining her, but she had locked it.

"Don't you dare come in here!" she shouted, obviously still embarrassed.

"Okay, sweetheart, I'll give you some space," I said, retreating to the bed to collect the rest of my clothes while trying not to think of the water running over her naked body. My cock ached, and so I concentrated on taking deep breaths and willing it to go down.

She could have her space for now. Soon, she wouldn't be locking me out of anywhere but instead would be begging me to join her. I'd make sure of it, I vowed. I slipped my jeans back on, leaving them unbuttoned to ease the pressure on my cock, and sat on the bed thinking about all the ways I was going to do that.

CHAPTER 23
GRACIE

SUNDAY MORNING - A TASTE OF ASH

After I woke up with Ash's head buried between my legs and the subsequent fantastic orgasm he'd given me, I shouldn't feel embarrassed at him seeing me naked. Yet I was.

I ran into the bathroom, holding his T-shirt up to cover my bare ass as best I could, and slammed the door to the sound of his deep laughter.

"No point in hiding from me, sweetheart; I have already seen what you've got!" he shouted, chuckling.

"Oh my god!" I groaned, making him laugh even harder.

Could I get any more awkward? Where had my sassy badass side gone? *Geez, girl, you need to get a grip!* My inner devil chastised me. She was right. I needed to get some of that sass back before I made even more of a fool of myself and put this guy off me for good.

After what we had been up to, I really shouldn't feel shy, but I couldn't help it. I wasn't used to such attention from men. I blushed when I remembered how he woke me up and his promise to wake me that way every morning.

Wow. Every morning? My inner devil was doing cartwheels inside at that thought, but the shy part of me couldn't understand his interest in me. I couldn't prevent my self-doubt from rearing its ugly head as I wondered. I knew I was pretty, but what did a sexy, rich, powerful, and dangerous man like Ash really see in shy, bumbling me?

I looked in the mirror and groaned. I was a mess. Shit. I had bed head and was sweaty from our exertions, and I had to have morning breath. The reason I panicked and ran to the bathroom in the first place, just barely avoiding his kiss.

I could still hear him laughing outside. The aggravating pig. His laughter was annoying, but it did provide me with some resolve. I narrowed my eyes as I looked at my reflection. I wasn't letting him away with it. I needed to clean up and then get out there and figure out how to win back some of my dignity. How? I had no idea, but I knotted my hair on top of my head, turned the shower on, and stepped under the water, determined to do just that.

He jiggled the door handle, but thankfully, I'd locked it because I was not quite ready to face him yet.

"Don't you dare come in here!" I shouted because, locked or not, the lock was flimsy, and I had no doubt that Ash would be able to shoulder it open easily if he wanted to.

"Okay, sweetheart, I'll give you some space," he sniggered, but I was really glad when he did just that. I needed some time to think clearly.

The fact he had wanted to come in gave my ego a boost. I quickly washed, dried off and brushed my teeth, all the while thinking things through. Ash liked me. He had to. Even I could see it was obvious. He had kissed me last week, and even though he'd acted like a jerk then, he had apologised now. Plus, he'd discussed me with his family, and Sonia had told me that he'd been looking for me since then. A guy didn't do that if he wasn't interested. Then, he had flirted with me and been all over me in my bedroom after we'd been attacked, and since then, he had been so attentive and had provided me with a couple of great orgasms.

So, whether I really understood it or not, it was obvious he was as attracted to me as I was to him. I was not going to keep second-guessing that. In fact, I was going to own it.

I wasn't quite sure how yet, but I was going to dig down deep and find the confidence I needed to keep a man like Ash interested. And there was no time like the present.

I didn't have any clothes but his T-shirt, so I put that back on. The funny thing was, just doing that and smelling him all over me again gave me a rush of wicked thoughts, and suddenly, it hit me, and I knew just how to regain my dignity.

Before leaving the bathroom, I smoothed my hair down and checked out my reflection one last time, glad to see I looked much better. Taking a deep breath, I pulled my shoulders back, lifted my head high and strutted out of the bathroom.

He was sitting back on the bed when I came out but jumped up when he saw me, his jaw-dropping as he took in my appearance. A surge of excitement ran through me at the awed look on his face as he licked his lips and looked me up and down. If there had been any lingering doubt of his interest in me before, that look blew it completely from my mind.

"You look stunning in my T-shirt, sweetheart," he said, giving me a slow, sexy smile.

As he checked me out, I did the same to him. He had put his jeans back on, but they were unbuttoned, and he was topless, of course. The sight of him nearly naked took my breath away. I stared at him as he stared at me.

My eyes roamed his body. Even though we had gotten down

and dirty before, I hadn't actually had the chance to look at him properly, so now that I had the opportunity to do so, I took full advantage.

He was still covered with bruises, of course, but regardless, he was gorgeous. His body was a work of art, all sinewy muscle and lightly bronzed skin. And those abs! I had never seen a six-pack on a real-life guy before, only in pictures, but this guy had an eight-pack. That was impressive as hell. He had to work hard to keep a body like that.

And that tattoo on his shoulder… Wow! I felt myself getting damp again just looking at him, and my eyes followed the eight-pack down towards the V-shape that led to the noticeably large bulge in his pants. I suddenly wanted to touch him and taste him so bad.

I strode over and sunk to my knees in front of him, slipped my hand inside his jeans and quickly pulled him free. Oh my god, his cock jumped in my hand, hardening before my eyes, and I couldn't help but gasp at his sheer size.

"Wow, big!" I heard myself say in awe.

And not just big. It was beautiful, too. I hadn't ever thought of a cock as being beautiful before, but this one was. It was long, thick, hard, and throbbing, and all mine. I licked my lips excitedly and looked up at Ash as I opened my mouth and licked the end, tasting him. Hmmm, salty but not too much. I kept my eyes on him as he watched me, his own eyes now heavy with desire.

I licked along his length before taking him into my mouth. I liked his taste. He cried out as I sunk down on him, taking him deeper inside. His groans of pleasure egged me on as I sucked and licked his cock. He didn't take his eyes off me, his face a mask of awed pleasure, as I moaned around his shaft.

I sucked him in deep. The look of desire in his eyes made me feel so powerful. I grabbed his ass to get closer. Taking one hand, I gently massaged his balls, moving my head up and down his shaft, finding my rhythm. He grabbed my hair then, unable to stop himself, thrusting into my mouth, going deeper and deeper each time while I continued to suck and massage him.

It wasn't long before I felt him getting close to his release. His moans were making me wet for him, and my pussy throbbed with need, but I ignored it. I was sure that it would get plenty of attention later, but this was about payback and dignity, so it would just have to wait.

His balls tightened, and he gave a final deep thrust which made me gag a little before shooting his cum down my throat. He tried to pull back, but I wouldn't let him. I gripped his ass with both hands and continued to suck hard, wanting to drink every last drop from him, loving how good he tasted on my tongue.

I felt elated as his legs wobbled slightly as he finished. He pulled my head away, sinking down on the bed before pulling me up onto his lap. He had a huge grin on his face.

"That was fucking amazing! Thank you, sweetheart!" he said before kissing me deeply.

My insides buzzed in triumph. I felt like a bloody sex goddess! Ha, dignity restored! *Go girl!* It seemed that inner devil of mine was very pleased with my efforts!

"Just paying you back for waking me up so nicely!" I told him with a grin.

He rewarded me with another lingering kiss before eventually pulling back to look at me.

"While I would love us to continue this, we have some calls to make, and I have a meeting to go to soon," he said, sighing, before gently moving me off his lap.

"Right, of course," I jumped up and headed to the wardrobe, looking for some clothes.

I bent over to pick up some underwear from the bottom drawer.

"Gorgeous!" he said, and his hand stroked my bare ass. I jumped and squeaked in shock.

He chuckled as I grabbed the rest of my clothes and ran for the bathroom, embarrassed again. I slammed the door and locked it again as he laughed loudly once more.

That bugger! I pouted as I dressed. He had me going from sassy and confident one minute to shy the next and then back again! I needed to stop getting so embarrassed around him. After all, the things we had been doing didn't feel embarrassing at the time, so why should I be embarrassed when we stopped doing them? It was stupid.

'No more embarrassment!' I thought firmly before striding out of the bathroom, head held high, sporting a haughty look, and tossing my hair as I threw his T-shirt at him. With my sassiness on full display again, and before I could chicken out, I walked straight over to him, pulled his head towards me, and kissed him hard on the lips, loving the shocked look on his face.

"Let's go make those calls!" I called over my shoulder as I flounced out the door, leaving him standing staring at me. Another score for my dignity!

He caught up to me as I flounced along the hall and grabbed my hand in his.

"You continue to surprise the hell out of me, Gracie," he said, winking as I peeked up at him from under my lashes.

I couldn't help the big grin I sported as we headed downstairs, but I was pleased to see that it matched his own.

We had a quick breakfast and then headed to Ash's office. As soon as we got there, I called the Bell Tavern, pretending to be sick. I hated letting Gina down at short notice like this, but luckily, another staff member who'd been on holiday had returned, so it wasn't an issue.

Then we chatted about what we should tell Derrick, and I agreed wholeheartedly when Ash stated he should talk with him first. I was more than okay with that because it meant he could tell Derrick as much or as little as he was comfortable with, and I didn't need to worry about divulging too much information.

CHAPTER 24
ASH

As soon as we got to my office, Gracie called in sick at work, and then we discussed what to say to Derrick.

She agreed to let me talk to him first, and so I gave his mobile a call.

He answered immediately.

"Where the hell is she? She'd better be okay, or you will be dealing with me!" he ground out.

"She is with me, and she is safe," I told him firmly.

"Give me your address; I am coming over now to see for myself," he stated.

"No need," I said, but he was insistent. I thought he would be.

He was determined to ensure Gracie was safe, and I respected him all the more for that, so I told him our address.

While we waited for him to arrive, Gracie and I talked about our lives and made out like teenagers as I sat in the chair behind my desk with her on my lap.

I listened to everything she told me, but it was hard to concentrate at times as all sorts of wicked fantasies ran through my mind. Oh, the things I planned on doing to her in this room when I was back to full health.

Fantasies, similar to the things we had done earlier, plus so much more!

I loved seeing her wearing my T-shirt this morning. It was so hot! I loved the sight of her in my clothes almost as much as I loved the sight of her naked. I hadn't been able to stop staring.

As she told me about what she had been doing this week, I fantasised about her slipping into my office while I worked late one evening, wearing only my T-shirt, before I pulled it off her, turned her over to my desk, and took her from behind.

Then I had a flashback to when she had been on her knees in front of me, sucking greedily on my cock. I was planning on having her do that in here, too. Oh, and anywhere else I could get her to do it. I closed my eyes and nuzzled her neck as I imagined it all.

I nipped her earlobe, blew inside her ear, then ran my tongue down her neck from her ear to her collarbone and nipped at the sensitive skin where her neck and shoulder met. She shivered in delight, and goosebumps spread over her skin. I loved how she reacted to me. She was so sensitive to everything I did to her, and it made everything feel so much more erotic.

We were so wrapped up in each other that we barely noticed the time passing before one of my men knocked on the door announcing Derricks's arrival.

Reluctantly, we pulled apart, and I gave her a quick kiss on the lips before helping her stand. I quickly adjusted myself in an attempt to hide my obvious erection before I went to the door and opened it.

"What the hell is going on?" he asked the minute I appeared.

Gracie slipped out of the office as I ushered him inside. We had agreed to let me talk to him first, and although he narrowed his eyes at me when I told him this, he didn't protest.

"I'll ask again, what the hell is going on?" he stated with a voice that demanded an answer.

He might have acted somewhat submissive and called me Mr Rominov before when he was working, but the way he spoke to me now made it plain that he wasn't intimidated by me in his personal life. I found my respect for him growing even more.

I sat down and motioned for him to do the same. At first, I thought he might protest, but after a second or two of deliberation, he sat.

Before I got down to my explanation, I thanked him for fixing me up. He nodded in acceptance but didn't say anything. His eyes were watchful, and I could see him weighing me up in the same way I was him.

There was much more to Derrick than he let on to most people, and I was pleased with what I saw.

I spent the next few minutes explaining what had happened.

Keeping it simple at first, I simply stated that I had been kidnapped. I suspected the men involved were planning to rob my family's businesses as they had been attempting to beat information out of me.

Thankfully, Gracie had seen them taking me into a building near the Bell Tavern and came to my rescue. Which had both surprised and delighted me.

However, unfortunately, we must've been followed as the two guys broke into Gracie's house the following morning and attacked us again. We had fought them off until my brother and cousin arrived to help. After that, we'd come here to ensure Gracie's safety. I also assured him that we were dealing with the situation and didn't want police involvement at this time. Not too far off from the truth!

It was a deliberately vague explanation. I watched Derrick intently to see how this information, or lack thereof, affected him.

He looked at me just as intensely, and I could tell he saw way more than I would have initially given him credit for. My respect for him went up another notch. It appeared he was exactly what I was looking for.

"What happened to the men?" he asked.

"They are no longer a problem," I replied.

He nodded approvingly, and I could see his mind working.

"But you're still in danger, and Gracie too, I take it?" he asked after a moment of silence.

"Yes, it seems they were part of a larger threat, but we are dealing with that and will have it eliminated soon," I said, emphasising the word eliminated to gauge his reaction.

Again, he said nothing, simply nodding his approval, staring at me long and hard. At that moment, I could tell that behind the usual upbeat, slightly diva-type persona he wore on a daily basis lay a strong, powerful, and dangerous man.

A lesser man might have squirmed under his gaze, but I didn't. I was used to strong, powerful, and dangerous men. Indeed, I was one. So, I simply returned his stare with the same assessing intensity until he smirked, nodding again, and I guessed that I'd passed whatever test that was.

"What can I do to help, Mr Rominov?" he asked.

Ah, the respect was back. However, I wanted to get Derrick onside, so the barrier between us needed to be lower. I leaned forward.

"Please, call me Ash, Derrick," I said with a grin.

He smiled. "Ash," he said with a slight nod of acknowledgement.

"I meant what I said. What can I do to help?" Derrick

repeated the question. Yes, I liked this guy, but would he be the right fit for my family? I wondered.

"Nothing yet; we have enough security here with our own men plus a few additional guys from Anton. However, we may need a medic at some point whom we can call on to be discreet," I said, once again gauging his reaction, and once again, he didn't disappoint.

"Ah, then I take it that you are likely going to be dealing with matters in a less than legit way?" he raised his eyebrows in question.

As I suspected, this man could be a great asset. A friend too, I suspected, if I could secure his loyalty and get him onside. Time for a final test.

"Derrick, I am aware you are a man who understands that sometimes things are not black and white in this world, and things are not always done to the letter of the law. My family are Russian businessmen, and the majority of our business is fully legal and above board, but there are aspects of our lives that are a bit darker. This situation is one of them," I said, giving him just enough of a hint as to what that meant without actually confessing anything as such.

I could see he understood exactly what I was saying, though.

"I have a good idea exactly who and what you and your family are, and so long as you look after Gracie and ensure she comes to no harm, I have no issue with that," he stated.

"I will never let anything happen to Gracie, and I assure you her safety is my first priority," I told him truthfully.

"I like Gracie a lot, more than a lot, and I am hoping that she will be a permanent fixture in my life in the future if she agrees to that," I confessed, and his eyes widened.

"I am aware that you take the safety of the women you

know very seriously and that you have taken care of Gracie, but that job is mine now," I told him firmly.

I wanted this woman, and he needed to know that I was serious about her.

He narrowed his eyes, obviously unsure about that.

"Gracie is an adult, and so as long as she is happy and agrees to, and wants, a relationship with you, then I will be happy for you both," he said, with just a hint of a warning in his voice.

I nodded. I totally respected that.

"I have no intention of forcing Gracie to do anything. I have genuine feelings for her, and I believe she is developing the same feelings for me, too. It is early days, but like I said, I am hoping she will become a permanent fixture in my life, so you can rest assured I will do everything I can to make her happy and keep her safe."

He stared at me for a few seconds. This serious, dangerous side of Derrick was a man of few words, and I liked that.

Finally, he nodded. It seemed we had come to an understanding."

"Like I said, as long as she is happy, I have no objections to you pursuing a relationship with her, Ash," he said.

I stood and shook his hand, thanking him again for his help the other night.

"Anytime," he said with a grin.

I got the feeling that Derrick meant that, and from what I knew of him, I believed that he might even enjoy the opportunity to skirt the law once in a while.

"I'll send Gracie in," I told him, feeling pleased.

Getting him onside was definitely a plus, and his willingness to help us with any follow-up to this situation boded well for my long-term future plans for him.

I grinned back at him. Yeah. I liked this guy.

CHAPTER 25
GRACIE

As expected, Derrick wasn't satisfied with a phone call and insisted on coming to check on me himself. He acted like an overprotective big brother at times, and I loved him for it. I thought that Ash admired him for that, too.

We'd chatted about our lives while we'd waited, in between bouts of making out like a couple of horny teenagers. So, by the time Derrick arrived, my lips were swollen from Ash's kisses, my pussy throbbing, and I was about ready to jump the guy's bones and demand he take me right there on his desk.

So, thankful that Ash had wanted to talk to Derrick alone first, I gladly slipped out of his office as soon as he opened the door to let Derrick in. I took a few steadying breaths and tried to calm my overheated body. I needed to get a hold of myself before I talked to him.

A short time later, Ash emerged and told me to go in. He looked relaxed, and since there hadn't been any shouting or crashing, and he wasn't sporting any more bruises, I assumed it had gone well. I sighed in relief, not realising just how anxious I had been about that until now.

Derrick immediately stood up and hugged me.

"You okay, sweetie?" he asked.

"I'm fine," I reassured him.

"Ash seems to like you a lot," he stated.

I noticed it was Ash now and not Mr Rominov. That pleased me because I knew that if Derrick were unsure of Ash, he wouldn't want to be on first-name terms with him.

"Yes," I said, feeling a bit shy again.

"How do you feel about that?" he prompted.

"I really like him, too," I said with a grin.

"Girl, it looks like you two have got it bad for each other!" he grinned back.

"So, have you gotten laid yet? Is he good? Bet he is!" he smirked and winked.

"No, I have not, Derrick Reid! And the rest is none of your business!" I exclaimed in shock, feeling the heat rising in my face.

"Liar! That blush tells a different story!" he chuckled, then sobered up, giving me a searching look.

"As long as you are happy with things and want to stay here, that is fine with me, Gracie, but if you have any doubts, I will take you back home with me right now. You don't need to feel you must stay if you don't want to, despite what Ash says."

I smiled, "I know, but I do want to stay."

"Alright, but if you change your mind or need me for anything, you know where I am," he said, hugging me tightly.

I nodded, pleased to have such a great friend caring for me.

With nothing more to say, he told Ash to let him know if there was anything he could do to help before leaving.

As soon as he had gone, Ash pulled me to him for a kiss. It was threatening to turn into someone far more, and I was definitely up for that, but unfortunately, the phone rang, and Ash needed to answer it. After that, he had some work stuff to do but asked me to remain in the office and keep him company.

I was more than willing, so I quickly retrieved a book from my room, then returned to settle down to read while Ash checked his emails and did whatever else he had to do.

The book was good, and, normally, I would have been engrossed and in my own little world while reading it, but I couldn't help glancing over to my Mr Sexy Voice and comparing him to the hero. And oh, my, did he compare!

Of course, every time I checked him out, Ash either caught me at it or was already doing the same to me. As the morning wore on, we spent a lot of time simply grinning at each other like a couple of fools.

After lunch, Ash finished up some important paperwork and then, unfortunately, had to leave for a meeting with someone to get more information about the ongoing threat. He reluctantly kissed me goodbye and headed off with Romi, leaving me in his office reading. I was glad to see he had learned his lesson and wasn't going to this meeting alone.

With him gone, I daydreamed about him for a while. Everything was so new between us and very exciting. Eventually, for my own sanity, I decided to push all thoughts of the man aside and try to read again. Otherwise, I would need to head to my room and take care of my needs because just the thought of the sexy Russian had me feeling rampant.

A short while later, Miki entered the office."

"Hey, Gracie", he greeted me."

"Hey," I said back, feeling a little awkward around the big boss guy. Even though I had accepted that Ash was part of the Russian Mafia, it still felt strange, and I wasn't yet used to the fact. I also wasn't yet quite sure how to behave around them, but more so their pakhan, Miki.

I studied him. I don't know what I would ever have expected the pakhan of the UK Bratva to look like, but it wasn't him. He was a very good-looking man, slightly taller than Ash and a bit bulkier. You couldn't fail to see the family resemblance between the two. In fact, all the brothers looked very alike, with just slight differences in skin tone and build. Although Ash and Marko were usually clean-shaven, Miki sported a well-groomed beard.

As he walked towards where I was sitting on the couch, I couldn't miss the air of authority in his confident swagger. Oh, yes, this was a man used to being in charge and a very attractive man indeed. All the brothers and Romi were attractive. Still, to me, Ash was the most handsome of them all.

He stopped before me and smiled. What a smile! If I hadn't been so enamoured with Ash, I would very much have developed a sudden crush on Miki just from that smile alone. Of course, Ash had all of the same qualities as his brother, and his smile hadn't just given me a crush on its owner but a full-blown obsession. My core was dampened at the thought of that obsession. Oh, my. I squirmed, feeling suddenly very hot.

Thankfully, Miki didn't seem to notice that I was a bit uncomfortable.

He thanked me again for saving Ash, telling me how glad he was that I'd come into Ash's life because Ash was so much happier with me around than he had been in the last couple of years."

"You seem to be good for him, Gracie," he said, smiling.

I smiled back, but I found his words strange. I didn't know Ash well yet, but apart from initially seeming like a jerk—I couldn't believe he'd ever seemed that way to me—he had always been flirty and smiled at me. I hadn't seen him unhappy. I guessed he must have been, though, because both Sonia and now Miki had commented on it.

I couldn't help wondering what had made him that way. I also couldn't help feeling a little thrilled that I seemed to have helped. I wasn't sure how I had helped, but I was glad I had, and I hoped I could continue to help him in the future. Oh, I can think of lots of ways you can help Ash in the future! My inner devil purred.

I bit my bottom lip to stop the smirk that threatened me as I thought about making out with him in his office earlier. I glanced at the desk, and I felt my cheeks heating as images of all the things I would dearly love Ash to do to me on that desk flashed through my mind.

You go, girl! My inner devil shouted in glee, my thoughts pleasing her greatly.

Thinking of Ash made me realise how much I was looking forward to his return. I hoped his meeting didn't take long because I was looking forward to another make-out session this evening and whatever else it might lead to.

Oh my! I felt my temperature rise further at these naughty thoughts.

Miki had been rummaging around in the top drawer of a filing cabinet while I'd been deep in thought, and I was startled when he asked, "You all right, Gracie?"

I dragged my eyes from the desk and looked at him.

"You look deep in thought. And a bit red," Miki said, raising an eyebrow, and I could hear the smirk in his voice.

"I'm fine, yes! And hot. Just hot. It's hot in here," I said, clearing my throat.

Shit, I was rambling and could feel myself reddening further in embarrassment at being caught in my dirty thoughts.

I fanned myself with my book to try to dispel the heat from my face.

He looked at me intently, glanced at the desk, and grinned. I hadn't known the guy long, but I already knew that Miki didn't miss anything, and I had an idea that he knew exactly where my thoughts had been.

To his credit, he didn't say anything and, after a quick goodbye, he left to go to a meeting of his own.

As soon as he was out of the door, I hid my face and cringed. Geez!

It could be worse; at least he didn't catch you and Ash doing anything. Yet! My inner devil said.

I groaned at the idea. It was bad enough that Miki might have realised I'd been thinking dirty thoughts. I didn't think I could survive the embarrassment of being caught in the act with Ash by Miki, or anyone else, for that matter. I made a mental note to ensure the door was locked the next time Ash and I were making out.

As the embarrassment finally eased, I settled back down to finish reading the last few pages of my book. It didn't take long, and when I finished, I was feeling restless. I needed to do something to keep my mind off one sexy Russian, and suddenly, I had the urge to write.

I took a pen and blank notepad from the desk and started jotting down some ideas. It seemed that the events of the past week were inspiring me to create my own story at last, and soon, I had the plan set for my very first book. I felt incredibly pleased with myself. I looked at the plan and thought that I finally had a story worth telling.

While I was so inspired, I grabbed my laptop and headed to the library. I set myself up a little writing corner and got to work.

It was going to be a mafia romance, obviously, as that was what I loved to read and what I always wanted to write anyway. I had the basic concept for a story already in my head but hadn't been able to write it until now. This week had certainly given me plenty of material to work with.

I wrote for a couple of hours and got the story synopsis done, the character synopsis for the main characters, and even the first chapter written as well. I was so pleased with how much I had achieved. I was finally writing my own book! I felt elated and couldn't wait to tell Claire and Marcie when they got home. They'd be so proud of me.

This time last week, I was a somewhat shy and pathetic person just getting over being sacked, a disastrous waitressing gig, and a messy kiss from a sexy Russian stranger I didn't expect to ever see again. This week, I was a sassy badass with a sexy Russian boyfriend on my way to achieving my dreams!

I headed to dinner feeling like I was walking on clouds.

CHAPTER 26

ASH

After leaving Gracie to read her book, I'd run into Miki on my way to find Romi, and he remarked at my whistling. I hadn't even realised I'd been doing that.

"You seem happy," he said.

"Kissing a beautiful woman would do that to you," I told him. Especially when that woman was Gracie.

I couldn't help the smile that played on my face as I thought of her while Romi and I drove back into London to meet with Sean and Juana. I was hoping they had some useful information for us so we could get a plan together, finally putting an end to the Malia Boys and Broxy's threat.

As we approached the rendezvous point, I found that I really wanted to get this whole thing out of the way, not just the meeting but the whole situation. I wanted it to end as quickly as possible so that I could focus my attention on wooing Gracie. I felt bereft of her company already and had only been away from her for about an hour.

I grinned. I couldn't wait to get back. I felt physically better today. I wasn't in as much pain with my ribs, and my face wasn't swollen any more. I was determined to continue exploring the delights Gracie had to offer again tonight.

Of course, I'd need to brief Miki on whatever information we got and probably spend some time discussing a plan of action before I could see her again. I huffed at the thought. The quicker this meeting was over and a plan formed, the better.

We parked and headed to the meeting on foot.

"Hey, Ash. I'm glad you are okay," Juana said when we arrived.

"Thanks," I replied before she continued.

"Sorry, it took me so long to get back to you. Siri has been keeping an eye on everybody since those idiots jeopardised his plans by kidnapping you. It took me until now to sneak out," Juana said.

"No problem. What have you got for us?" I asked.

She bit her lip and glanced at Sean, who I noticed looked uncomfortable. Warning bells went off in my head.

"Some information you're really not going to like," she told me, shifting on her feet anxiously.

"Maybe we should get Miki and Marko on the phone first and tell everyone together?" Sean said.

I felt myself wanting to spiral. Shit, I could tell by the look in his eyes this had something to do with the incident. I didn't know how, but I could tell.

"Just spit it out, no matter what it is," I said through gritted teeth.

Sean took hold of Juana's hand in support. Yep, there was definitely something going on there.

She glanced at him, then took a deep breath.

"What happened with Krissa was initially random, as we were all led to believe, but then Siri became involved."

"What the fuck?!" Romi said, resting a hand on my shoulder in support.

Jesus, I knew it! I couldn't breathe. I took a few deep breaths to steady myself. I couldn't let myself spiral.

"What do you know?" I said in a low voice. I was barely in control but forced myself to keep it together. This was important. I needed to know what had happened.

"I better start at the beginning. Yesterday, Siri had a secret meeting; I expected it to be about the attacks on your family, so I followed him. It turned out to be that big-shot criminal lawyer dude, the one who defended Lev Petrov. I heard him tell Siri that Petrov was getting released early after making a deal to rat out somebody he had been sharing a cell with."

"That fucker!" I shouted.

"Yeah," she agreed, "Anyway, he said he would be out in a few days and would be getting picked up by some undercover agents from the National Crime Agency to be taken into witness protection. The lawyer dude told Siri to make sure that didn't happen and to get rid of him instead, as his boss didn't need him anymore and he was a liability."

That made me pause.

"Why would he, and whoever his boss is, want his client dead?" I asked.

"Wait, there's more," Sean replied grimly.

"Apparently, the lawyer dude's boss is orchestrating the alliance between Siri and the Broxy's, and so he wanted Siri to do the honours and frame you guys as part of the plan."

What the fuck?

"Siri asked if he should obtain any information on Glowacki's operations from Petrov. The lawyer said no, as it would be out of date and of no use. He just wanted Petrov gone before either you or Glowacki got a hold of him, as the boss didn't want you learning that he was the one who had ordered Krissa to be killed."

Shit! Fuckers!

"What the hell does that mean?" I asked, enraged.

"I'm sorry, Ash, I have no idea. That is all they said about Krissa," she said apologetically.

"Any idea who the lawyer's boss is?" Romi asked.

"No," she shook her head, "But I did find out a bit more about the plan against you guys."

I wanted to scream and throw things, but I knew I needed to calm down and focus. I needed to know what else Juana had to say.

"What?" I ground out, trying desperately to keep control.

"Siri said the Broxy's had an informant inside the Bratva who found out the location of your lab. Ivor, he called him. Apparently, he followed one of you guys there one night."

Ivor had only been with us a year or so. He came to us directly from Russia after a fallout with another member of our Brotherhood over there, and we took him in. This was obviously how Ivor repaid us, fucking traitor! Well, he would soon see what we did to traitors.

"Ivor told Siri you get your shipments every third Friday. He said the next one is due next week. They will attack then. Siri will be doing that and, at the same time, the Broxy's are going to hit your home. Siri and the Broxy's don't trust each other, so they are splitting up the attacks."

I snorted. They were right not to trust each other. They would no doubt be planning to double-cross each other as soon as they could anyway.

"I thought they had wanted to frame the Albanians and then get Glowacki and us fighting each other as a distraction. What happened to that?" Romi asked.

"They will be doing more about that starting tonight. They have a couple of Broxy's who are dressed up as Albanians, sporting fake tattoos, and they are going to be going around your dealers, making as much trouble as possible. They also have another couple of Glowacki's men onside who will be with them so that it looks like the Albanians and Glowacki are working together," she said.

Shit, more traitors! Glowacki would be just as furious as us. It looked like we all needed to clean our houses. Because where there was one or two, there could very likely be more.

Unfortunately, that was all the information Juana had for us. However, it was more than we had known, and I was grateful to her for her continued help.

When Sean and Juana left, we headed back to the Estate.

Romi was driving again as I was too on edge.

I called Miki and told him to get Glowacki to meet us as soon as possible at the Estate; we needed to talk. I cautioned him to ensure that Glowacki used the back entrance when he arrived so no one saw him.

Then I told him about Ivor. He would keep the guy occupied somewhere away from the Estate and have him watched at all times. The bastard would be killed soon, but we didn't want to show our hand yet, so that would have to wait.

By the time I ended the call, I felt like I was climbing the walls.

My breathing was harsh, and my fists opened and closed with the need to hit something as I went over everything Juan had said. Especially the information about Krissa. I had thought there was only one other person to kill for closure; now, there were at least another three.

"Fuck!" I shouted, hitting the dashboard with my fist.

"Shit. We're taking a detour to the office so you can beat the shit out of something other than my car," Romi exclaimed, taking a sharp left.

He was right. I desperately needed to hit something without breaking everything in sight or taking my fury out on some random person. I needed to blow off steam in a controlled environment. Since it would likely take a couple of hours for Glowacki to get to the Estate, we had time.

A few minutes later, we pulled up outside our office in the city centre, where we conducted our legitimate business and where most of Marko's legitimate IT staff were based. There was also a fully equipped gym like the one we had at home, but bigger and better. This one had a boxing ring, targets, and bags. Just what I needed.

I put in my earphones and started punching a bag to a background of heavy metal. I punched and punched until I was dripping with sweat. The more I punched, the more pain I endured, the more controlled I became.

By the time Romi said we needed to leave, my knuckles were raw despite the boxing gloves and strapping on my hands, and my ribs were bloody aching, but I felt calmer.

———

We met Glowacki as he arrived with his second oldest son, Dariusz. Dariusz was his second in charge and set to succeed him in place of his older brother, who was murdered by the Albanians at the same time our parents were.

We headed into the office where Marko and Miki were already waiting.

I filled them in about the traitors and the planned attacks against us first. Glowacki was bloody fuming when he heard he had another two traitors in his organisation. I couldn't blame him. He had been getting men sent straight from Poland over the last few years to rebuild his numbers since our war with the Albanians, but they were obviously not trustworthy. Something he would need to deal with soon, but not quite yet.

After updating them on our current issues, I finally told them what I'd learned about Krissa's death and the fuckers responsible. The room went deathly silent as everyone processed the information.

"We take out Petrov, then we take down the Malia and Broxy alliance, and then we will deal with the lawyer and whoever his boss is," Miki stated with barely concealed fury. Miki's anger was different than mine. Mine was red hot. When I was angry, I railed loudly, shouting and lashing out uncontrollably. Meanwhile, Miki's anger was the white-hot type. Controlled, planned, and deadly. I was dangerous. Miki was so much more so.

"Agreed," Glowacki stated.

Then, the discussions started in earnest.

Our first issue was what to deal with Lev Petrov. We needed to get to him before he was taken into witness protection.

Petrov had been Glowacki's top enforcer, but two years ago, he and two of Glowacki's soldiers, brothers Piotr and Szymon Nowack, had been out partying and randomly snatched a young girl off the street. The bastards then raped and murdered her before dumping her back in the alley near where they had taken her.

That alone would have made Glowacki furious, but the fact that the girl happened to be our sister, Krissa, had sent him mad like the rest of us.

Unfortunately, the police had found Krissa before any of us did. The three idiots had been so drunk and drugged at the time that they had left behind some DNA evidence. They were picked up by the National Crime Agency before we could get to them, and as the officers involved were not on the payroll of either of us, we couldn't cover things up and had to allow the due process of the law to take place.

Glowacki had managed to get the brothers out on bail and then handed them over to us, making it appear that they had gone on the run.

We took our time torturing and killing them, but they stuck to the story that the attack on Krissa was random, and none of them knew who she was.

Petrov was remanded in custody and eventually pleaded guilty to manslaughter for a ten-year sentence. Ten fucking years! And now the fucking bastard was getting out early for being a rat. Double fucking bastard!

Before we could even put a plan in place, I was spiralling again. I wanted to kick the shit out of someone so badly. I needed to calm down. I had too much pent-up energy and emotion ready to explode inside me if I didn't do something about it.

Suddenly, Gracie's image flooded my mind. I needed her desperately. She had a calming effect on me, and I needed her badly at that moment. I would never hurt her, but I could think of some very pleasurable ways of using this excess energy with her instead of my usual fallback of punching things. After my time at the gym earlier, I doubted my body could handle that kind of workout again. However, a different type of workout was exactly what it needed.

"I need some space," I said and immediately left the office.

I knew Miki and the others would sort out a plan to deal with the bastard and another plan to bring the alliance down, so he could fill me in later.

I ran to Gracie's bedroom, hoping she was there. I needed her. Now!

CHAPTER 27
GRACIE
LATE SUNDAY - THE INCIDENT

t was getting late. I was lying on my bed, trying hard to distract myself by reading another book, but it wasn't working. I couldn't help wondering where Ash was and whether or not he was safe. I missed him. It was funny how quickly he had become someone I missed.

I worried about him on and off since he had left. Whenever I wasn't replaying our earlier intimate exploits over in my mind like my very own porn show, or making up some new ones, of course. It had me feeling as horny as hell, and I really wished he would hurry back so that I knew he was alright and he could give me another taste of things to come.

As if he heard my thoughts, he burst into the room, slamming the door behind him. His gaze landed on me immediately, and I couldn't miss the desire flaring in his eyes. I gulped and licked my lips in anticipation. His eyes flared again as he followed the action.

"I need you, now!" he stated, his Russian accent thick with emotion, his chest heaving with each breath.

My eyes widened.

Wow! I can see that, was all I could think as he strode towards the bed, tearing off his shirt.

He looked like a man on a mission. A predator and I was definitely the prey he was after. My pussy throbbed at that idea. It wanted to be preyed on by Ash. In fact, it longed to be.

My eyes roamed his body, taking in his muscular frame, tight abs, and the bulge in his pants.

I dropped my book, and my mouth went dry, making me lick my lips again.

He stopped at the bottom of the bed and pulled off his shoes and socks.

I wondered if I should get up and strip off my own clothes or wait for him to come to me.

I decided to be bold and get naked for him, but before I had time to react, he was on me, pressing me back against the pillow, kissing me like a man possessed. And it was bloody great!

He was frantic as he peeled my top and bra off before his mouth latched on to my nipple. He sucked hard, and I bucked into him.

Dear god, this guy's touch just got better and better. He moved to the other nipple, giving it the same attention while one hand slipped inside my waistband. He groaned when he found me already damp and continued to kiss me hungrily. I couldn't believe that such a hot guy wanted me this much.

He pulled my yoga pants off, then my panties, and I was naked before I realised it. Somehow, so was he. How the hell he managed to undress us both and keep touching me and kissing me, I would never know. The guy definitely had skills! Yai for us! My inner devil shouted, and I grinned at myself. Sometimes, I thought that I could very well be nuts. I certainly seemed to be whenever I was around Ash.

He was kissing all the way down my body. I squirmed,

eager for him to get where I knew he was headed. Thankfully, it didn't take him long. I gasped in pleasure as his tongue licked my folds and then flicked inside. Oh my god! He licked and sucked at me like he was devouring me; his groans of pleasure made me even wetter. He continued his assault, directing his attention to my clit, sucking and nibbling, licking, and rubbing until I was out of my mind with pleasure, chasing the high I could feel building inside me. I mewled as he thrust two fingers inside my hole. A few more thrusts, and I was done for. I came on a long moan.

He didn't stop there, though. He kept up his ministrations until I was squirming and bucking into him again. Oh, the things this man was doing to me were way better than my imagination could invent, and certainly way better than my previous two sexual partners had been. I couldn't get enough of what he had to give me. I was almost on the verge of coming again when he stopped.

I moaned in protest, but he quickly climbed up my body, positioning himself between my thighs. I opened my legs further as he settled between them. My heart raced, anticipating what was about to happen.

"I want you, Gracie," he said, and my core clenched at the thought.

Such a sexy voice! My inner devil purred dreamily.

"Tell me you want me, too," he said.

My breath hitched as I looked into his eyes. Oh, I so did! I wanted him badly, so badly I couldn't think straight, never mind form a coherent sentence. Besides, I was shy, and it was difficult enough for me to form a coherent sentence in the presence of a young, hot guy at the best of times; in such an intimate situation, it felt nigh impossible.

So, instead, I leaned towards him, intent on kissing his sexy mouth.

He held himself just out of reach. Damn it!

"Tell me," he demanded.

Of course, I wanted him. Wasn't it obvious?

He was gazing at me intently, his muscles straining as he held himself still above me, and I could see the effort it took him to do so. We were both breathing heavily with our need.

I leaned towards him once more, but again, he pulled back. That's when I recognised the vulnerability in his gaze. This wasn't just an ego thing; he really needed to hear me say the words. He really needed to know that I wanted him. How could he doubt it? I didn't know, but just like I had my insecurities, I guessed deep down that Ash did, too.

"I want you," I gasped.

He smirked, but I could see the relief in his eyes.

He leaned down and finally kissed me. Our tongues danced together in perfect sync. He moved us so we were lying on our sides while we continued to explore each other's mouths. We kissed until we finally had to break apart to breathe. As we frantically pulled air into our lungs, he reached for his jeans on the floor and pulled a condom out of the pocket.

Putting it on the bed beside us, he leaned over me again, and his hands started working their magic on my body once more.

His touch sent little sparks of electricity straight to my core.

"You are so wet for me, Gracie. Just perfect," Ash said.

Then he tore open the condom with his teeth and, in one smooth motion, pulled it on.

He lined his cock up with my entrance, and my breath hitched in anticipation.

This was it. This was really happening. I was about to have sex with Mr Sexy Voice.

I was so excited. I couldn't wait. I moved my hips up, but Ash hesitated.

"If I take you, you're mine, and I'm never letting you go," he stated possessively.

Oh my god! He wanted me. He really, really wanted me. And not just for now, but forever!

And in that second, it was clear I felt the same way. It should have been too much, it should have been too soon, but it wasn't. It should feel wrong, but nothing had ever felt so right.

"Do you want that?" he whispered in my ear.

His hot breath and that accent were my undoing.

"Yes!" I cried and then grabbed his head and kissed him.

That was all it took, and he plunged into me.

My whole body tensed at the invasion.

I was wet, but nevertheless, he was a big guy. It was a tight fit at first, but after a few seconds, I felt my pussy relax, and he started to thrust. He was straining, all his muscles tense, and I knew he was desperately trying to keep himself under control. Not only that, but I guessed he had to be in a bit of pain from his injuries, too. He was obviously not going to let that stop him. Ash was one powerful male, and if I had doubted it before, I could never doubt it now with this obvious display of strength. And somehow, that turned me on even more.

I gushed, my juices running down my thighs as I wrapped my legs around his waist. I tried to get as close to him as possible without putting pressure on his ribs, and I was rewarded when he slid even deeper inside me. His thrusts filled me deeply and stretched me to the fullest.

"That feels so good," I told him, and that seemed to set him off.

He pounded harder and faster, losing all control. The whole bed moved with his effort. We were both sweating and moaning loudly with pleasure. For a brief second, I worried about someone hearing us. Then he kissed me deeply again, and I decided I really didn't care. All I cared about was Ash and the pleasure he was giving me.

I was soon on the verge of coming again. One more thrust, and I felt myself clench around his cock as I came, shouting his name.

"Gracie!" he grunted loudly as he followed close behind with his own release.

He didn't pull out straight away but stayed leaning over me, looking into my eyes as we tried to catch our breath. I could get lost in those eyes. My inner devil purred.

After a few seconds, he moved off me and lay on his side, pulling me close to him.

"That was awesome, sweetheart", he said, still panting heavily, but I noticed his accent wasn't quite so thick and his eyes not quite so wild.

"I really needed you, Gracie," he stated, and I could hear the truth in his words.

He got up, removed the condom, and wrapped it in a tissue from the bedside table before heading into the bathroom to bin it.

I stifled a girlish giggle. Oh wow, oh wow, oh wow! I couldn't believe how good that was. And it was just the start of something I knew was going to be amazing. I was buzzing with excited expectation.

However, reality was hitting me, and I realised I was lying there naked and exposed. So, I quickly pulled back the covers and climbed beneath them.

I bit my lip to stop grinning at him like an idiot as he returned to bed. Wondering what he would do next, I was pleased that he got into bed beside me. He pulled me to him again, cuddling me.

It was lovely, but I wondered what had made him so upset before. So, I asked.

He didn't reply, and I began to think he wasn't going to, but eventually, he began to speak.

He told me that Janusz Glowacki was the head of the Polish Mafia in the UK and a close ally to the Bratva. However, two years ago, three of his men had raped and killed Ash's sister Krissa. Obviously, the family had been distraught over this, but so had Glowacki.

The three men involved were caught by the police before the brotherhoods could get to them, but Glowacki had managed to get bail for two of the men. The other had prior convictions, so he was remanded in custody.

As soon as Glowacki picked up the two who had been given bail, he turned them over to Krissa's family. Ash watched me intently as he told me that they had killed the two men, and Glowacki had made it appear as if the men had simply gone on the run to avoid a trial.

The other man, Lev Petrov, had pleaded guilty instead of going to trial and was given a ten-year sentence. However, they hadn't killed him in jail, even though he said they easily could have because they wanted to make him suffer themselves. So, they were biding their time.

Woah, this was serious stuff, not fiction, but real life. I should be terrified of what I was hearing. I should be terrified of Ash. I should be, but I wasn't.

"Does it bother you what we did or what we plan to do?" he asked, still watching me closely.

"No," I said, immediately realising the truth of my words.

These guys were rapists and murderers, after all. So, I kind of felt that they had deserved it. And Petrov would, too.

Did that make me a bad person? I wasn't sure.

If it did, then I guessed I fit with Ash better than I'd thought. I smiled because I couldn't seem to be bothered by that.

Although I didn't believe Ash was a bad person. In fact, I

was pretty sure he was a good person. A good person who sometimes did bad things.

If I was going to be with him, and I knew I really wanted to be, then I needed to know exactly who he was and what I was getting involved with. I needed to know that I could stand by him no matter what.

"When you hurt or kill someone, is it always because they have done something terrible like that?" I questioned him, wanting to understand this man better.

"Not always something as terrible, no, but we never hurt or kill anyone who has not proved themselves to be a threat to our family and whom we can't deal with through more legitimate means," he explained.

"We are Bratva, and we run illegal operations, but we never directly hurt women or children, and we do not get involved in human trafficking nor running girls. Glowacki is the same in that respect, and that is why we are allies. We are not good men, but we are not truly bad men either."

I nodded. I thought that was true of many people. Nothing in life was ever truly black and white. We all lived in a world with varying shades of grey, though we didn't always recognise that. Some people simply had more grey in their lives than others. Nobody was truly pure, and thankfully, very few were truly evil; most folk tended to sit somewhere in between.

Ash continued talking. He told me about Petrov's imminent release to go into witness protection after ratting on a cellmate. He also said that tonight he learned that while they had all thought Krissa had simply been in the wrong place at the wrong time when she was taken, while that was true, the family now knew that her identity had been discovered, and the three had been ordered to kill her by another party. Whether they would have any way or not didn't matter; someone else had made sure of that.

I could see him getting angry and stressed again when he confessed that he believed what happened to Krissa was his fault.

He was supposed to pick her up from a restaurant where she had been having dinner with friends to celebrate her graduation from college, but he was late. He had been kept behind at a business meeting and then was held up in traffic. It had been a lovely warm evening, so rather than wait inside for Ash when her friends had gone home, she had chosen to stand outside in the street by herself instead. She had then been snatched.

He'd arrived to find her missing. Despite searching for her, the family had been unable to find her, eventually discovering her death when police informed them of the situation, and the subsequent arrest of the men involved just a few hours later.

The more he told me, the more I could see his stress levels building. I could even feel the heavy weight of the guilt he carried. He blamed himself. He said that if he hadn't stayed late at a business meeting, putting business before his sister, and then got caught in traffic, she would never have been snatched, and so her murder was his fault. Of course, it wasn't, but he had obviously been blaming himself for her death since it happened, so telling him that wasn't really going to help. However, I felt compelled to say the words anyway.

"What happened to Krissa wasn't your fault, Ash. The only people responsible are the men who hurt her. I am sure she would hate for you to blame yourself. You said the traffic was heavy that night, and that was pretty much out of your control, so I doubt that the extra five minutes you were detained at your meeting would have made any difference."

He had gotten up while talking and was pacing up and down the room, shaking with anger. He didn't even seem to notice that he was naked. I could see him starting to spiral out of control again. I knew he heard me speak, but I wasn't sure he was fully listening. I kept trying anyway.

"You should also remember that Krissa chose to wait outside instead of staying in the restaurant. While she should have been safe either way, she wasn't. Fate conspired against you both, and neither of you were to blame. When you finally get your revenge, you need to forgive yourself. I am sure that is what Krissa would want if she were able to tell you," I said in earnest, hoping at least some of my words were hitting home.

He was still pacing about the room, obviously still distraught, his fists opening and closing and his eyes wild.

I didn't know what to do, but distraction worked for him before, so I decided to try that technique again.

I walked to him. He stopped pacing and stood still, all his muscles tense, breathing heavily with anger. I wrapped my arms around him and held him, looking into his face and watching his reaction. His eyes slowly focused on me, and I watched them soften.

I simply stared at him for a moment, waiting for him to calm down a little. Once he did, I dropped down to my knees and took him into my hands. He immediately started to harden, and I licked my lips to moisten them and then kissed his tip softly before licking the slit there.

He hissed in a harsh breath, and his cock jerked in my hand. I licked it again, and it hardened fully.

Opening my mouth as wide as possible, I drew the tip of his penis into my mouth and sucked. Then, I withdrew my lips and did it again and again, drawing him in deeper and deeper each time. Sucking harder and faster with each movement. He was still panting heavily but no longer in anger. I looked up at him, and his eyes were closed, his head tilted back, a look of ecstasy on his face.

I felt myself relax. It looked like it was working, so I

continued with gusto, licking, sucking, and moving back and forth along Ash's swollen shaft.

He brought his hands up, tangling his fingers in my hair as he started to thrust, and I let him, aware of how much he needed this. He continued thrusting deep, and I concentrated on breathing deeply through my nose to control my gagging reflex. I was so not used to this, but I didn't want to stop. Not in the least.

My eyes were watering, but I was not going to stop him from thrusting into me, taking what he needed. I loved that he needed me this much, that he was now thrusting with abandonment and out of control with lust. He was fully in control of me, however, but that was okay because I was really very happy that he was so obviously enjoying this. It made me feel powerful, and I knew that if I did want him to stop, he would.

He thrust one more time before roaring, "Fuck!" as his cum ran down my throat.

Until Ash, I'd never swallowed before, but I found where others had tasted too salty; he didn't. I loved his taste, and drinking him down was not at all awful. In fact, I enjoyed it, and I could tell he liked me swallowing by his groan of pleasure as he watched me. So, I would happily do it again and again.

When he was finished, he helped me to my feet and wrapped his arms around me, embracing me tightly.

"You are bloody amazing!" he whispered, and I could hear the satisfaction in his voice.

I walked him over to the bed where we crawled back inside, wrapped in each other's arms, and that's how we fell asleep.

CHAPTER 28
ASH

woke up with Gracie lying across my chest and smiled at her sleeping form in my arms. I felt more relaxed than I had since Krissa was murdered. Last night was amazing. She was amazing!

I thought back over it.

After I had told Miki and the others everything I'd learned from Sean and Juana, I knew I was beginning to spiral again. Unable to cope, I had been desperate to get to Gracie. I was sure she could make it all better, and she did.

And now she was mine!

I felt like I was bursting with joy. I stroked her soft blond hair, which was splayed across the pillow. She was gorgeous, and I marvelled at how lucky I was to have found this woman. I didn't know how I deserved such luck, but I wasn't going to question it.

She moved slightly, and a little moan escaped her lips. My cock jerked at the sound.

Plunging into her wet pussy last night had been utter ecstasy, and my cock was ready to beg for more.

I thoroughly enjoyed our first time together, and I couldn't wait to explore her body more as our relationship developed. Of course, she was so much more than just a body to me. I thought about how she calmed me and how easy it was for me to open up to her in a way I hadn't been able to do with anyone else.

I was amazed that she had taken it in her stride.

The fact that she seemed to be able to accept me for who and what I was was an immense relief.

However, talking about everything had started me spiralling again before Gracie took me between her lips, and the warm wetness of her mouth brought me back to the real world once more.

Releasing my cum down her throat was like releasing all the anger, guilt, and frustration that had been raging inside me for the last two years. It had left me with an overwhelming sense of calm, which I still felt even thinking about Krissa and those bastards.

Oh, there was still rage, but it was buried deep inside for now, much more controlled.

I was still longing to get a hold of that asshole Petrov and make him pay, slowly, but the anger I felt towards him wasn't as all-consuming as it had been.

For once, I could think more clearly about things, and that was down to Gracie and not just her fantastic mouth; I grinned at my wicked thoughts. Just being around her helped me; she grounded me.

I remembered her words last night.

My family had said that what happened to Krissa wasn't my fault, but I had never believed them. Something Gracie said made me think, though.

She'd said that Krissa would not want me to blame myself. I believed that, but it didn't stop the guilt.

However, she'd also said that fate had conspired against us

that night and very little that happened had been within my control.

It had finally sunk in that she was right. Several things had conspired to create the terrible tragedy that took Krissa from us. It wasn't all down to me.

Yes, I'd stayed at work to finish my meeting, but it had only run over a few minutes. Traffic was heavy that night, and whether I had left those few minutes earlier or not, I would likely still have been late. If traffic hadn't been so heavy, I could easily have made those few minutes up, and she might be alive now, but that wasn't the case.

Krissa's friends had needed to get a taxi to the train station. They had wanted to wait for her to be picked up first, but she'd insisted they left so they wouldn't miss their last trains home. Normally, taxis took a while to come, but on this occasion, one had just dropped passengers off at a nearby club and so arrived at the restaurant quickly. If it hadn't, she might not have been alone when the bastards had passed by, and she might still be alive, but that wasn't the case.

Krissa could have chosen to remain in the restaurant to wait for me or even go back inside when her friends left, but she hadn't. If she had, she might have been alive now.

But fate ensured that I was late; her friends left promptly, and she made that fateful decision to remain alone outside.

It was not really my fault, or her friends' fault, or Krissa's. It was simply down to fate and those three bastards, of course! And then Siri and anyone else who caused her death. All of whom would pay for their part in it soon.

I finally felt things shift in my mind.

Perhaps it was time to start healing and forgive myself? Gracie said I should. She told me that's what Krissa would want.

I sighed. I knew deep down Gracie was right, but I wasn't quite ready to do that yet.

The weight of guilt that I had carried around the last two years had certainly lifted, but it wasn't yet gone. Not completely. I'd been living with the blame too long. It had become a part of me, but perhaps when I got my revenge, I could finally let it all go.

I looked at the beautiful woman sleeping on my chest and knew I wanted to. I needed to be the man she deserved. A man that wasn't eaten up by useless guilt. A man who didn't allow himself to be consumed with impotent rage. A man who could control himself. Like the man I had been before. Resolve settled in me. I would be that man again. Every day, I would work a little more towards him, for Krissa, for my family, for Gracie, and for me.

I kissed the top of Gracie's head, but she didn't stir.

I continued watching her for a long while, thinking of everything that had happened between us since we'd met at Glitz. I couldn't believe it had only been just over a week. Life had got a whole lot more exciting for me since she entered it. I had begun to feel alive again, not just going through the motions.

I wanted to get all this Bratva shit sorted out as soon as possible so we could explore our relationship properly. I always knew that if I fell, it would be fast and hard, and it certainly had been. I'd already told her she was mine, and she'd agreed, but I wanted to make sure she never regretted that. I wanted to make up for our difficult start, but we hadn't even been out on a date yet.

While I had tended to keep things casual in the past, I wanted to have a real relationship with Gracie, starting with dating and hopefully leading to something more serious in the future. The near future! She was the one for me, but I didn't want her to ever feel like she'd missed out on anything. So, as soon as things had calmed down and were safer, I was going to whisk her off to somewhere nice and bombard her with one date after another to be sure she never did.

In the meantime, I would have to continue to woo her with my sexual prowess. I laughed to myself at that and bent down to kiss her forehead, then her nose, her mouth, her cheeks, her chin. Soon, she was awake and smiling up at me. My cock was already hard by then, and so I got down to business and showed her again just how much I wanted her. Several times!

Much later, we headed down for breakfast, fully sated, hand in hand and grinning like a couple of idiots. I could get used to this.

———

When we finished eating, I headed to Miki's office to discuss the plans he'd put in place after I left last night. He briefed me on things, and we then sorted out some more of the finer details.

Apparently, last night, another of our dealers and one of Glowacki's were attacked. Ours wasn't killed outright this time but stabbed and left for dead. Thankfully, he was now recovering in one of our safe houses. However, Glowacki's guy was shot dead.

More attacks, just like Juana had said.

Of the four traitors we'd discovered within the Bratva, Ivor was the one we'd let get closest to us. The others were merely foot soldiers who hadn't proved themselves enough to go up the ranks yet and now never would.

Ivor, however, had been sent to us from Russia by Uncle Maxim. He'd worked as a bodyguard there, though not one of

Uncle Maxim's own, but had gotten into trouble by sleeping with a police officer's wife, so Uncle Maxim had sent him to us to get him out of the way. Despite his penchant for chasing the wrong kind of women, he'd been thought of as loyal and trustworthy, so we'd taken him in and allowed him into our main security team.

I fumed with rage just thinking about how we had allowed him access to our home and family. We'd treated him well, and he had betrayed us, providing Siri with details of the Lab's location and our drug shipments. He would pay dearly for that, but not yet. Unfortunately, if he disappeared at this point, it would cause too much suspicion, and so we needed to let him live. For now!

He would be one of the ones we'd deal with at the last minute. In the meantime, he'd be kept busy with other things that took him away from the Estate as much as possible. That way, we could make the required arrangements to defend ourselves, and he'd be none the wiser.

So, the first part of our plan was to create a fake war with fake attacks being staged tonight and over the next few days, using our most trusted men. We were going to make it seem that some men were killed on both sides. This would give the impression that our forces were being weakened. In reality, we'd fake their deaths, then hide them away in some abandoned farm buildings within easy reach of the Lab and use them against the Malia Boys when they attacked.

The next part of the plan was to grab Petrov on Wednesday when he was due to get out under his witness protection deal. We needed to get to him, incapacitate the National Crime Agency officers, and then snatch him before the Malia Boys could. We didn't want to kill the officers unless we had to either, so that had to be taken into account. We would, however, be killing Petrov, but not until we got any information we could out of him.

I was to oversee his capture. Marko had already hacked into the National Crime Agency database and was monitoring it. He'd let me know when he got information on the route they'd take so we could pick the best spot to intercept them.

On Thursday, Glowacki and his family will be coming to the Estate in secret. Although we knew the Estate was to be attacked, we were not sure if any attacks were planned on Glowacki's home. However, with so many of the traitors being his men, we weren't taking any chances. When the attacks took place, his daughter would be staying at our house with the rest of the women in the panic room, along with Glowacki's younger son, Sebastian.

Miki had brought in a couple of our lower-ranking soldiers yesterday to guard the Estate gates over the next few days. They weren't involved with the Malia Boys or Broxy's, but they were disloyal and a pair of thieves. The idiots had thought we didn't know they were stealing from one of our money laundering businesses. They worked security there and thought we were too stupid to notice. Stupid fuckers now thought they'd been promoted. They had, to cannon fodder!

When the attack happened, it was expected that the guys at the gate would be taken out first. That would get rid of another issue for us while keeping our loyal guards safe. We weren't planning on sacrificing any of them.

Miki and I had discussed bringing in Anton for some additional help, and I had initially been reluctant to get him involved but eventually capitulated. We needed people we could trust guarding the Estate while we were elsewhere, so it made sense. Nevertheless, I hadn't wanted to involve him but, in the end, he insisted. As a Bratva Blood Brother, he said it was his duty to help protect us, our home and our family. We might have made the oath when we were just kids, but we all took it seriously.

Anton's guys were ex-military, and most had been special forces trained. That gave us a great advantage over our opponents. The Broxy's had a few ex-military in their ranks themselves, but not as many and not so well trained. They wouldn't be a match for Anton's men, or even our own for that matter. The hope was that our combined force would take out as many Broxy's as possible before they reached our home, women, and children. However, if anyone did get too close to the house, Romi, Marko, and a few of our most loyal guys would be waiting.

In order to give us the element of surprise, we planned on keeping up the pretence of war and our seeming ignorance of the planned attacks until the last minute. Therefore, Romi would leave early Friday night with a couple of men and put the word out that he was going to attack another of Glowacki's businesses. In the meantime, Dariusz would be doing the same, saying he was about to attack one of ours. That way, our enemies would think that we were too distracted and short of men to protect ourselves properly.

In actual fact, once the word was out, they would all head back here via our secret back entrance to be ready for when our enemies appeared. They'd also bring Derrick with them to ensure a medic was close at hand if needed. I'd called him, and he had agreed to help out. He was already planning on helping anyway, apparently, because Anton would be here along with Derrick's boyfriend. I knew I liked the guy.

Marko would remain here to monitor police activity and the phones of Siri and the Broxy's leader, Scot Maitlock. He'd successfully hacked them already, and we were keeping tabs on both. That should give us the heads up on when the attacks were about to happen and where exactly we could find Siri. We wanted to capture him. We had a lot of questions to ask him.

Although our Estate was out in the countryside, it wasn't that far from civilisation that the noise of an attack would go unnoticed, so I had some of our guys set up traps around the grounds to help take some of the Broxy's out as quickly and quietly as possible.

Also, in order to help cover up any noise from their gunfire, we rigged up some fireworks. Miki called the local police station with a cover story. We told them we were having a party for guests visiting from abroad that night and would be letting off fireworks in case there were any complaints about noise. Naturally, the sounds of extensive gunfire would be a concern to our neighbours, but the sound of fireworks hopefully wouldn't be. Besides, complaints of fireworks being set off were far better for us to deal with than complaints of a gunfight.

However, if there were enough complaints, the police would likely come to investigate. So, to be sure they couldn't, Sergei and his dealers were ready to create as much mayhem on the streets on Friday night as possible. That way, the police would be too busy dealing with more serious issues to worry about a few noise complaints.

Hopefully, that would apply to them attending any noise complaints at the lab location, too.

When Miki spoke to Uncle Maxim about Ivor, he also arranged for some of our relatives to visit. That way, we would indeed have guests from abroad, making our cover story of a party seem more plausible.

Miki, Glowacki, his son Daniel, a few of their most trusted men, and I would slip away late Thursday night and join a few of our men who were hiding out at the C. We'd join up with the rest of the men we had hiding out in the abandoned buildings nearby the following evening, and together with the few guards we had at the Lab itself, we'd be the defence team for the Lab attack.

Glowacki believed some of the traitors in his brotherhood had been discovered. He had a plan in motion to ensure they were eliminated by his loyal men just as soon as the attacks began. The two who'd been working with the Malia boys and Broxy's hadn't been found yet but were being hunted down, and Glowacki was determined to make them pay when he found them.

So, those of us at the C would wait until the Malia Boys arrived to attack the Lab, and then we would advance from the rear once they'd passed us. The men we had already planted in the abandoned farmhouses would approach from either side, and with the few guards based at the Lab itself and the drivers for the drug shipment all in front, we would surround them.

Hopefully, we could then deal with them and capture Siri before they breached the Lab and caused any damage.

I smiled. Miki, as always, was so thorough. There was really nothing else I could add to the plan.

There was just one thing I was uncomfortable about.

"Why are we taking Glowacki or any of his men to the farm and Lab? We have some hiding out on the farm, but they don't have any idea there is a lab located there. However, when they have to defend it, they soon will. Once they know the location of our lab, we can't take that back. They may be allies, but what if that doesn't last? They would know exactly where and how to hit us," I asked.

"Also, why reveal anything about the C to Glowacki and his sons at all? Only family and the closest of our men know about either location?"

Glowacki was a good friend and ally. However, the secrets of the C and the lab location had been kept for a reason, and I didn't know why he was divulging them to Glowacki at all.

He looked at me thoughtfully, obviously weighing up whether or not to tell me what he had up his sleeve.

The longer he looked at me, hesitating, the more I thought that I knew why he was trusting Glowacki so much. I shook my head.

"No."

"It's a good match," he told me, and I knew I was right.

"Like hell! Do you want an arranged marriage?" I asked him.

"Listen, our parents had one, and it became a love match. Glowacki had one, and he and his wife respected and cared for each other. Most of our family had arranged marriages, and they worked out. I'm sure Sonia's will work out too," he said in defence of his decision.

"That was all years ago. We don't do that so much now. I, for one, don't want an arranged marriage, so don't even think of that," I exclaimed.

He laughed.

"Don't worry, little brother. I know you have it bad for Gracie, and I am assuming if there is any woman that will get you into a marriage with them, it will be her," he smirked.

"You should re-think this," I said, shaking my head and pursing my lips in annoyance.

He was my older brother, but he was also our Bratva Pakhan and, in the end, his word was our law, so I could only try to appeal to his good nature.

"We need to ensure this alliance of ours stays strong and marriage ties both of our families together. Anyhow, we shook on it, so the deal is done," he told me firmly.

Shit, I was not pleased about this. I couldn't imagine Sonia would be either.

"I take it the arrangement is with Dariusz?" I asked, annoyed.

"Yes, he is the better match and will eventually take over from Janusz," he replied.

"I also take it that you haven't told Sonia yet?"

"Nope," he said quickly, "I haven't had time to discuss it with her yet. Dariusz is also unaware," he stated.

Bloody hell. Sonia would flip. She was a romantic at heart and would not want an arranged marriage. I doubted Dariusz would either. Miki was making the wrong decision. I knew it.

"She's not going to like it," I said, stating the obvious.

"She doesn't have any choice," he said.

"We all have to help the family in our own way. This is hers," he stated with finality.

I huffed out a breath. I felt strongly against this proposed marriage and would back Sonia up if she was adamantly against it, but that needed to wait for another day. We had too much to deal with right now. I only hoped that Miki hadn't sealed the arrangement and there was a way out of it. Otherwise, this family was in for a great deal of strife in the near future.

"I'm not happy about this. You've made a mistake, Miki. However, this isn't the time to deal with that," I said, shaking my head in disgust as I got up to leave, turning my back on him. I was bloody angry with him.

"It's done!" he practically shouted.

I turned around and looked him in the eye, and when he broke contact first, I sighed. He might have made the arrangement, and he might have had the final say as our pakhan, but Miki, our brother, was uncomfortable with his decision. The fact that he had made such an arrangement showed that he was more concerned with our current issues than I had realised.

He leaned back and sucked in a deep breath before leaning forward, rubbing his forehead and squeezing his eyes shut as if he had a headache coming on. He looked like a man with the weight of the world on his shoulders, and I guess, in some respects, he probably did. I didn't envy him.

I let out a long breath, releasing the tension in the air.

"I need to go; Gracie's cousin Claire and Marcie are due back from their spa trip today, and we are going back to Gracie's so I can introduce myself."

"Good luck with that," he called after me, chuckling.

CHAPTER 29
GRACIE
MONDAY - INTRODUCING ASH

After having such great sex with Ash, I spent the morning absolutely glowing. I wrote some great scenes, too, after all of that inspiration. My first sex scene was in the bag, and I couldn't wait to get down and dirty with Ash again later, solely for research purposes, of course.

After Ash had finished talking with Miki, we headed back to Claire's house so I could introduce him to her when she and Marcie got back from their trip.

I couldn't believe how everything in my life had changed since they went on their trip. I had become a badass with a sassy attitude and had a Bratva boyfriend to rival any book boyfriend written by my favourite authors.

On top of that I was writing.

Wow! In the space of a week, my life went from zero to almost perfect.

I just hoped Claire and Marcie agreed. Things had moved so fast. I knew they might have concerns about that, but I hoped they would still be happy for me. I also hoped that they wouldn't worry too much about Ash's dodgy side. I knew Marcie might not have picked up on it when working for this family on the legal side of their businesses, but Claire, with her uncanny ability to see through anyone, definitely would.

Before we reached the house, Ash told me about the expected attacks. He kept details quite vague as he didn't want to worry me, but I wished he would tell me more. I didn't push him for more information now, but I would definitely do so later. I knew he just wanted to protect me, but I wasn't planning on being kept in the dark.

However, at the moment, I was more concerned with other things.

Ash had said that although the two guys who beat him up were now dead, their boss, Siri, wasn't, and he could pose a danger to me and possibly even to Claire and, by extension, Marcie. Although I felt safe with Ash, especially when we were at the Estate, I needed to know that Claire and Marcie were safe, too.

That's why we planned on spending the next couple of nights at Claire's. Firstly, to introduce Ash to Claire and Marcie as my boyfriend and secondly, to make sure that they both remained safe.

Ash had arranged for several of his men to keep a watch on the house and also on the girls whenever they went out. I was aware he had a couple watching us, too.

It helped that Marcie's flat was being re-decorated and wouldn't be complete for another few days, so she would be staying in the spare room at Claire's. That meant both girls were predominantly in the same space whenever they were home.

I was glad that he was ensuring they stayed safe, and it made me fall for him a little bit more.

We'd be returning to the Estate in time for the plans to unfold, whatever they were. Ash had only told me that there were two attacks planned and, therefore, two plans of defence, one at the Estate and one elsewhere. As I would be at the Estate when it was under attack, Ash said he'd tell me what I should expect nearer the time. I was a bit worried about that, but I trusted the guys had everything under control. Ash certainly seemed confident enough.

On Wednesday, Ash was hoping to arrange for Marcie to go to one of his clubs, Platinum, down south in Ripley, Surrey, for a couple of days. He was planning on encouraging her to take Claire, too. He was going to get Luca Orlov, the manager for Glitz, to go with them. Luca oversaw all of the clubs for their company, Platinum Entertainment, and would be getting Marcie to look at the club for an event they had planned in a few months. He was also Bratva and so could take care of business while protecting the girls by keeping them out of harm's way.

We reached Claire's house before the girls returned and were in my room making out again when they arrived home a short while later. The look on their faces when they saw me come down to the living room hand in hand with Ash was priceless. Marcie did a double take and exclaimed, "Mr Rominov!"

"Marcie," he said, nodding his head at her in greeting.

Claire looked shocked before she narrowed her eyes, looked him up and down, then looked at me, "Well, I guess you have something to tell us."

I swallowed, suddenly unsure where to start. Ash took a step towards her, coming to my rescue.

"Hi, you must be Claire; I have heard a lot about you," he said, holding his hand out.

Being the up-and-coming lawyer she was, she took it and shook it firmly while looking him in the eye, then stepped back to appraise him from a distance.

"How do you know our Gracie then?" she asked.

"We met at the event Marcie's company ran for us at my family's new club, and we kept bumping into each other, then we had our first date last Friday night," he told her, smiling charmingly.

Smoothly done, I bit back a smile.

"Oh, so I brought the two of you together, you could say!" Marcie exclaimed, delighted, clapping her hands excitedly.

I laughed. I guessed Marcie did.

"About time you got laid, girl!" she nudged me and winked.

"Oh my god, you did not just say that in front of Ash," I stated, totally embarrassed.

He just laughed and hugged me and told her she no longer had to worry about me having any problems with that. Marcie squealed in delight, and Claire frowned disapprovingly. Oh my god! I needed the floor to open up and swallow me.

"Yeh!" Marcie clapped again. "I can't believe that while we were away, you got yourself a rich and handsome boyfriend!" she squealed.

Claire's lips were pursed, and her eyes were narrowed again. She was looking at us like she was assessing the situation and finding it wanting. I could tell she was desperately struggling not to bombard Ash with questions.

"So, what have you guys got planned for tonight then?" she simply asked in the end.

"We are planning a quiet night in," I told her. "You?"

"Same," Marcie said.

Claire was looking between us both with a frown on her face and a look in her eyes, which told me she was trying to decide if what was happening here was a good thing or not. I smiled brightly at her, hoping she would decide it was the latter.

She never said anything, and I was relieved when they left to take their bags upstairs.

I could hear Marcie gibbering excitedly all the way.

"So far so good. Claire's obviously cautious of me, but she hasn't tried to kill me, so that's good," he whispered, chuckling.

"Cautious! Did you see the way she was looking at you?"

"She is a bit terrifying!" he grimaced, and I laughed because, well, she was.

I frowned and bit my bottom lip. I was worried. Claire was the only real family I had left, and I really needed her and Ash to like one another.

He smiled.

"It'll be fine!" he stated with such confidence that I couldn't help but believe him.

He took me into his arms and kissed me gently on the lips.

It soon developed into something much deeper and continued to get even more heated until we were interrupted by giggles. I jumped back from Ash, my face heating as I saw both Marcie and Claire standing in the doorway watching us.

"Wow, Mr Rominov, you and Gracie need to get a room!" Marcie winked at him.

"Later," he told her and winked back. "And you should call me Ash. That goes for you too, Claire," he said with a genuine smile.

I had to give it to him; he was trying hard to put Claire at ease.

She pursed her lips.

"Well, Ash," she said, "I was about to open a bottle of wine, and we were actually planning to order some pizza for dinner. Would you both like to join us?"

She was looking at him in that assessing way again, and I could tell that the answer to that question was a make-or-break for her.

"I certainly would love to if that suits Gracie?" he replied without hesitation, looking at me for my agreement.

"Absolutely," I said, grinning up at him.

Out of the corner of my eye, I noticed the first hint of a

smile from the ice queen. I was filled with hope. It looked like Ash might just be able to thaw her out after all.

We ordered some pizzas and sides from the local takeaway to share between us, and Marcie poured the wine as they told us all about their spa trip.

We had a good evening eating and drinking, getting tipsy and laughing at Marcie's stories about the hunky masseur and the male yoga teacher that she said Claire was so into, but Claire totally denied it.

Around 10 p.m., Ash got a call from Miki. He excused himself and went outside to take it. As soon as he was gone, Claire rounded on me.

"Spill it!" she said firmly, "All of it!"

So, I did! I told them a condensed version of pretty much everything, only leaving out the Bratva involvement and the larger situation with the Malia Boys and Broxy's.

"Wow! You are one badass chick!" Marcie squealed in awe. "I can't believe you took on those guys and rescued Ash!"

"Me neither!" Claire said, looking at me with a newfound respect.

"At last, my little cousin is coming into her own!" she hugged me and looked proud.

"I've been watching you both together, and it is obvious your feelings are genuine, but there is one thing bothering me," she told me seriously before continuing, "I'm a defence lawyer, sweetie; I'm around guys who skirt the law every day, and I can tell them a mile away, and Ash is one of them."

"I know," I replied, looking her directly in the eye. "He has told me, but I know that he'll never hurt me, and I am okay with that," I said, ensuring that I sounded it.

She pursed her lips, and her gaze was assessing again. I met her eyes squarely, and after a few seconds, she sighed.

"Well, as long as you know what you are getting yourself

into," she stated, pulling me into a hug. "But if he does hurt you or gets you hurt in any way at all, he will have me to deal with!"

She lifted her glass, "Cheers to the new and improved Gracie and her sexy boyfriend, Ash!"

We all clinked our glasses, and just like that, Ash and I were accepted.

"Yes!" my inner devil shouted.

When the man in question returned, we said our goodnights and headed to bed.

I was blissfully happy and couldn't stop smiling.

As soon as we were inside my room, he pulled me close. His lips brushed feather-light kisses on my forehead, nose, mouth, cheeks, and chin. I smiled up at the handsome man bestowing them on me. I loved these little kisses, but I needed more. So much more!

I pressed my body against him, desperately wanting to be closer. I felt the rigid length of his cock. Hmmm. I grinned wickedly and reached down and wrapped my hand around it. He responded with a groan, and soon, the feather-like kisses became more and more frantic as our excitement built. I stroked him up and down a few times through his trousers.

It wasn't enough for me, though. I needed to feel Ash. Quickly, I unzipped his trousers and took him in hand. I loved how hard he was. It made me feel so powerful to know that this magnificent male was filled with desire for me. I stroked him a few more times while we kissed before I bent down and licked at the precum on the tip. I lapped at him, enjoying his taste. I moaned around him, and it was obviously more than he could take because a few minutes later, he pushed me down onto the bed, climbed over me and proceeded to remind me that it wasn't just the taste of his cock I liked.

CHAPTER 30

ASH

TUES/WEDNESDAY - GETTING TO KNOW
GRACIE'S FAMILY

Gracie and I spent a leisurely day on Tuesday sleeping late after a night of blissful sex, then showering together before spending the rest of the day snuggling and talking about anything and everything.

She told me all about her mother and being a young carer. I now understood where she got her love of reading and her ambition to be a writer. I intended to help her make her dream come true. I wanted all of her dreams to come true. She didn't have the best start in life, and I wanted to ensure that she had a much better life from now on. With me.

She had already agreed to move in with me, and I couldn't be happier about that, but I wanted even more. When the next few days were over, I was going to pull out all the stops to ensure that she felt the same. She deserved to be treated like a queen, and I'd make sure that she was.

We spent more time with the girls in the evening. Winning Claire over wasn't as hard as I thought it might be. Marcie, I knew, would be a piece of cake, and I think the fact we worked together, and she liked me went a long way towards getting Claire on the side.

I invited Marko over to join us, supposedly to introduce him to Claire and Marcie, who were the only real family Gracie had. In reality, however, I wanted him to help me watch over the girls while our guys were busy with other things.

While Marko was here and the girls were busy, I grilled him on what he'd found out about the lawyer Juana had told us about. He'd been looking into him and trying to get some dirt on the guy in case we needed to blackmail him for any reason in the future. The lawyer would pay for whatever part he had played in both Krissa's death and our current situation, but since he was a well-known lawyer, we needed to tread carefully. So, any information we could get on him would help.

Also, we needed to know who had been pulling his strings. We had to find the prick, who was our unknown enemy before he could cause us any more damage. And if he also had anything to do with Krissa's murder, he was a dead man.

So far, the information he had on the lawyer was pretty basic and mundane stuff. There was nothing we could use against him, but Marko assured me he'd keep digging. A guy like that definitely had a lot to hide.

We also discussed our search for Juana's sister, but unfortunately, we were no further on in finding her, which was disappointing. However, we believed Siri likely knew where she was, so capturing him remained high on our agenda for many reasons.

For dinner, we got a takeaway and played some drinking games with shots. Then Gracie made us cocktails. I wasn't usually a cocktail fan, but even I was tipsy enough to enjoy them. Besides, the ice queen was watching me like a hawk to see if I was game enough, and I knew the challenge in her eyes was another way of testing out my suitability for Gracie. So, I drank them with gusto, and as the evening wore on, Claire began to thaw.

Marko enjoyed the cocktails, too. I hadn't pegged him for a pina colada drinker, but he had several and didn't even bother when Gracie topped one with a mini umbrella. In fact, Marko stuck it behind his ear and left it there for most of the night. I think he was just enjoying being away from all our usual Bratva stuff. Being here with the girls gave us a glimpse into a different type of life that we rarely got to enjoy. One where we were free to be normal guys enjoying the company of normal girls without the darkness of our usual lives interfering.

Later we watched a horror movie. Gracie spent most of the time curled up on my lap, hiding behind a cushion and peeking out every now and then. I found it adorable.

Marko fell asleep in the chair. I guess it wasn't gruesome enough for him. When he woke up, I teased him, saying, "Hey, Marky, was that too scary for you? You had to pretend to be asleep, huh?"

"Funny," he said, throwing a cushion at me.

I ducked, and it hit Claire smack in the face. She looked shocked, and I wondered if the ice queen was about to resurface. We were all holding our breath as Claire sauntered over to him, looking pissed off. He started apologising, "Sorry I…" but she whacked him over the head and burst into laughter.

She didn't stop there, though. She just kept laughing and whacking Marko until he grabbed another cushion and whacked her back. A full-blown pillow fight ensued, with us all joining in until we were exhausted from it. I had to admit I hadn't had so much childish fun in a long time, well, apart from my food fight with Sonia, of course.

It was a good night and definitely helped break the ice between us all. It felt good to just relax and let loose for once. I could see Marko felt the same way, too, as he was relaxed and smiling when we said goodnight, leaving him to sleep on the couch. I went to bed with Gracie wrapped in my arms and a grin on my face, feeling happier than I could remember.

———

We were all up early on Wednesday morning, and despite the amount of shots and cocktails we'd consumed, none of us seemed to be suffering too badly from their effects. The girls were excited to be off to Surrey.

I had managed to convince them to go Wednesday through to Saturday on the pretext of them combining business with another short holiday. Claire was still off for a few more days, so it worked well. Of course, it helped that I told them the trip was an all-expenses paid one.

I was pleased they had agreed. Luca was taking them, and he already knew Marcie well so he would be able to conduct the business side of things while also ensuring their safety. It was the perfect solution to keeping them safe and out of the way of the unpleasant business ahead.

When Luca arrived to collect them, we had a quick chat. Miki had already informed him of our plans, and I updated him on some of the finer details. He needed to know exactly what was going down in case things went wrong, and he needed to help us out in some way or keep the girls away longer if necessary.

As he took the girls' bags to the car, I noticed him checking Claire out rather thoroughly. He saw me smirking at him and grinned. I chuckled. He would need to work hard if he wanted to charm her. We watched them leave, and then I helped Gracie pack up some more of her things while we waited for Romi to arrive to pick us up.

Before we returned to the Estate, we stopped at the airport to pick up our relatives. Romi's mum and brother, and our aunt

Marta had flown in from Russia for our pretend celebration. We all embraced. Aunt Letitia smothered Romi in kisses until he pushed her off, embarrassed, and we all laughed.

I introduced Gracie to them as my girlfriend and my aunts gushed all over her, grabbing one of her arms each and bombarding her with questions as we walked back to the car. Gracie blushed but answered them happily and seemed to be content to continue chatting with them as we returned home.

When we arrived back at the Estate, Glowacki and Dariusz were already there. Miki made the introductions, and I couldn't help but notice the way Janusz Glowacki looked at my aunt Marta or the way he held her hand a tad lónger than he did anyone else's. I understood Janusz's interest; my aunt Marta was a lovely-looking woman.

Miki noticed, too, and his eyes narrowed, a thoughtful look coming over his face before he schooled his features again into his usual poker face.

Nonna appeared, and the women flocked to her to say hello.

While they were busy, our chat turned to the reason the Glowacki's were here. Lev Petrov was getting released later this afternoon, and each of us relished the prospect of finally getting our hands on the bastard.

We couldn't take the risk of stopping the National Crime Agency officers ourselves and snatching Petrov, so instead, we did something we usually wouldn't do and hired a gang of local thugs to do it for us. We rarely hired out, but these guys came recommended by the MacArthur gang from Glasgow, whom we had some dealings with and trusted to some extent.

Marko had given us all the details we required, so the task was simple enough. There were only two officers involved as Petrov was being secreted off on witness protection, and so we'd provided the thugs with some tranquiliser darts. That way, the officers could be dealt with quickly and easily without the necessity of killing them, and Petrov could be knocked out ready for us to collect him.

While we waited for word that the job was done, we had a quick lunch Nonna had prepared, chatted with our guests, and created an alibi should we ever need one.

A little while later, we received word that Petrov had been acquired and went to meet up with the guys at a rendezvous point not far from where they'd picked him up. Miki and I quickly moved his unconscious form into the boot of our vehicle and headed to the C to meet up with the others.

CHAPTER 31
GRACIE

WEDNESDAY - HEAD OVER HEELS
FOR ASH

fter lunch, Ash and the guys headed off to deal with their business. Ash's aunts went to their rooms to unpack and rest, and I headed to the library to do some more writing.

I hadn't done any writing while we were staying at Claire's, and I was longing to get more done. I was bursting with new ideas. I just needed to get them down on paper. Unfortunately, no matter how hard I tried to focus, my mind kept distracting me with thoughts about the last few days. So, eventually, I gave in and allowed my mind to wander back over them.

After spending one of the best days of my life with Ash on Monday, we had a night of sex that rivalled anything I have ever read about. It had certainly given me some great material for my own book, and I told him as much. He had grinned and looked smug at my words, and while I knew he didn't need me to inflate his already large enough ego, frankly, he deserved it. Anyway, expressing your appreciation for someone is the right thing to do. In this case, I was certainly glad I had because he decided he liked being my muse and was taking the position very seriously. Something we were both enjoying immensely.

It wasn't just the sex that we had enjoyed the last couple of days. It had been utter bliss to spend time together, just snuggled in bed, talking for hours about anything and everything, learning about each other. Ash made me feel important and treasured.

We also had great fun with the girls and Marko. Ash had invited his brother Marko around last night, and I was surprised at how well everyone had gotten along. Marko was funny when he was a bit drunk, and he seemed to enjoy my cocktails, especially my pina coladas. He even wore the little cocktail umbrella behind his ear, which made him look really cute. Not that I would tell Ash that, of course.

It was nice to see both men looking relaxed and happy. I didn't think they got to just let loose and act like normal guys very often. Something told me that their world weighed heavily upon them.

I must admit that I had a moment of concern when Marko threw a cushion at Ash, hitting Claire by accident instead. However, she surprised us all when she walked over to him and started smacking him with it. Eventually, he picked up another and whacked her back and then all hell broke loose as we all joined in, hitting each other repeatedly until we all finally collapsed, laughing hysterically.

Of course, the drinking games we'd played and my cocktails might have had something to do with that. There was nothing like a few good cocktails to loosen things up and liven up any event.

I loved seeing both the men and my girls enjoying each other's company. We felt like a family. It was so nice, and as I watched them, I knew I was doing the right thing by getting involved with the Rominovs, especially Ash.

Each day I spent with Ash, I felt happier and more content

with my life. I knew it was fast, but I was well and truly head over heels for the man.

Claire seemed to have quickly gotten over her reserve about him as well, which helped when I told her I would be spending a lot of my time with him at the Estate.

Actually, I was moving in there permanently today. However, I wanted to keep that knowledge to myself for now. I planned on simply letting Claire get used to my absence before I told her. I'd lived with Claire for so long, and she had always felt so responsible for me that I knew my leaving would be hard on her, so I thought it was better to ease her into it.

To be honest, I hated to leave her alone, but I couldn't let it stop me from taking my relationship with Ash to the next level.

Although, her being alone might not be a problem for long. I grinned as I thought about how Luca had been eyeing her up like she was a dessert, and he was ready to dive in with a giant spoon.

I saw her glancing at him when he wasn't looking, and her slight blush told me of her interest in him, too. Ooh la la! Maybe I wouldn't be the only member of the family getting it on with a hot Russian.

It would be great if Claire and Luca became an item, too. He was Bratva as well, but according to Ash, he had less to do with the illegal side of things than any of them. Luca mainly ran their legitimate entertainment businesses, but since he was also Miki's best friend, he helped him out with less legitimate stuff when needed. However, I thought that if he stepped away from that side of things even more, he might just be perfect for my cousin. Luca looked just her type and seemed really nice. His Bratva links could be a problem for her, but perhaps not. Time would tell, I guessed, but I was secretly rooting for him.

After the girls had left with Luca, Romi picked us up, and

we collected the family who were visiting from Russia. I'd been nervous to meet them, but they had been so nice to me, and their teasing nature quickly put me at ease. We ended up chatting away like long-lost friends all the way back to the Estate.

They seemed like such a close family. I couldn't help laughing with Ash as Romi's mum kept kissing him and fussing over him while his younger brother Dimitri called him a "mummy's boy!" to his great embarrassment.

I thought it was lovely. Letitia made me think of my own mum. I missed her so much. I wished she could have met Ash. I believed that despite his background, she would have approved.

I quickly found that I had a lot in common with both aunts, who were avid readers, too. Letitia was a bubbly woman who reminded me of Marcie. She had a wicked sense of humour and a dirty mind. I really liked her. Marta was quiet and stunning, and she was a huge dark contemporary romance fan, like me. In fact, some of the books I found in the library were hers. The aunts were easy to be around, and I looked forward to spending more time with them.

They weren't the only new people I'd met today. When we finally arrived back at the Estate, Janusz Glowacki and his son were already there, apparently finalising plans with Miki.

He was definitely not what I'd imagined. Ooh, daddy! sprang to mind, and even though I wasn't into daddy doms, I thought that Janusz Glowacki could just change my mind. If I wasn't already head over heels for Ash, of course.

Glowacki was a handsome man and a lot younger than I had expected. I had only really heard his name before, but for some reason, I had thought he would be much older and definitely not as hot. I was so wrong about that. Phew!

He looked to be around the late 40s or early 50s, and he was tall, like the other men, probably around six feet or so and just as powerfully built. With his buff body, silver hair, styled short at the back and longer on top, and a well-groomed beard, he was what my romance authors would describe as a silver fox!

He oozed power. I could see he was a man who was used to being in charge by the way he quickly assessed his surroundings, taking note of everything and everyone. I suppose the air of absolute authority the man projected was a must for a Mafia boss. Miki projected the same sort of air. In fact, all of the guys did, though to a lesser extent.

Glowacki was dressed in a dark, well-fitted, and incredibly expensive suit, with a white shirt and blue tie to match his icy blue eyes, which I swore could freeze you on the spot if he wanted them to. Thankfully, those same eyes warmed when he was introduced to us ladies, and there was a definite playful twinkle in them that spoke of all sorts of naughty things.

Glowacki's son Dariusz was a younger and darker version of his father. He was another handsome man, but he had a more open, relaxed air about him. I found I liked him instantly. It was obvious Ash liked him too by the way they embraced in a man hug, clapping each other on the back.

Both Glowacki and his son were charming to all of us ladies when introduced, but I couldn't help noticing the way Janusz Glowacki looked at Marta or the way he clasped her hand a tad longer than he did anyone else's. I also didn't miss her sharp intake of breath or how she blushed when she looked at him.

It looked very much to me like Glowacki and Marta had an instant and mutual attraction. That might be a good thing; he was a widower, and she was a widow, so they already had something in common.

Marta was Ash's youngest aunt, only thirty-eight years of age. Marta was the daughter of his grandfather with his second wife, and so was his dad's much younger half-sister. She lived in Russia with her older brother, Maxim.

Apparently, she was married when she was very young and

lost both her husband and son in a car crash a few years later. She had never quite gotten over it, Ash said. I couldn't even begin to imagine how losing your husband and child in such circumstances would affect someone. Glowacki lost his wife to cancer, but his son was murdered as well, so that was something else they had in common.

I was definitely basing one of my characters on Janusz Glowacki. In fact, I decided he'd make the perfect love interest for my female lead's older sister. Actually, I thought I might base her on Marta. Oh yes, I couldn't wait to make that a nice side story. They had looked so good together. It would be a tragedy if they didn't somehow get together, even if it was just in my book.

Although, from the way it looked, they could very well write a story of their own. Perhaps it was my newly loved-up state, but suddenly, I was noticing little hints of attraction between people. Romi and Sonia, Claire and Luca, and now Glowacki and Marta. It could just be me projecting. However, I hoped I was right, and at least some of the people got it together. Being in love was wonderful, and I wanted everyone to feel as good as I felt.

The mere thought of love had me thinking of Ash and wondering how he was coping. None of us women said anything when the guys headed off to attend to business, but we all knew what that meant. Lev Petrov was being released, and that meant the guys would be dealing out some of their brand of revenge.

I couldn't help feeling nervous and worried for Ash. I knew Miki would have it all under control, but I didn't know if Ash could keep himself under control.

I looked at the blank page on my laptop and sighed. I badly needed to distract myself from my worries about how Ash was coping, and I really wanted to get some writing done, but my mind wasn't cooperating. It just wasn't quite ready to write anything yet.

So, instead, I took a quick run to the kitchen and grabbed a coffee and a cute little cupcake before returning to the library and curling up on the sofa there. Once I was comfy, I sipped my coffee, nibbled my treat and thought about the last time I enjoyed cupcakes. Naturally, this brought my thoughts back to Ash again. He rarely seemed to be out of my thoughts recently.

He would find today difficult, I knew that, because no matter how good it might be for him to finally get revenge on Lev Petrov, he still carried so much guilt inside. Then, of course, the family now knew there had been more people responsible for Krissa's death than they had initially thought, and that meant the closure Ash had expected to find by killing Petrov wasn't going to happen.

I wondered how he would deal with it? Even if everyone, including himself, believed he was more in control of his anger recently, he could still easily spiral out of control. I'd been able to soothe him before by distracting him. I decided it might be a good idea to plan a few diversionary tactics for later in case they were needed. Great idea! My inner devil shouted. I smiled, lay back against the sofa, closed my eyes, and let my imagination wander free as I planned exactly what some of those tactics would be.

An hour or so later, I was frantically typing my first sex scene. All that thinking about Ash and planning an evening of intimacy for us inspired me to create another for the characters in my story. Initially, it had been a bit strange and awkward writing that kind of scene, but I soon got into it and quickly lost myself in my writing again for a few hours.

CHAPTER 32
ASH

Once we arrived at the C, we retrieved Petrov's unconscious form from our vehicle. He was hidden in a body bag, which was how we usually brought our live victims to the C. That way, if anyone saw us, they would believe we were simply staff moving a dead body into the crematorium.

Vlad and Marko took him from us into the main room. They had arrived previously and were already in disposable suits.

We quickly changed ourselves and entered the main room, glad to see Petrov had been woken up. I was excited to finally have this bastard under our control. It was way past time he was made to pay for what he and the Nowack brothers had done to Krissa. I couldn't wait to get started on my revenge. Unusually, though, I realised that I wanted it over with quickly.

I didn't want to prolong things. I had always envisioned spending hours over days torturing Petrov and thoroughly enjoying my revenge. Yet, as I saw him strung up before us, I found that I no longer wanted that.

Instead, I wanted to get back to Gracie, get the rest of this shit over, and then focus on spending the rest of our lives together. I no longer took any pleasure from any of this and realised that just killing the fucker was enough. Gracie had given me something more in my life than the revenge that had kept me going these last two years, and although I still needed the revenge for a certain level of closure, I no longer craved it in the same way I once had.

I felt myself wishing to just slit the bastard's throat and have done with it. However, we needed information from him, so I took out my favourite stiletto knife and got started on making the rapist bastard sorry for ever touching my sister. It didn't take long, and he had spilt everything he knew.

Once we had all the information we could get, Miki and Marko got in a few hits. Then Glowacki and Dariusz took turns punching and cutting him. He had been planning their downfall and to take over their business, so they had a right to their revenge, too.

Finally, we were done, and he had succumbed to blood loss. It only took a few hours. In the end, I wasn't the only one who did not want to draw things out.

I was pleased that I handled it all without spiralling out of control. Gracie's presence in my life made me a calmer person. So much so that I managed to remain in control despite everything we had learned from Petrov.

Even though it had been awful to hear, I was glad we now had the full story about Krissa's kidnapping and murder.

The Nowack brothers had assumed the girl they picked up was just a random girl off the street, but Petrov had recognised her and called Siri.

At the time, Petrov had formed an alliance with Siri to take down Glowacki. They had planned to kill him and his sons and put Petrov in charge in his place. Then, the Polish Mafia and Malia Boys would have worked together and opened up the human trafficking route through Polish territory. With the Polish

Mafia under new rule and in a new alliance, our own alliance would have ended, weakening us, and making it easier for them to go up against us. Apparently, Petrov and Siri had decided that killing Krissa was a bonus. Another chance at weakening us while they put the rest of their plans into action. Fucking bastards!

However, we also learned that the alliance between him and Siri had the backing of some "bigwig" who was financing the takeover. Although he was unable to tell us who that person was, he did know that his own lawyer worked for him. That same lawyer who had instructed Siri to kill Petrov to ensure we couldn't find out about his boss.

So, we had known there was some anonymous bigwig behind the Malia Boys/Broxy's alliance, and the lawyer was acting as a go-between. Still, now we also knew that this secret person had been plotting our downfall for at least a couple of years. Now, we just needed to find out who he was and what he had against us. Then, we would end everyone involved. Nobody threatened our family or our allies.

That bastard lawyer would be getting a visit from us soon.

In the meantime, it was time to head back to my Gracie.

As we jumped into the car for the drive home, I smiled at the thought of all the delicious things I was planning on doing to her.

CHAPTER 33
GRACIE

By the time Ash returned home, I'd finished writing for the day and had begun to put my plans for the evening ahead into action.

Up until now, Ash had been the one to take care of me, running baths, washing my hair while we showered and delivering snacks to our room whenever we got hungry after our antics, but not this time. Tonight, I planned on pampering him.

I brought some massage oil that I had in my bedroom at Claire's house back with me, and I had it ready. I had also brought several candles, which I arranged around his bedroom. Our bedroom now, I reminded myself. I ran a warm bath. Like the one in the guest room I had first stayed in, it was big enough for two, just like the shower. However, while we had enjoyed a number of showers together, we hadn't yet bathed together, and that was something I was hoping to do soon. Although not tonight. Tonight was all about Ash.

After that, I changed into a skimpy black lace nightdress with a matching thong, put some romantic music on in the background on a loop, and waited.

I heard him saying good night to Marko before he entered the room. He stopped and gulped as he took in the sight of me. A slow smile spread across his face. He looked calm. It was not what I'd expected, but I was glad.

I walked over to him, and he took me in his arms, kissing me fiercely. I returned it with equal enthusiasm while unbuttoning his shirt.

He undressed quickly.

"You look gorgeous, sweetheart," he said as I led him naked into the bathroom and made him climb into the tub.

"Strip," he said to me, looking me over with heat in his eyes.

I shook my head.

"I'm going to bathe you, then massage you," I told him.

"And that sounds great," he said with a smirk. "But you can do it naked."

I hesitated, suddenly shy at removing my clothes while he watched. I knew it was silly because he had seen me and touched me everywhere, but I still felt shy about stripping.

"Strip for me, Gracie," he demanded again.

"You are beautiful, and I want to see you." And the look he gave me made me feel beautiful.

I slowly shimmied the lace up and over my head and dropped it on the floor. I felt exposed and vulnerable, but I forced myself to stand there as he perused me.

He licked his lips, and his eyes filled with lust. His hot look made my shyness evaporate, and I suddenly felt powerful. When he looked at me like that, I felt so special, like I was his everything. It was enough to bolster my courage, and I pulled off my thong. He reached out for me, pulled me towards the tub, and kissed my navel.

"Gorgeous," he murmured, then let me step back so I could sink to my knees and start washing him.

He watched my every move, his breathing becoming more laboured with each stroke of the cloth over his skin. I very slowly stroked over his chest and then down his abs, admiring them as I went. I took my hand lower and lower towards his cock, which was straining to break free of the water. I moved the washcloth over it, rubbing gently, and he closed his eyes and groaned.

I dropped the cloth and cupped him with my hand. His cock jumped at the different feeling and sprang fully to attention. I smiled and started moving my hand up and down. He moaned, and his hips bucked involuntarily into my hands. I loved being in control. I continued moving my hand up and down for a while, enjoying teasing him.

I was so engrossed in watching my hand squeeze him that I didn't realise his hands were on me until it was too late, and I landed in the bath on top of him. Water sloshed over the sides as my head went under. I came up soaked with my hair all over my face and gasping for breath. He laughed, pulling me against him until I was straddling him.

"Playtime is over, sweetheart," he said, kissing me passionately and sinking his finger deep inside me.

His lips kissed along my jaw and down my neck. He continued his assault on my pussy, dragging me close with his other hand on my ass so I was pressed higher up his chest, giving him easy access to my nipples. He took one in his mouth and sucked, and I would swear there was a direct line from there to my core as I felt it clench and gush wetter. Oh, but that was so good!

I rode his hand, bucking my hips against his fingers, and pressed his head closer to me. I continued like that as my orgasm built. His groans told me how much he was enjoying this, too. He murmured something in Russian, and I shivered at the sound. God, his voice did things to me that should be illegal.

"You are so wet for me, sweetheart. You feel so good." The Russian accent with the English words was my undoing. I came, gasping his name and shuddering.

That accent got me every time!

I was still high with the aftermath when he moved me over him and impaled me on his cock. Wow! He thrust me up and down on his shaft, and I moaned as my walls fluttered around his length.

"I can't wait any longer," he gasped with need, his accent thick.

Oh my god. I exploded again, clinging desperately to Ash's shoulders for purchase as my whole body convulsed. He pumped into me another couple of times, then followed me into bliss; my name was torn from his lips as his cum shot inside of me.

We lay there, unable to move until our breathing slowed to normal before we climbed out of the tub. It took a while to get us both dried off because neither of us could keep our hands to ourselves or our mouths.

Finally, I led him back into the bedroom.

"Playtime again," I told him as I turned the music down a bit and got him to lie down on his front.

I massaged his back and shoulders, loving the feel of his hard muscles under my hands. I continued down to his buttocks and then his legs.

His breathing was slow and steady.

"That's great, Gracie!" he moaned, sounding very relaxed.

But I'd lulled him into a false sense of calm; this was not that type of massage. He always managed to make me lose all control, and it was my turn to repay that compliment.

I made him turn over and rubbed more oil on my hands before straddling him. His breath hitched at the sight of me kneeling above him naked. I gently stroked his shoulders and down his arms, then picked up the oil again. This time I poured it all over my tits and rubbed it in, half-closing my eyes, mirroring the look of lust on his face. He reached up to cup my breasts, but I grabbed his wrists.

"Uh uh!" I said, moving his hands above his head.

"They stay there!" I warned him, pulling away and shaking my head as he tried to reach for me again.

He smirked but dutifully moved his hands back into position. Good boy!

I lowered myself towards him, using my oiled tits to massage his chest while I kissed my way across his body. When I looked up at him, he was staring at me, and I could see he was desperately trying to lie still. I smirked and started my torture again, circling my tits over his chest while I kissed and sucked on his neck.

"God, Gracie!" he moaned, his voice strained with the effort it took for him to lie there and allow me to tease him.

That accent and his restraint made me so wet. I couldn't keep this up anymore. I wanted more; in fact, the thing I wanted was currently poking me in the ass, and I knew it was time to give us both what we needed.

I rose up, positioned myself so the tip of his cock was aligned with my pussy, and sank straight down. My channel, still wet with my juices and his cum, took him in easily.

I moved up slowly, determined to tease him further, but he obviously had no restraint left and grabbed my waist as I started to ride him.

"Yes, sweetheart! Ride me, Gracie!" he gasped, and I did, bringing myself up and down on him, moving faster with each stroke, feeling him filling me up so well.

After a while, my strength began to wane, but he helped me, moving me up and down on his cock until we were both panting and sweating and on the verge. Dear god! I needed this as much as he did. I'd already had two orgasms in the bath, but my body craved another. I sunk down one more time and felt myself coming all over that hard Russian cock of his, crying out his name.

"Gracie!" he shouted before doing the same, releasing hot cum into me.

When he was empty, he stayed inside me but pulled me against him and buried his face in my neck, murmuring incoherently in Russian, totally lost in the moment.

We stayed like that for a long while before he eventually pulled out of me. Moving me to his side, he wrapped his arms around me and kissed my forehead. I would never get enough of this.

CHAPTER 34

ASH

THURSDAY - PREPPING FOR WAR

woke with a smile and a feeling of lightness I hadn't felt in a long time. Last night had been bloody amazing.

It was early in the morning now, and I was lying in bed with Gracie. Despite the events that lay ahead in the next couple of days, I felt happier than I'd ever been.

I kissed the top of Gracie's head. She slumbered by my side, looking so peaceful, and I determined to ensure that she always felt that way. As soon as this war was over, I wouldn't let anything disrupt her peace ever again.

The next couple of days would be hard for us, and I longed to get them over with. However, I revelled in the quiet contentment of this moment.

I closed my eyes and let my mind wander back to last night's events, replaying them like my own private porn show.

When I got home, I couldn't believe the beautiful sight before me as I entered our bedroom. Gracie was dressed in a piece of black lace that barely covered her ass, with a matching thong underneath.

I hadn't imagined she could get any sexier until that

moment. She literally took my breath away each time I saw her and constantly surprised me, too.

Her lingerie had been gorgeous, and I loved seeing her wearing it. I'd get her to wear it again soon, but right then, I needed to see her naked.

When I demanded she strip, she slowly shimmied the lace up and over her head and dropped it on the floor; oh my god, I had nearly come right then.

Sitting in the bathtub while she stroked the washcloth over me had been sheer torture but of such an exquisite kind. The kind of torture any man would gladly endure.

But a guy could only take so much. I chuckled as I remembered how adorable she had looked coughing and spluttering water with her hair plastered all over her face. That was my Little Miss Hot Mess!

Oh, and that sexy massage! The little minx had certainly got me all hot and bothered with that. I'd never had any sort of massage before, but I was certainly looking forward to my next. I grinned, my cock hardening at the memory.

What a night! I was looking forward to many more nights like that in the future.

We really were great together. I would never get enough of Gracie.

I sighed. I would love nothing more than to spend the rest of the day and night in bed with her.

However, there was a lot to do today if we were going to successfully bring down the Malia Boys and Broxy's alliance and end things without any real casualties on our side. That would be difficult, but if all went according to plan, we might just pull it off.

I didn't have the time to indulge my all-day fantasies, so a quickie would just need to suffice. I smiled wickedly and ducked down under the covers to wake up my gorgeous girlfriend in the best possible way.

An hour or so later, we were both showered and dressed, and I'd let Gracie know the basics of our plans for each location.

She had wanted to come to the lab location with me to, "keep you out of trouble," she said. My heart swelled when she said that. I loved that she cared so much that she wanted to be there and put herself into another dangerous situation to look after me. But hell no!

While, on the one hand, I wanted to have her with me and was unhappy about leaving her care to anyone else, on the other hand, I knew that on this occasion, it was necessary. Taking her with me would be far too dangerous, even if it was possible. I wouldn't be able to focus on anything but looking after her, and that could prove fatal for both of us.

Also, she didn't know how to shoot, something I intended on remedying at a later time, and as guns were definitely going to be used, she could end up shot. I couldn't bear to lose her, so I eventually managed to convince her to remain at the Estate with the other women and lock herself in the panic room with them if the need arose. I prayed it wouldn't, but it was always best to be cautious.

Being cautious had been drummed into us by our dad. That was why I still bristled a bit at Miki giving up some of our family secrets to Glowacki. He was a friend and ally, yes, but nevertheless, it worried me. Still, it was done now, and that was that.

Gracie, Dimitri, and my aunts met Glowacki's younger sons and his daughter at lunch. The Glowacki family had arrived in the early hours of the morning under the cover of darkness through our secret back entrance that only our family, and now Glowacki's family, knew about.

Daniel was twenty-three, like Sonia, and next in line after Dariusz. He was another geek like Marko and ran the IT side of things for his dad the way Marko did for us. So, naturally, they were good friends. He was coming with us to the C on this occasion, though.

Sebastian was Glowacki's youngest son. He was only seventeen and was remaining here with the women. He hadn't been happy about that at first, but Glowacki had given him a gun and instructed him to protect the women and his sister, and that seemed to have appeased him.

Magdalena was the baby of the family and Glowacki's only daughter. He absolutely doted on her. She was a pretty girl who had inherited her long auburn hair from her deceased mother and her piercing blue eyes from her dad. She was also highly intelligent, as could be witnessed whenever she talked about something that had piqued her interest.

She looked at Aunt Marta with awe. I could understand why. Aunt Marta was a beautiful woman, slim, around Gracie's height, with a sweet personality. Her long white-blond hair and sparkling green eyes gave her an other-worldly air.

Magdalena was carrying her tablet, as she always seemed to be whenever I saw her. She told Aunt Marta that she was researching Russia for a school project and wanted to ask some questions. Aunt Marta beamed at her, and they both settled down on the sofa to chat.

I noticed the way that Glowacki looked at the pair. The unguarded expression that crossed his face for a second told me that he found my aunt intriguing. My gaze sought Miki, and I saw that he had noted Glowacki's interest, too. I wasn't surprised as very little escaped Miki's attention. Glowacki, however, seemed oddly oblivious to us as he crossed the room, sat on the other side of Magdalena, and joined their conversation.

I watched them closely. I wasn't sure how to feel about Glowacki's obvious interest, but I put it out of my mind when Daniel approached to go finalise some of the details for the evening ahead. I had more important things to think about than Glowacki's attraction to my aunt.

A few minutes later, Daniel left, and I looked around for Gracie. She was still in conversation with Aunt Letitia, and as I walked towards her, I noticed Miki having a heated discussion with Sonia. I guessed by the way she kept glancing at Dariusz and glaring at him that Miki had finally told her about the arrangement, and she was definitely not keen.

Luckily, Dariusz himself seemed totally oblivious to the daggers she was shooting him. I doubted he would even understand the reason for them if he saw them. I didn't think Glowacki had told him about his part in the impending marriage yet. I was hoping that when he found out, he would rebel too, and the arrangement would be called off. I would certainly back them both up with that.

As I headed over to Miki, Sonia turned and ran out the door, looking distraught. I felt bad for her, but unfortunately, there was no time to address this issue with Miki again. It would have to wait; we had bigger issues to deal with today.

Still, I couldn't help taunting my brother.

"Dumb ass!" I said, shaking my head.

As expected, Miki practically froze me with his cold stare before crossing to Glowacki and tapping him on the shoulder.

It was time for us to leave.

I kissed Gracie goodbye. Then Miki, Glowacki, Daniel and I slipped out of the Estate. On our way to the C, Miki and Glowacki checked in with the guys we had hidden away while I confirmed that Sergei had everything arranged to cause mayhem for the police the following night.

Our elderly medic, Dr Rawlins, was already there when we arrived. He had set up a small makeshift hospital area ready to tend to any casualties if required.

All of our plans were set, and all that was left for us to do was to bide our time and wait for the following evening, our drug shipment to arrive, and the attacks to commence. Easier said than done! I had a feeling it was going to be a long night and an even longer day.

CHAPTER 35
GRACIE

THURSDAY NIGHT/FRIDAY - THE ESTATE
ATTACK

When Ash left yesterday, I pretended he was just heading off on a short business trip and not to prepare for one part of this two-part war we were all about to be involved in.

He'd sent a good night text late in the evening, and it was all I could do not to call him and beg him to come home. I missed him and was worried about him, but I was determined not to be a distraction, so I refrained from calling him and just sent a quick good-night text back instead.

It hadn't been easy, but I knew I needed to be strong and supportive and not act like the clingy, scared female I was.

So, I managed to keep my mind off things for the most part by writing more of my book. I'd been on a roll with that and was about three-quarters through, so I wrote until the early hours of the morning, and exhaustion set it.

However, today was the big day, and my nerves were through the roof. I tried to lose myself in writing again, but I just couldn't concentrate.

I spent some of the day chatting with Sonia and Marta and

the rest of the time wandering aimlessly around the house worrying about things.

The men had all been buzzing about and having hushed conversations in corners, obviously doing their best to prepare for whatever was to come while trying to pretend everything was fine. They seemed to think they needed to keep us women sheltered from the worry of the situation.

They were acting a bit over-protective, archaic even, and I didn't like it. I would rather know what was going on because not knowing made me feel worse. Also, I didn't like being treated as if I was incapable of dealing with this situation or helping out. It frustrated the hell out of me.

Eventually, I couldn't take the not knowing any longer and went in search of Marko with a plate of food as a bribe for information.

He was muttering away to himself when I found him in his computer lab, which was in a separate wing of the house.

"Hey, everything alright?" I asked as I entered.

"Yeah, I'm just getting impatient, like everyone else, to get this show on the road. The sooner it starts, the sooner it will be over," Marko replied, looking up.

"Great, food! I'm starving!" he exclaimed, his stomach growling in agreement as he reached for the plate.

Before he could grab it, I quickly moved it out of his reach.

"Hey!" he protested.

"Not until you tell me what is happening," I shook my head, moving the plate behind my back.

He laughed.

"I take it nobody is bothering to tell the little women what's going on? Quite right!" he stated, smirking.

"Guess you aren't that hungry after all," I pouted in annoyance.

He tried to make another grab for the plate, but I jumped

back away from him so quickly that I practically tripped over my feet as I went.

"Alright, don't drop it," he laughed as he lifted his hands in a placating gesture.

"I know how you like to roll around in food, Little Miss Hot Mess, but you've got the wrong brother for that," he said, waggling his eyebrows at me and grinning.

"Very funny!" I glared at him, and he laughed.

I narrowed my eyes and grinned wickedly at him as I reached towards the bin under a nearby desk as if to throw the food into it.

"Okay, okay, I'm just teasing!" he cried, "I'll tell you whatever you want to know, no need to take it out on Nonna's food!"

"Talk," I said, giving him the plate and sitting down beside him.

"We are all concerned that there has been no communication about tonight from either party yet. It's almost like they are on radio silence. That could mean that they are aware we know something, or it could just be them being cautious, but we can't be sure, and it has us on edge," Marko said between mouthfuls.

"Either way, it shouldn't be a huge problem. Miki has thought about pretty much everything in the defence of both sites. Nevertheless, we were hoping for the element of surprise for our retaliation to avoid unnecessary casualties on our side. If we lose that element, it will mean things could also take longer to get under control, which makes keeping things secret from the police and other possible witnesses so much harder." He frowned.

"I guess the guys downstairs think that telling you women will only make you worry more about a situation you have no real control over, and that's why they are being so secretive. They should know better," he chuckled.

"I would much rather be told than be kept in the dark." I pouted and huffed out a frustrated breath.

"I can understand that; sometimes, not knowing only allows the imagination to run riot."

"Rest assured, though, everything is still going according to plan, and they still have plenty of time to start up communications. I will keep monitoring them and will let everyone know when they do."

"And if they don't?" I asked.

"Well, the plans to defend both sites will take place as expected as soon as the attacks start, which is liable to be around ten pm when the shipment is due, and no matter whether they are aware we know they are coming or not, we will win," he said decidedly, before adding ruefully, "Just perhaps not quite as easily as we hope."

I felt a little bit better knowing what the others knew, but I so wanted to be with Ash and not stuck here at the Estate. I hated that we were split up at this time, and neither of us knew how the other was doing.

As the day wore on, I felt more and more helpless. My whole body was fraught with tension, and I couldn't keep still. I paced up and down our bedroom, staring at the clock, willing it to move forward but fearing it doing so. I longed to get this night over with, but I worried about what lay ahead and how we would all cope with it. I also worried about how many people would die tonight.

My stomach churned at the thought of anyone I knew being hurt or, worse, killed. I prayed everyone would be okay. Especially Ash. I didn't know what I would do if I lost him. In such a short time, he had become the most important person in my life. I was terrified he was going to be hurt and feeling pretty helpless right now.

I wanted to contact him and hear his voice, but I forced myself not to. It was excruciating being apart from him. He had assured me that everything would be fine and their plan was a good one. But no matter how good a plan they had, anything could happen.

An hour later, I was lying on our bed, my mind tormenting me with all the possible things that could go wrong, when a text came through.

ASH

I miss you, sweetheart.

It was him. My heart did a little jig. He missed me as much as I did him!

I quickly replied.

ME

Miss you too, Ash. So much!

I even added a heart emoji and kiss for good measure.

We spent the next twenty minutes or so sexting, getting raunchier and raunchier with each reply we sent. It was fun and helped pass the time even though my stomach was still tying itself in knots the nearer we got to the time the shipment was due.

ASH

Got to go, sweetheart, that's Marko confirmed. The chatter has started, and they are on their way. Take care, hide in the panic room with the others if necessary, and I will see you when this is all over!

That was his last message, and I felt sick.

I checked the time. It was just after nine p.m. This was it. It was really happening.

ME

Be careful!

I replied and prayed that he would be.

Just as I pressed send for the final time, Sonia burst into the room then.

"It's time!" she cried. I nodded solemnly, and we headed down to the basement to join the others.

Anton was there with a man called Nicholas Wright, whom I learned earlier was Derrick's boyfriend and several other men. The door to the panic room was open, and I saw that Sebastian had already taken Nonna, Letitia, Marta, and Magdalena inside. They were playing card games and, thankfully, looked quite calm.

Sebastian was armed, and it looked like Marta was too. So, not all the women were expected to be completely useless in a fight then. That was good to know because when this was all over. I was getting Derrick to give me more fighting lessons and Ash to teach me how to shoot.

The few civilian staff who worked at the Estate had been given a couple of days off to ensure they were not involved. So, it was only family, Bratva or Polish Mafia soldiers, Anton, and his men here now.

Sonia greeted some of the men and quickly introduced me before we took seats in front of the monitors with Vlad so we could watch the security feed. Just as we sat down, we saw Romi and Dariusz returning with Derrick. They came in via the secret entrance, and as soon as they got to the underground car park, Sonia stated she needed to talk to Romi and rushed back into the main house to meet them before anyone could stop her.

A few minutes later, Derrick and Dariusz came down to the

basement to get an update from Anton. Sonia and Romi didn't follow them, and I wondered what they were up to as Sonia had promised Ash she would stay downstairs with Nonna. I'd only known Sonia for a few days, but I already recognised her to be a bit impulsive. I'd thought I had been nervous, but she had been like a cat on a hot tin roof all day. I hoped she wasn't going to do anything stupid and put herself at risk.

Thankfully, she reappeared around ten minutes later. She seemed a bit calmer, although she did look a little red-faced. Just as she sat back down next to me, the first shot rang out. Then another. It had begun. Shit!

The rest of the men left Nicholas watching over us and went to join the fight.

"If they get anywhere close to the house, you all get inside with Nicholas, lock the door and only open it when it is all over," Derrick said, gesturing to the panic room, before following the others up the stairs so he could be on hand if there were any casualties.

I watched the attack begin, my eyes glued to the monitors, with my stomach churning. I didn't think I had ever felt this worried or nervous.

Then all hell broke loose. Guns fired and men shouted, and all we could do was sit and listen, our eyes glued to the security cameras as they streamed the live footage from around the Estate.

Every now and then, a figure passed one of the monitors, but it was hard to tell if they were friends or foes most of the time. Watching everything through the monitors didn't make it less frightening. Gunshots, fireworks, and mini-explosions were going off. It was hard to tell what noises came from the battle and what was part of the defensive cover-up. All I knew was that it was loud and utterly terrifying.

The battle raged on for what seemed like hours but was

probably only around forty minutes. The various sounds became louder as the enemy neared the house but more sporadic as time went on until, eventually, there was silence.

Everyone held their breath as Romi radioed Nicholas to say it was finally over. As soon as the words were out, we all let out a collective sigh of relief.

Then Derrick appeared with the first of the wounded, and Sonia and I went to help.

All of the Broxy's were dead, including their leader. Vlad had killed him, but not before he was wounded himself. Luckily, the bullet just entered his shoulder and went clean through, so Derrick made quick work of cleaning and dressing the wound.

As he did so, more of our wounded came for treatment. A large number of the men were injured, but none were badly hurt. There were a few knife wounds that needed stitches, but the rest of the injuries were bullet grazes, a few broken bones and cuts and bruises from hand-to-hand fighting. I cleaned up the lesser injuries while Sonia helped Derrick with the others. I couldn't help noticing that she was especially attentive to Romi, cleaning his injury and fussing around him like a mother hen.

I definitely had my suspicions about those two. I hoped that if something was going on with them, and it was serious, Sonia's brothers wouldn't cause any issues over it. They were so overprotective of her that it was almost suffocating. Although after what had happened to Krissa, I could understand it.

Thinking about her brothers had me worried again. We had been told the battle at the lab location was still underway. We had been exceptionally lucky. Only a few of our men had died, but they were the traitors, and their deaths had been planned. I hoped that everyone at the lab location was just as lucky. I sent up another silent prayer for their safety.

CHAPTER 36

ASH

THURSDAY NIGHT/FRIDAY - THE LAB
ATTACK

'd never slept at the Crematorium before, thankfully, because it was bloody uncomfortable on the concrete floor. It didn't help matters that Glowacki's men were creeped out by the whole idea of sleeping here, and their constant grumbling had kept the rest of us awake. Only when Glowacki finally lost his temper and told them to "shut up and stop being such pussies!" did they stop their incessant complaints.

I'd woken at dawn after just a few hours of sleep, and I was stiff, sore all over, and moody as hell. After several coffees and a long shower, I'd finally perked up and was feeling my usual self.

I couldn't say the same for Glowacki's men. Although they hadn't said anything else after being told to shut up during the night, their body language showed their continued unease. Some people were just superstitious, I guessed.

Glowacki didn't seem to be bothered by being here, nor did his son Daniel either. Or maybe they were. It was hard to tell with those two. Both were adept at hiding their emotions. Daniel, even more so than his dad. Daniel rarely showed any emotion at all. To be able to hide his feelings so well, I knew there had to be a story there. I wondered if I would ever find out what it was. Maybe it was best not to, I mused as I watched him sitting quietly by himself. I had enough issues of my own to deal with.

As the day dragged slowly by, I felt myself becoming more and more anxious. However, the impending attacks weren't the reason my stomach was churning. It was the fact that Gracie wasn't beside me and wouldn't be with me until it was all over. I missed her.

I needed everyone at the Estate to remain safe, especially Gracie. I didn't know how I would cope if anything happened to her. She had become my everything in such a short time, and I couldn't imagine life without her now.

I had wanted to call her so badly last night but had restrained myself. I was concerned that if we talked, she might be upset or worried, and I'd end up heading back to the Estate to be with her instead of sticking to my part of the plan here. I wanted to be with her, but for her safety and the safety of my family, I needed to stick to Miki's plan. I needed to play out my role like everyone else, stay focused, and get back to her in one piece.

Instead, I simply sent her a goodnight text, so she knew I was thinking of her.

The rest of the time, when I wasn't going over the plan again and again with the other guys, I was daydreaming about my Little Miss Hot Mess, replaying every intimate encounter we'd had in our short time together.

I did the same today. I managed to get through until the evening before I contacted Gracie. It had been a difficult task, but I was proud of how long I held out. I'd finally relented around eight thirty pm when I knew it was too late for me to do something stupid like try to head back home before the attacks commenced.

I'd texted her again. I missed her too much and needed the connection, but I hadn't wanted to hear her voice because if I had, I would definitely have done something stupid.

We spent the next half hour or so sending raunchy messages to each other.

It was fun.

I had sent the odd sex-laden text to women in the past but never done what could be considered sexting until now. I'd never felt inclined to do so with other women. However, with Gracie, I found that it was incredibly enjoyable.

Although it made me horny as hell, it was a good way to pass the time. Gracie seemed to thoroughly enjoy it if her responses were anything to go by. It helped keep our minds off what lay ahead.

However, it was now time to focus again.

I read her last text before turning my phone to silent.

GRACIE

Be careful!

Count on it, sweetheart! I replied in my head.

I might not have been too careful at times in the past, but with Gracie in my life, I vowed to myself that I damn well would be from now on as I checked my weapons and readied myself for the battle ahead.

We were all wearing vests and night vision goggles, and I was glad. It might be early July, but the sun had already set and being the UK, the cloud cover was blocking out much of the moonlight. Without any streetlights out here in the countryside, it was pitch black at this time of night.

We watched via the hidden security cameras used by our RomCore firm as the van containing our drug shipment drove along the private access roadway between the C and the farm. A short while later, the vehicles carrying our enemies followed, and we waited until the last vehicle had passed, then crept out behind them.

We took a shortcut through the grounds and soon caught up with them. They were moving slowly with their lights out to keep from being detected until the last minute. They obviously didn't know about our cameras or that we were aware of their plan.

All that boded well for us. Although the number of vehicles was a concern, It seemed that there were more Malia Boys than we knew existed here tonight. From my approximation, they outnumbered us by about two to one with weapons and night vision goggles on a par with our own. That level of equipment was highly unusual for them. I guessed the bigwig funding them was sparing no expense.

Nevertheless, we still had the element of surprise and a number of traps set up, which I expected would help even the odds out a bit.

Indeed, they did help. We managed to plough through a good number of the bastards before they knew what had hit them. Our timing was perfect, too, and with each of the teams in position, we quickly surrounded them, trapping them. Everything was going according to Miki's plan, and we hadn't lost any of our own guys or Glowacki's yet.

Well, the three Polish traitors Glowacki killed didn't count. We'd taken them to the C with us last night, and he had put a bullet through their heads. They were the last of the traitors he knew about, apart from the two who were working with the Malia Boys. They were still missing, but it seemed likely that they were already dead. Once the plan to break down our alliance had seemed to be working, their involvement wouldn't have been needed, so Siri had probably killed them off.

I ducked to avoid a bullet as it whizzed over my head, startling me out of my thoughts and back to the present. That was close. We had been doing well up until now, picking the enemy off from a distance, but now their numbers were dwindling, and we had started to close in.

Despite the fact that it was becoming glaringly obvious with every second that passed that they were losing, they still seemed intent on gaining entrance to the lab. I wasn't sure what they believed they'd achieve now. However, it was likely they just wanted to do as much damage as possible by destroying the lab, its contents, and as many of us as they could before they died.

They were acting desperate. That could prove in our favour, as desperate people often make mistakes. However, it could also prove to our detriment because desperate people had nothing to lose, so they often fought harder.

Shots rang out around us. It was pandemonium. However, there was less shooting now and more hand-to-hand fighting.

I stabbed one guy in the stomach. He fell to his knees. I bent, grabbed his head, and slit his throat.

Another guy ran towards me, his raised hand holding a large machete. I feigned a step to the right, then moved quickly to the left, caught his hand, and knifed him under the arm. He staggered, and I stabbed him again in the side of his neck. His dead body crumpled to the ground.

Daniel stumbled past me, fighting the biggest guy I'd ever seen. He was a giant and built like a brick house. I had no time to move out of the way as the pair tumbled into me. We all fell to the ground in a heap, and my head banged hard off the ground.

I tried to get up. I felt nauseous and dizzy, but I needed to get to my feet because Daniel was in trouble. The Brickhouse knelt over him, his hands around Daniel's throat. Daniel's arms were trapped by the guy's legs, and so all he could do was try, uselessly, to buck him off.

I forced myself to stand and reached for my gun, but I must

have dropped it when I fell. I couldn't see it. So, I did the only thing I could and jumped on the guy's back. I plunged my knife deep into his throat. The guy didn't let up his stranglehold on Daniel, so I pulled the knife and stabbed him again and again. Blood splattered everywhere, but finally, his hands loosened, and he fell forward, dead.

I helped Daniel push the big fuck off him. His neck would be bruised, but thankfully, he was alive. That could have ended so badly.

I located my missing gun and then glanced about, checking on how things were going. Glowacki was fighting a guy several yards away, and Miki was doing the same not far from him.

Pockets of men fought all around us. Up this close and personal, it was easier to get injured or killed. This was getting out of hand. It was time to end this before we started losing men. Miki must have had the same because as soon as he had despatched the guy he was fighting, he gestured for us to close in tighter.

We fell into position beside one another and headed towards the others.

A guy ran at me from behind, taking me down to the ground. Daniel pulled his gun and shot him.

Glowacki caught my eye as I straightened. He gestured towards the back door of the farm building that housed the lab. Six guys slowly made their way towards it. I nodded to him and held my gun at the ready again. We left them to it as we quietly made our way over to where Miki was fighting off several attackers. Miki punched one, and he fell to the ground. Glowacki shot him in the face at the same time as I knocked another over the head with the butt of my gun, then shot him in the head, freeing Miki to finish off the third.

As soon as he had despatched the guy. I tapped Miki's arm

and pointed to the figures before the three of us silently moved forward.

They were a lot further away than the rest of the guys who were fighting, so we crept nearer to get within easy firing range. Unfortunately, one of the figures turned and spotted us. He lifted his firearm and aimed, but Glowacki took him out with a shot to the head before he could fire. Miki and I took out another two, but the others managed to get inside.

The few guys we had in the building were all currently focused on the front, which left the back of the building vulnerable to attack. The fools were sitting ducks. Shots rang out, and we knew we were too late.

There was a small explosion. The lab entrance had been breached. They were inside.

We entered the building cautiously and headed towards the lab.

There was only one way in and out of the underground lab, so these guys were never getting out of there alive, but if we weren't careful, neither would we.

They had closed the door behind them, so we positioned ourselves on either side and readied ourselves to provide cover as Glowacki opened the door. As soon as he did, we were met with a volley of gunfire. My ears rang with the noise. Miki grimaced. Glowacki tried to tell us something, but the sounds were so loud neither of us could hear a thing.

The door opened up into a long hallway. There were doors to several small rooms and two large lab areas leading from it. Two of the enemies peeked out from doors at the far end. The other guy had taken cover in a room nearer the middle of the hall. That was good because although there was a lot of fire, we were predominantly out of range of the two furthest away.

Not even bothering to talk this time, Glowacki gestured to us that he was going in and wanted us to provide cover. We both nodded and began to shoot through the door as Glowacki made a run for it.

As soon as he was inside, he took cover in the nearest room on the right-hand side and then provided cover for us to do the same on the left side.

Shots were fired back and forth for some time before we finally managed to hit the guy nearest us, but not before he got a shot at Miki. My heart raced as I saw him hit the ground.

"You okay?" I shouted at him.

He nodded.

"Got my vest!" he yelled back, sounding a bit winded. It probably hurt like hell, but at least he wasn't dead. Thank fuck!

We weren't that far away from each other and could probably have simply spoken, but since our ears were still ringing, shouting was the only way we could hear a bloody thing.

Glowacki shot again but missed. I did, too. Our adrenaline was high, and even though we had managed to move closer to our two remaining enemies, it was really hard to shoot straight. That was the case in these kinds of situations; no matter how well-trained you were or how good a shot was, and we were both very good shots, it wasn't as easy to hit a moving target as films made it seem.

It was also tiring to be this high on adrenaline for this long, and it showed in all of us on both sides.

Glowacki peered out of his doorway, ready to make another shot just as one of the enemy shot at him. I sucked my breath in because, god damn, it was so close I swore I saw the hair of his head move with the force of the air as it whizzed past him, just barely missing him.

His eyes met mine, and I saw the shock of his near-miss register. Then his eyes turned cold. He radioed, and within a couple of minutes, one of his guys threw a backpack through the doorway. Miki grabbed it and chucked it to Glowacki, who opened it.

I grinned when I saw the contents.

A moment later, Glowacki threw a canister along the hall. It hissed, and as smoke billowed out, Glowacki took off running and shooting. We quickly followed. Although we could breathe easily through the masks he'd given us, it was difficult to see through the smoke. However, coughing alerted us to where the enemies were, and we just fired towards that direction.

A moment later, Miki lifted his hand, and we stopped shooting. We were no longer being shot at either. In fact, apart from our own breathing, it was silent.

We stood still and waited for the smoke to lift. As it did, we saw the bodies of our enemies lying on the ground.

"Looks like we got them all!" Glowacki said, just as one lifted a handgun and fired at point-blank range, hitting him in the chest.

Shit! I fired back, killing the guy, but Glowacki was already down. Down but still alive. Thank God. However, he wouldn't be for long if we didn't get him help soon.

Miki radioed the rest of the men for an update. Unfortunately, even though our men were winning, the fighting above ground still raged on. It wasn't possible to move Glowacki, so we had to hold up where we were.

Miki kept an eye out to ensure no more enemies were trying to breach the lab. I stripped my vest off and then the t-shirt underneath and used it to help stem Glowacki's blood loss. The bastard bullet had gone right through his vest!

It was a while before we got word that the battle was over. As soon as we did, Daniel ran in to check on his dad, who had now passed out with blood loss. He'd already sent for a vehicle, and it came tearing across the field towards us as we carried Glowacki out of the building.

We bundled him into the back, and Daniel jumped in, holding my now blood-saturated T-shirt over his dad's wound. I stepped back, and the vehicle sped off towards the C, where Dr Rawlins was already waiting with his makeshift hospital prepped and ready to operate.

Thank God we had that set up. There was no way Glowacki would have made it to either of our homes, and we couldn't have taken him to a hospital under the circumstances. So, without our makeshift set-up at the C, he would be dead. Of course, he still could be. That was a huge worry, but if anyone could help him now, Dr Rawlins was the man. I just hoped that he could.

One of Glowacki's men updated us on the situation with Siri. Apparently, he and a small handful of his men had escaped.

Although several of our men had given chase, they'd been too late to stop the men taking off in a helicopter that had landed in a field nearby.

"A helicopter? A fucking helicopter!" I fumed.

The Malia Boys didn't own a fucking helicopter. Obviously, that had to have been another thing supplied by this "big wig" enemy. We really needed to find out who that fucker was!

At least most of Siri's men were dead.

We would just need to catch up with the slimy bastard himself another time, and we would. We had questions he needed to answer, and then his life was forfeit.

As the rest of the injured were transferred to the C for medical treatment, we began the arduous task of the clean-up operation, which needed to be done as quickly as possible.

To speed the process up, our guys were split into teams. I oversaw the one who collected the dead bodies. We loaded them into a truck, which we had previously hidden in a farm building for just that purpose, to be transported to the C for cremation.

Miki oversaw the other teams. One got to work fixing the lab door and the damaged farm buildings, while another collected discarded weapons, cleaned up blood, covered up bullet holes, and generally removed all signs of the fight that had raged only a short while before.

It took some time, but just as dawn broke, we took one last look around. The lab location had been compromised, so we had already moved our operation to a secondary location. This one would need to be destroyed, but not yet. We would deal with it later once things had calmed down. Meanwhile, we just needed to ensure that there was no evidence left of what had occurred.

Finally satisfied that we could do no more, we returned to the C to collect our vehicles and head home.

Glowacki was still being operated on. It would be a while before we knew the outcome. Miki decided to remain at the C with Daniel and wait.

He sent me home.

"There's nothing we can do but wait, so there's no point in all of us being here. Go home to Gracie," he told me.

I pulled Daniel in for a bro hug and clapped him on the back.

"Glowacki will be fine. If anyone can survive being shot, it's that cantankerous old bastard," I said affectionately.

He nodded.

I climbed into one of our vehicles and nodded to the driver to take us home. I'd managed to give Gracie a quick call earlier when I'd had a spare moment. It had been a relief to hear her voice. I couldn't wait to get back to her. I had missed her and planned on showing her just how much as soon as she was back in my arms.

In the meantime, I lay back against the headrest, closed my eyes and let the tension drain from my body. Thank God that was over.

CHAPTER 37
GRACIE

My phone rang, and I answered immediately, recognising Ash's ringtone. I knew he was okay, but I was glad to hear his voice.

"Sweetheart how are you?" he asked.

"Fine, now I can hear your voice," I told him, and I finally was.

The churning in my stomach settled as soon as he spoke.

I sighed as the tension drained from my body, and I couldn't stop smiling as he told me how much he had missed me.

"I love you, Gracie," he said.

"Love you too, Ash," I replied shyly.

Wow, we just confessed our love! Yeh! My inner devil was delighted. I knew it was early days for something like that, but it just felt right, and so I refused to second guess it.

He gave me a brief rundown of what had happened at the lab. It seemed to have been a much fiercer battle than we'd had here. I was so glad Ash, Miki, and Daniel were okay. I worried about Janusz, but at least he was still alive, and the Doctor was operating on him. That had to be a good thing. I just prayed that

Glowacki had the strength to recover, but having met him, I had a feeling it would take more than a bullet to stop that man.

I felt lighter after our phone call, and with the wounded, all tended to, Sonia and I went to help with the clean-up operation that was underway. It would be some time before Ash got home, so in the meantime, I was happy to keep busy.

Romi and the other men were doing a great job clearing things up quickly. The bodies from the Estate grounds had already been transported to the C for disposal.

Derrick and his boyfriend were cleaning blood up from the porch and rinsing it off the gravel driveway. Men were moving around outside, picking up discarded weapons and debris from the fireworks and the traps that had been set and loading them into bags. Romi told me they would be taken somewhere to be crushed.

None of the enemy had got close enough to the house to do any damage, but there were traces of blood throughout the hall and down to the basement. It was the blood of our own men when they came to be treated, but nevertheless, it needed to be cleaned up.

Sonia and I grabbed some mops and got to work.

While we did that, Romi had the men go around the grounds again to ensure nothing was missed.

They had taken a lot of precautions when they prepared for this mini-war, and they were taking the same amount of precautions during the clean-up. I was glad. I had no doubt that Ash and the others would be involved in a number of dangerous situations in the future, and it made me feel better to know that they had taken their lessons in caution from Ash's dad so seriously.

I was startled from my thoughts by Dariusz Glowacki shouting into his mobile as he hurried along the hall. His face was flushed with anger. Romi asked what was wrong.

"They bombed our fucking home," he spat out, then yelled something else in Polish before hanging up.

He gave us a quick rundown of the situation. Apparently, someone had left a bag in Magdalena's room. Worried that Magdalena had left behind something she might need, one of the guards who had stayed to protect the Glowacki home opened it. He had radioed to his colleagues that there was a bomb and that it had a timer, but he hadn't been able to get away before it went off. He was tragically blown up along with part of the house, but thankfully, he was the only casualty.

We were all shocked. Thank goodness Miki had taken the precaution of having the Glowackis come to the Estate while the attacks against the Bratva took place. There had been no intel that anything had been planned against the Polish, but Miki had felt that it was a strong possibility under the circumstances, and Glowacki had agreed.

I didn't want to think about what would have happened if Magdalena and Sebastian had stayed home. Of course, the enemy wouldn't have known they weren't there. The fact that the bomb had been placed in Magdalena's room suggested she was the target. Glowacki would go off his head when he found out, and rightly so.

After filling us in, Dariusz called someone else and fired off instructions in Polish to whoever was on the other end of the call before hanging up.

He was absolutely furious. I understood. It was hard not to be. I couldn't believe that someone had tried to murder a child. Poor Magdalena. Thank goodness she was here with us and safe!

Dariusz said that they had some of the local police and fire crew in their pockets, and with the help of the few men they'd left at their Estate, a cover story of a gas explosion had been concocted.

When he left us to call Daniel and update him on the situation, Sonia asked to speak to Romi alone. I took the hint and made myself scarce.

I decided to get some air and see if there was anything else that needed to be done outside.

Everything was pretty much done, so I sidled over to some of the men who were having a smoke and chatting and listened to their conversation.

Since the battles were over, they didn't feel the need to be so tight-lipped as before, and I learned pretty much everything that happened both here and at the lab.

I discovered that the remaining Bratva traitors had been killed tonight, except Ivor, who had escaped. I hadn't liked him. He was a good-looking man, but he had cold eyes, and the way he sniffed around Sonia was creepy. If I had been asked to name the traitor out of all of the guys I had met, it would have been him.

He was often paired with another guy, Igor. I hadn't liked him much either.

It turned out that he had been another traitor. Romi had put a bullet through Igor's brain as soon as the attack had started. The guys talked of him doing that so casually that I should have been shocked. Yet I wasn't. I didn't feel bothered by it at all. I had no sympathy for them.

I wondered if that made me a bad person. Was I too accepting of death now because I loved a man capable of killing? Or maybe my dark romance novels had literally romanticised this lifestyle for me? I mulled that over.

No, I didn't think so because I would feel bothered and upset if it were other people, good people, but these weren't good people. These were bad people who were willing to sell out their friends and brotherhood to the enemy for money. They didn't deserve sympathy.

A lot of people had died tonight. I did feel sad about the few Bratva men who had been killed at the lab location, even though I didn't know any of them. However, the rest of the men deserved to die. They were people who would easily have killed me or any of my friends, so I couldn't bring myself to feel sympathy for them either. If anything, I was grateful that they couldn't hurt us anymore. Shades of grey!

Thinking about all of that had me worrying again about Glowacki, and I decided to seek out Magdalena and check she was okay.

Dariusz had told her and Sebastian what had happened to both their dad and their home, and although Magdalena had been distraught when she first heard, she had calmed down by the time I saw her.

After a while, Marta took her up to bed and assured her that she would remain with her and keep her company until her dad was better. That seemed to settle the girl who had taken an instant liking to Marta.

It had been a long and exhausting couple of days, and everyone was tired, so once Magdalena and Marta headed to bed, the rest followed quickly, and I headed upstairs, too.

I knew I wouldn't be able to sleep until Ash was home, but at least I would be waiting for him in bed when he arrived. I planned on showing him just how much I missed him after I checked every inch of his body to ensure that he hadn't been hurt, of course.

Hell yeah! My inner devil squealed, pleased with my thoughts.

CHAPTER 38
ASH

SATURDAY MORNING - HOME

Miki called during the drive home with some good news.

Glowacki was finally out of surgery but couldn't be moved. So, Miki, Daniel, and a couple of our men were remaining with him until he could be. Miki said they hoped it would be by the following evening.

Once he could travel, he would be taken to our Doctor's private clinic for some scans before he was brought back to our Estate. Since his house had been partially destroyed by the explosion and would need some rebuilding, he and his family would stay here at the Estate with us until he'd recovered and the repairs were completed.

It was a relief to know he had survived the operation. It would take time for him to recover, but we'd have his back and keep his family safe until he did.

We had lost several good men tonight, but not as many as we could have, and for that, I was thankful.

I let out a long breath. I was exhausted and longed to hold Gracie in my arms again.

The minute I entered the house, I headed straight for our bedroom. When I opened the door, Gracie was lying on the bed, awake and obviously waiting for me.

She smiled when she saw me, and I crossed the room and took her lips, kissing her deeply. I loved kissing Gracie; she always tasted so good.

We clung desperately to each other as our tongues explored each other's mouths in that time old fashion. We'd been apart less than two days, but it had felt like a lifetime. I was so glad we were together again, and Gracie was safe.

She moaned into my mouth, and my already swollen cock jerked in response, straining to break free from the confines of my pants. My exhaustion was completely forgotten.

I wanted to take her right now but held myself back. Instead, I led her into the bathroom and turned on the shower. We continued kissing just as desperately as we stripped and climbed into the cubicle. As the warm water cascaded over our bodies, I kissed her everywhere, then followed my lips with my hands, lathering her with the soap.

I washed her thoroughly. I loved doing so. It somehow felt even more intimate than sex. Probably because it was about more than just sexual release; it was about showing her how much I cared. I needed her to know I'd always take care of her needs in every possible way.

When I had finished rinsing out her hair, she took the soap and washed me just as thoroughly as I had her. By the time she had finished, I was so hard it was painful, and I couldn't hold back any longer.

I hugged her to me, revelling in the sensation of her luscious curves pressed against the length of my body. After a quick kiss on her lips, I turned her to face the wall. Pulling her back against me, I positioned myself behind her, the bottom half of our bodies pressed tightly together so that she could feel my hardness against her ass. I curved my body over her and kept one hand around her waist to keep her where I wanted her while I let the other hand wander over her body.

She sighed and shuddered in pleasure, and I brought my hand up to lightly hold her throat as I nuzzled her neck.

I turned her back around and grabbed her tits.

"So soft," I said, fondling them.

My breath hitched in anticipation as her hand reached between us, and I couldn't stop the hiss of appreciation as her hand circled my cock. She stroked it a few times, making me harder with each caress of her hand, and I leaned forward to kiss her.

I whispered endearments into her ear as we fondled each other.

She felt so good, and the feelings she invoked in me with her hands on my body were like nothing I'd felt before. This woman set me on fire. Wherever she touched, her fingers sent small currents of electricity through me.

I shuddered as her hand moved and cupped my balls, squeezing gently. While she showed them the attention they desired, I gave my attention to her breasts. She moaned and arched into me, thrusting her chest closer to me.

I admired her gorgeous tits as I circled her areola with my thumb before taking her nipple into my mouth and sucking hard. I didn't want the other to feel left out, so I gently pinched and tugged on it while she continued to stroke my balls.

I nibbled, licked, and sucked on one breast and then the other, making sure both had equal attention. Gracie's hand moved again, and she clasped her palm around my length lightly, teasing me.

"Gracie," I pleaded.

She took pity on me and began stroking in earnest, but her teasing deserved a response, and I decided to give her a bit of her own medicine. I pinched her nipple, making her gasp, and as her mouth opened, I thrust my tongue inside her mouth; at the same time, I thrust a finger into her warm, wet channel, then another. I let my thumb put gentle pressure on her clit while I matched the rhythm of my tongue with my fingers and proceeded to fuck her mouth and pussy.

Then I stopped.

I let my fingers hover over her entrance, and my lips hover over her mouth and did nothing. Right at that moment, doing nothing was the hardest thing I had ever done. But I wanted to increase our pleasure by driving us both wild with need, so I forced myself to remain still. We were both panting heavily, but apart from that, neither of us moved as we looked into each other's eyes.

"Ash?" she questioned.

"What do you want, Gracie? What do you need?" I asked her, my voice barely a whisper, my Russian accent thick.

She shuddered, thrilling me with her reaction. I knew she liked my voice, especially when my accent showed, and I planned on using it to my full advantage.

I leaned close and whispered in her ear, "What do you want, moya Lyubov?"

"You," she gasped, leaning forward to kiss me, grabbing my hand and pushing it between her legs.

"Now fuck me like the best book boyfriend ever and stop playing games," she said, pouting with annoyance, and I couldn't help chuckling.

"Yes, moya Lyubov," I laughed gently as I nuzzled her mouth teasingly and let my fingers dip back inside her.

Her fingers reached down and gently brushed over the head of my cock, which seemed to lean into her touch of its own accord. She circled its length and stroked. Every touch was like molten lava, and as my fingers increased their pace inside her, hers increased theirs on my cock.

Soon, she was writhing and bucking against me, and my dick was pulsing with its need to release. Neither of us could take this much longer.

"Please, Ash," she whimpered.

I needed to be inside her, and she needed me there just as badly.

I picked her up quickly and pushed her against the tiles, hooking her legs around my waist. I rubbed my cock through her folds, coating it with her juices, then pushed into her.

She was so wet for me but so tight. I only got partway through the first thrust. I stopped and held myself back from pushing her any further until I could feel her channel adjust to my girth. As soon as her muscles began to relax around me, I rammed in deeper, right to the hilt. God, it felt so fucking good!

She groaned with a mixture of pain and pleasure, and I slowly moved in and out of her, getting faster with each thrust until her moans of pleasure resonated around the room.

"Yes, sweetheart, take all of me! I want you to come all over my cock, baby!" I said, my accent thick with emotion.

She turned me on so much that I had to fight hard to stay in control and not come right away. I pumped into her a few more times, stroking her clit at the same time. She was so close I could feel her pussy clenching around me.

"Ash!" she screamed, and I continued thrusting while she came, her juices running over my shaft.

I didn't let her regain her equilibrium as I continued thrusting, riding her until I felt her building towards another orgasm.

"Oh god, Ash!" she cried, her voice filled with emotion that her whole body seemed to vibrate with.

I loved how she reacted to me. I felt like a bloody god whenever I was buried inside her, and that thought sent me into a frenzy, pumping harder and faster until she released again.

"Love you!" I grunted out as I shot my seed into her, filling her with cum so much it ran down our thighs.

I stayed locked into her for a while, mumbling endearments in Russian as the aftermath slowly faded, and our breathing returned to normal. Every time I spent with her, it seemed to get better and better. I was so sated I could barely hold us up.

The warm water ran over us as we clung to one another, enjoying the feeling of being in each other's arms.

Finally, I let her slide down my body, moving back just enough to kiss her.

"I love you too," she said with a smile, finally responding to my earlier declaration.

I grinned back, feeling smug and winked, replying cockily, "Of course you do; what's not to love?"

She laughed and rolled her eyes before leaning forward to give me a kiss.

My heart swelled with love for her, and I pulled her from the shower and wrapped her in a towel. We took turns drying each other, and when we were finally dry, I dragged her to the bed. I wanted to go for another round, but I suspected that neither my body nor Gracie's was up to it. We were both exhausted.

There would be plenty of time to enjoy each other from now on anyway, I reminded myself.

"Let's get some sleep," I said before pulling her under the covers and wrapping my arm around her.

She snuggled close, and I noted how our bodies melded together perfectly, just like we did in life. We were a perfect match, and I still couldn't believe how lucky I was to have found her.

"I am so glad you are home safe," she said, kissing and nibbling my chest.

My cock shot straight up again. I grabbed Gracie and pushed her back into the pillows, capturing her lips, all thoughts of sleep going right out of my head.

EPILOGUE
ASH

TWO WEEKS LATER

t had been a couple of weeks since the attacks, and we were yet to find Siri, but we would. The guy's death was inevitable. He had been involved in Krissa's murder and had been conspiring against us for the last two years; there was no way he could be allowed to live. So, no matter where he was hiding, we would eventually find him. When we did, it wouldn't be a quick death either. That male had questions to answer, and we would make sure he did before we finally put an end to him once and for all.

Marko was in charge of finding him, and not a stone was being left unturned. His bank accounts had been accessed, and the money moved from those in his name. The ones he had under an alias that he didn't know we knew about were being monitored, and if there was any activity, Marko would know. At some point, he'd eventually need access to his money, and if we hadn't found him beforehand, we would then.

Ivor was also still missing, but he would be found and dealt with, too. There was nowhere either of the bastards could hide from us for long.

Despite them still being at large and the lawyer and his boss still being an issue, life felt good.

With the Malia Boys and Broxy's practically wiped out, we had fewer enemies to worry about for now, and our operations were running smoothly again without any more interference.

We'd spent the last couple of weeks cleaning up the mess their demise had left behind. Between ourselves and Glowacki's family, we'd temporarily taken over their territories and were in talks with the Irish Mafia regarding that. Out of all the criminal families and organisations with a hold in the UK, they had a moral code similar to ours. They were the only ones we could see as another possible ally for both us and the Polish, so we'd been negotiating a deal with them.

Miki was also talking to several other likely candidates to take over the activities we were planning to offload, and some of them looked like good prospects, at least for the arms and drugs route anyway. The Irish Mafia were interested in that too, but there were also one or two gangs further north and up in Scotland who might want a bit of the London pie and who might work out for us. We'll see. There was time to deal with that.

Uncle Maxim was happy about how everything had been handled, but we needed to be sure on whoever we got to take over running drugs and arms routes. Hopefully, at some point, our own drug distribution operation was someone he and our US cousins would happily deal with.

Otherwise, it could be a no-go, and we could find ourselves stuck in this life forever. Miki was determined we'd succeed in getting out of this side of things, and I knew if anyone could make that happen, it was him.

The only cloud on the horizon was the arranged marriage

set up between Sonia and Dariusz Glowacki. Sonia was completely against it. I hated to see her so unhappy.

Marko and I had made it very clear to Miki that we were against the arrangement, but ultimately, he was Pakhan, and there was little we could do about it. He was wrong to have made such an arrangement in the first place, and he knew it, but once these kinds of arrangements were made, they couldn't easily be broken without all parties concerned losing face, and in this business, losing face was a big no-no.

The situation had been put on hold for the time being, however, because Glowacki was still recovering, and Miki wouldn't discuss the matter with him until he was well enough. The operation had been a success, but Glowacki had somehow developed an infection, and while he was doing better now, he was still very weak.

In the meantime, I guessed Miki was probably wracking his brains for a viable alternative. I didn't envy him. I'd tried thinking of one myself but couldn't come up with anything. I was so glad I wasn't in Miki's shoes right now. Sonia was so angry with him that she could barely even look at him. It served him right, but I hated seeing my family split like this.

Dariusz wasn't really on board with the idea himself. He wasn't completely against it and said he would go through with it if his father insisted, but I knew Sonia hoped that when Glowacki found out that neither of them was keen on the match, he would agree to some other kind of arrangement. I just hoped that was the case for Sonia's sake.

Aunt Letitia and Dimitri returned home a couple of days after the attacks. Aunt Marta stayed behind to look after Magdalena. The pair have developed a strong bond and appear inseparable.

The rest of the Glowacki family have remained with us, too. Their home is being rebuilt, and the younger boy, Sebastian, had taken the lead on that while Dariusz and Daniel kept on top of their business interest in Glowacki's absence.

It was nice having them all here, but any time we found it too crowded, Grace and I would disappear to the library or our room. Our relationship was going from strength to strength, and I was ready to take things further.

After checking my emails, I made a quick call to ensure everything was ready.

It was Gracie's birthday, and I was taking her on a short break.

She didn't know where that was a surprise. She also didn't know that I had another very special surprise in store for her when we got there.

I turned off my computer and headed up to the bedroom, filled with nervous excitement.

Gracie

The last couple of weeks flew by. I'd spent most of it writing my book or cuddling up somewhere with Ash and getting to know him better, and the rest of the time indulging in "research," as Ash liked to say, for my sex scenes. He took his role as my book-boyfriend muse very seriously, and I was more than pleased to let him.

I finally finished my first book and was looking into publishing it. I had found my groove, and my second book was also underway. Yey for me! Claire and Marcie were so proud.

I had been trying to write this morning, but I was too excited. It was my birthday, and Ash was taking me away for a short break. I knew he had been planning something special for days because he had been very secretive at times, and at others, he had been asking a lot of questions. For example, a few days ago, he asked me if I had ever been to a castle. I told him that I hadn't but would love to visit one. I really hoped that was where we were going. I would love to stay in a castle. It was such a romantic fairy-tale-like thing to do.

Ash entered the room, looking as excited as I felt.

"Ready?" he asked.

"Definitely," I practically squealed in delight.

He grabbed our suitcase, and we left our room hand in hand and headed out to the car.

My excitement racked up a notch when I saw the red convertible that sat waiting for us. I'd never been in an open-top car before, and I was bursting with excitement.

"Wow, what kind of car is this?" I asked in awe.

Ash proceeded to inform me that it was a Mercedes-Benz E-Class Cabriolet, which was apparently one of his favourites. I knew the family had a garage full of vehicles, but I'd hardly ever seen them use anything other than black SUVs.

As I sunk back into the plush red and black leather seats and checked out all the latest gadgets, I was glad he'd chosen to drive this one today. I felt like a celebrity and couldn't help the huge grin on my face as I thought of how jealous Claire and Marcie would be.

The wind blew gently through my hair, and I was glad that it was a decent enough day. It was July, but since this was the UK, that didn't guarantee good weather like it did in some countries. It could have just easily been raining, and I would have had to forgo this pleasure.

After about forty minutes, we stopped at Battersea heliport. I knew that was where we were due to the sign, but I had no idea why.

"What are we doing?" I asked, but he just smiled.

I had assumed we were driving to wherever we were going, but by the look of the helicopter sitting about a hundred feet away with its propeller blades whirring noisily, that was not the case.

As we parked, Marko ran towards us. He whispered something into Ash's ear and winked at me.

Obviously, they were up to something.

Ash slung his arm around my shoulder and led me towards the aircraft. Oh my god! I was going to fly in a helicopter! My inner devil was doing a jig while mumbling something about joining the mile-high club! Uh-huh, not in a helicopter, I told her, bursting her bubble.

Ash helped me climb in, and Marko handed the suitcase to him before taking Ash's car keys.

"Have a great time!" he shouted over the noise, grinning widely as he waved us off.

The view was utterly breathtaking. Thank God I wasn't afraid of heights!

A couple of hours later, Ash pointed to a spot ahead, and my breath hitched when I saw the most splendid, unique sight I had ever seen.

"Star Castle, Isle of Scilly," he shouted over the noise of the propellers. "That's where we'll be staying," he said, smiling broadly. Oh wow! Ash was taking me to a castle, after all.

I threw my arms around him and gave him a quick kiss of thanks before turning back to watch as we approached this majestic building.

"Look at the shape!" I cried excitedly.

It was absolutely stunning. The castle itself was a square building nestled inside a wall shaped like an eight-point star. The Bratva star. I smirked and raised an eyebrow at him.

"It seemed fitting," he said, grinning.

I chuckled. It did, indeed.

We landed a couple of minutes later in a special area within the gardens just outside the wall.

We were greeted by the hotel concierge, who loaded us into a golf cart and drove us into the castle and up to the grand entrance.

If I'd felt like a celebrity in the car and the helicopter, I now felt like a princess being taken to the castle of the prince for the first time. I was absolutely giddy with the excitement of it all. I couldn't stop beaming at Ash as he held my hand, and we enjoyed a tour of the main castle building. It was small but luxurious, as I expected a sixteenth-century castle turned hotel to be.

I was a little disappointed to find out that we weren't actually staying in the castle itself until I saw the suite Ash had booked instead. It was located within a newer building set within the garden grounds with its own private entrance and lawn area. It was beautiful.

I only had time for a quick freshen-up before Ash led me outside, where a table for two had been set up, complete with a bottle of champagne chilling in an ice bucket. Oh, this was just getting better and better, and the romance addict in me was so happy.

We indulged in a wonderful meal of mussels in white wine to start and prawn linguine for our main while listening to a string quartet playing discreetly in the background.

The waiter informed us that all of the seafood was caught locally and prepared in the hotel restaurant, and everything tasted so good. I was thoroughly enjoying myself and didn't think anything could top this, but I was wrong.

After clearing our plates away, the waiter whispered something into Ash's ear before he and the quartet disappeared.

As soon as they left, Ash reached under the table and pulled out a box. I swallowed hard when I recognised it was the iconic blue and white Tiffany's box. I'd never had one before, but I knew what they looked like. My heart pounded as I realised that he had bought me a very expensive gift and taken me on this wonderful trip. He had also had flowers sent to me this morning. I was being completely spoiled.

"Happy birthday, sweetheart", he said, passing the gift to me.

"Open it!" he urged when I simply stared in awe at the box.

My hands shook as I very carefully undid the ribbon. Before opening the lid, I stopped to admire the beautiful box which I intended to keep forever.

I gasped. Inside was a beautiful platinum necklace with a heart-shaped ruby pendant, which was my birthstone, surrounded by smaller diamonds and matching earrings. Oh my gosh, I jumped up and ran around the table, grabbed Ash, and kissed him soundly on the lips.

"Thank you, they are gorgeous!" I said, amazed by the generous gift.

"You don't have to spend so much on me, you know…"

I started to say, but he cut me off with a wave of his hand.

"I can afford it, and you deserve the best, sweetheart, and that is what I intend on giving you from now on," he replied, pulling me into his lap before whispering suggestively in my ear, "And you can always show me your appreciation later."

I laughed. Oh, I would definitely be showing Ash my appreciation. He certainly deserved it.

"Come on, time for dessert!" he said, swatting my backside and tugging me back towards our suite, grinning mischievously.

Inside, the staff had obviously been hard at work. A large area of the floor was covered in a plush-looking red rug over what appeared to be a red plastic sheet. At the edges, there were a couple of ice buckets filled with champagne and what looked like cans of skooshy cream. What?

There was also a very large cream cake sitting on a paper plate smack in the middle of the sheet.

Oh my gosh, was this what I thought it was?

"Strip," he said, already quickly divesting himself of his own clothes.

Oh, hell yeah! My inner devil shouted as I started tearing off my dress. When we were fully naked, Ash pulled me onto the sheet with a completely wicked grin on his face. He leaned into one of the ice buckets and pulled out yet another box, a smaller one this time, before bending down on one knee and holding out the box to me. Oh, dear sweet Jesus! My heart was pounding!

"Sweetheart, I have been in love with you since our first kiss. Will you marry me?"

"Yes!" I cried without any hesitation.

I leapt straight into his arms as he stood up, almost knocking us both over.

Only just keeping his balance, he held me as I clung to him and kissed him all over his face, repeating, "Yes, yes, yes," over and over again like a mad woman.

He gently set me down and opened the box. It was a gorgeous engagement ring, exactly like my necklace and earrings set.

"Now you have the whole set," he said, putting it on my finger.

"It's so beautiful, I love it!" I kissed him again.

As I held my hand up to admire it, something wet and sticky hit me in the face. I spluttered in shock.

"Ha, there she is, my Little Miss Hot Mess!" Ash cried, doubling over with laughter as bits of cake dripped down my face and chest in a sticky, clumpy mess.

"Pig!" I exclaimed, laughing back as I picked off some of the cake and rubbed it all over his cheeks.

He laughed again and grabbed me, pulling me to him and giving me a long, passionate kiss. When we finally broke apart, we said, "Sweet! I knew you would be!" And we both burst into fits of laughter.

We spent quite a while after that rolling around on the sheet, alternating between spreading cake, or skooshy cream, over each other's bodies and kissing and licking it back off again. I was so hot and horny by the end of that, not to mention sticky, that I decided we needed to clean up. With a wicked grin, I shook up a bottle of champagne, popped the cork, and sprayed it all over Ash, effectively rinsing the mess from him and shocking him in the process.

"Ha, cleaned you up," I laughed.

"You little madam!" he cried, lunging for me before taking me down to the ground and trapping me under him.

"We'll get clean later; I'm going to get you even more messy first," he growled, his voice so thick with lust that I could barely make out the English words in his Russian accent.

"You have a nickname for me, but I have one for you too," I told him shyly.

He raised his eyebrows.

"Oh yes, what is that, my Little Miss Hot Mess?"

"Mr Sexy Voice," I said, biting my lip. "I love your voice, especially when your accent gets thicker or when you speak in Russian."

He smirked.

"Oh, I know," he whispered in my ear, making me shiver before kissing my neck and murmuring what I recognised to be endearments in Russian.

I was so hot for him, listening to his accent and feeling his lips making their way across my body that if I had panties on, they would have melted off. Geez, this man was my everything, and I couldn't wait to marry him.

He slid easily inside me. I was so beyond ready for him. It only took several thrusts, and I was on the O train heading to heaven. He followed not long after, and we were both still riding the high as we curled up together on the rug while we tried to catch our breath.

"Time to clean up," he said when we were finally able to move again.

Lifting me up, he carried me into the bathroom.

After filling the bath, we climbed in. He sat behind me, encasing me with his big body as he took a cloth and started cleaning off the remnants of our messy romp. I had never felt so safe, happy, and loved in my life.

I sighed with contentment. I didn't know what the future held for me as the wife of a Bratva blood brother, but I did know that I loved this man and would do whatever it took to live a long and happy life with him.

"Love you," he said, kissing my neck.

"Love you too," I said and smiled, knowing my book boyfriends would have to take a back seat forever now because they just couldn't compare.

The real thing was far better!

ACKNOWLEDGMENTS

I would like to say a huge thank you to the fantastic team at Hudson Indie Ink for all their help and encouragement in getting this book finally published. Thank you to Stephanie and Blake Hudson for taking a chance on a newbie like me, and a very special shout-out goes to Libby Blandford for encouraging me to submit my extremely raw manuscript in the first place and to Claire Boyle and Sarah Goodman for their hard work in helping me turn that raw draft into the book it is today. Another shout out to the wonderful Xen Randall for her amazing covers and to all of the other Hudson Indie Ink authors who have been so helpful and encouraging and who accepted me into their little family and made me feel like an author long before I actually was one.

I would also like to thank the fantastic authors whose work inspired me and then encouraged me to write my own books: Sophie Lark, Maggie Cole, Eden Summers and Elodie Colt. Without you, I would never have found the courage to pursue a lifelong dream!

Next, I need to say a big thank you to my Mum and Dad, who always encouraged me to try new things and only ever expected me to do my best; my husband, who puts up with me constantly reading or writing; and my wonderful son, who believes in his "badass Mum".

Finally, to anyone who reads this book, you have done me a great kindness by doing so, and I really appreciate it; thank you.

My life has been a rollercoaster ride of ups and downs but

throughout it all, I have always lived by a few sayings that have been my life's mantra, "Reach for the Stars," "Never Stop Dreaming," "Fake it till you make it," and "Don't Quit!" and what a journey they have led me on with writing novels with Hudson Indie Ink being one of the next stops. I can't wait to see where it all leads.

So, for anyone out there thinking of pursuing their dream, remember these quotes and – go for it!

ABOUT THE AUTHOR

Jax Knight is a fledgling author who finally gave in to the voices in her head, letting them come to life in her first dark contemporary romance series.

Jax lives in Scotland with her husband and son. She enjoys martial arts, reading and coffee and can often be found hiding away in a corner, glued to her Kindle or with her head buried in a book while sipping a Mocha.

A sucker for sexy, protective villains with morals and feisty, fun females, all her books have them aplenty and a guaranteed happy-ever-after!

Ash is her debut novel and the first of six books in her Bratva Blood Brothers Series.

If you'd like to keep up with all of her new releases and more, please come and join her newsletter or follow her on social media to stay up to date!

ALSO BY JAX KNIGHT

Bratva Blood Brothers

Ash

Romi

Miki

Marko

Luca

Anton

www.ingramcontent.com/pod-product-compliance
Lightning Source LLC
Chambersburg PA
CBHW030554170726
48283CB00002B/326